Praise for

ADELINE

"*Adeline* is an intimate portrait of a sister, a wife, a woman, and most importantly, an artist. In this vivid, deeply moving novel, Vincent brings us beyond the world of legend directly into the passions, the struggles, the ambitions, and finally the genius that is Virginia Woolf."

— Alison Smith, author of *Name All the Animals*

"*Adeline* deftly walks the fine line between story and scholarship — an entirely fresh reading of Woolf's work, brought alive by a writer of considerable imagination, insight, and skill."

— Marya Hornbacher, author of *Wasted* and *Madness*

"Spare, exacting, deeply imagined, *Adeline* brings us as close as we are likely to get to the secret negotiations that fed Woolf's art."

— Kathleen Hill, author of *Who Occupies This House*

"*Adeline* is a singular feat of the creative imagination in which the reader is taken inside the consciousness of a major artist in a way that is both completely believable and commandingly compelling. It is wholly worthy of its great subject."

— Terry Teachout, author of *Duke: A Life of Duke Ellington*

"Readers in search of a crash course on the Bloomsbury circle and the machinations of Woolf's fevered mind will appreciate Vincent's attempts to illuminate both, but her dark portrait of Woolf's agonizing journey through a life marked by psychic pain will hold the most appeal for those already familiar with this sad story of genius and madness."

— *Kirkus Reviews,* starred review

"This beautifully written and penetrating re-creation of the life of a feminist icon will appeal to anyone with a passing interest in Virginia Woolf and the Bloomsbury Group. Readers will come away with a deeper understanding of both Woolf's brilliance and her suffering."

— *Library Journal*

ALSO BY NORAH VINCENT

Self-Made Man:
One Woman's Journey into Manhood and Back Again

Voluntary Madness:
Lost and Found in the Mental Healthcare System

Thy Neighbor

ADELINE

A Novel of
Virginia Woolf

Norah Vincent

MARINER BOOKS

HOUGHTON MIFFLIN HARCOURT

BOSTON · NEW YORK

First Mariner Books edition 2016
Copyright © 2015 by Norah Vincent

For information about permission to reproduce selections from
this book, write to trade.permissions@hmhco.com or to
Permissions, Houghton Mifflin Harcourt Publishing Company,
3 Park Avenue, 19th Floor, New York, New York 10016.

www.hmhco.com

Library of Congress Cataloging-in-Publication Data
Vincent, Norah.
Adeline : a novel of Virginia Woolf / Norah Vincent.
pages ; cm
ISBN 978-0-544-47020-0 (hardcover)   ISBN 978-0-544-70485-5 (pbk.)
1. Woolf, Virginia, 1882–1941 — Fiction. 2. Women authors, English —
20th century — Fiction. 3. Bloomsbury group — Fiction. 4. London
(England — Intellectual life — 20th century — Fiction. I. Title.
PS3622.I536A66 2015
813'.6 — dc23
2014026848

Book design by Chrissy Kurpeski
Typeset in Minion Pro

Printed in the United States of America
DOC 10 9 8 7 6 5 4 3 2 1

To Honor, who is her name

Julia [Prinsep Stephen]'s other sister, the melancholy Adeline Vaughan ... died on April 14 [1881]; Julia's third child by Leslie [Stephen] was conceived as soon as she came home, and named after her dead sister. But "as Julia did not like to use the name full of painful association" the name Virginia (after ... her posh aunt ... Lady Virginia Somers) was added, and the first name, shadowed by death and grieving, was never used.

— Hermione Lee, *Virginia Woolf*

Act I

NIGHT AND DAY

~

Saturday, 13 June 1925

8:23 A.M.

SHE IS LYING full down in the bath, with the tepid water hooding her head and lapping just below the vaulted arches of her nostrils. Her breath, shallow and short, ripples the surface gently. She can hear her heart galloping distantly, as it so often does when she is ill, thrumming weakly but so quickly, a soft insistence sucking at the drums of her ears.

The swells of her breasts rise from the water, glistening and cool, the nipples pruned in the morning air. Her long, exhausted feet rise, too, at the far end of her, well out of the water, lean-boned and pale, marred with the angry knots and weals of tortured walks in ill-fitting shoes. They clutch the livid brass spout, flexing and squirming like newborns of an alien brood, quailing under the light.

She drifts in the shallow dream of herself, the lulling of the water, her breath, her heartbeat, audible and palpable at once, the other life inside her going on moment by moment, beat by beat, and all the vying thoughts going with it.

Always the thoughts.

Does the heartbeat have its own thoughts? she wonders. Or does it merely drive and amplify the dread that is coursing through her so wildly these mornings, urging the breath on with it, faster, shorter, sharper? Then, too, there are the headaches mounting all day, clenching her skull from the nape of the neck to the roots of the eyes like a caul of barbed iron. Yet — and here she halts her own description, for the panic must stop. It must. She will not let this happen again.

There is the stall of recognition. She knows this feeling, this progression of decline, she knows it very well, the consciousness curling under the despair, helpless as a page in the fire, succumbing to the grey, darkening possession. Slowly, slowly comes the blackness with its burning edge-glow eating inward to the center until all the parchment of her right mind is consumed and there is nothing but ash. Flaked and so fragile, it trembles there, fluttering on the balance of the unbearable heat, until at last it collapses and disappears with only the faintest of whists.

She knows what this is like. She watches it, she thinks it. She watches herself thinking it, and that is perhaps — she remembers this particularly — her only defense.

She bends her knees slightly and lets her feet sink back into the water. The toes are cold, the injuries ripe. They melt in the vague warmth and comfort of the bath. She lets herself feel this, every blister weeping, every scar moistening, and she sighs.

Now think, she urges herself. Think it away. I know you can. Concentrate. She furrows her brow and frowns, narrowing her huge, sunken eyes at the bounding rim of the porcelain tub, as if conjuring out of its whiteness the necessary will that is already so weak.

This, at least, she can control, if only she thinks of it well enough, attentively enough, if she makes herself tall and bending like the pair of priestly elms in the garden.

Yes, she thinks, the elms. In the garden.

Her mind begins to coast, moving in the picture, the mood of the morning, through the opened window and the unasserted light, out into the garden, over the moistening grass, the vaporous earth, and the insects hard at work, then up, as groundwater in root and trunk and branch and twig, all through the fretwork of elms. She thinks of them, swaying softly, outward to the smallest filigree of veins, the harmless air gossiping through their varied separations, making the tender leaves susurrate.

Now, she enjoins herself, *as them*. Think as them. She loosens her grip, rolls her scapulae down flatter against the belly of the tub, closes her bulbous eyes, breathes in once deeply, then sighs slowly, very slowly, eking out the breath. She begins to glide into the vision, just there, on the shushing in her flooded ears. She breathes again, and the exaggeration of the sound fills her, releases her.

My branches, she thinks. My branches are wide and firm, yet delicate, intricate, sensitive as flesh, clean and open to the air as two clear ramifying lungs. I am these trees, these elms — she loosens, breathes again, enfolding and dispersing the breath.

"Breathe." She hears her sister Nessa's tender voice intoning out of the past. "Breathe, Virginia, breathe."

And she does, heaving her breasts high above the water line and down again; she watches their ringed shorelines advance and recede over the puckered skin. She listens to the breath slowing, deepening. She thinks as the elms, of being the elms, healing the air. She thinks of her sister's hands on her chest those days so long ago in the sickroom, lightly resting, the fingers faintly exploring, as if reading the Braille of her brocaded dress. Distress. She raises her mouth above the water and says this aloud, quietly, "Distress. The dress."

Then, as if startled by the sound of her own voice, she sits upright with a great sloshing urgency, her buttocks squealing on the porcelain, her knees bucking, legs tensing straight and splashing. She listens to the *esses* of the spoken words hiss as they race round the lavatory, and she says them again, louder.

"Distress. The dress."

She cocks her head to one side, considers the sounds and meanings of words, the one creating the other, the sound of the thing being the thing, the original thing, blazing through the world in true spirit — *dress, distress.* The sound of it and the light of it as one. The wavelengths traveling in tandem.

And yet, she squints disapprovingly, the wretched intellect at work. Always the masculine mind interferes, sucking the magic out of sounds and shutting it into words. The very word for this, the academic word — onomatopoeia — sounds like what it is, a chained sprite falling down the stairs. She laughs at this, and the sound of her laugh pops around the lavatory.

She is breathing harder again, she notices. Too animated once more by the thoughts. Too many thoughts. Too fast. She tries to think again of the elms and calm herself. Calm, she tells herself. Calm. You cannot brook all of this at once. Again she thinks of Nessa's hands on her and the voice guiding her. She folds her hands in her lap, in the pool of water there. She drops her shoulders, circles her neck.

She stops abruptly, midturn, and looks up.

"That's it," she says, too loudly now, the outburst crashing back and forth between the tiled walls like a dropped pot.

"Eureka in the bath, you infernal Greek! I have it."

This she has absolutely shouted, and she regrets it at once. She puts her hand over her mouth like a child caught in a gaffe, for the noise will bring concerned footsteps and a careful knock on the door. But she will finish this quietly first. She puts a finger to her lips: "Shhhhh."

She shoots her eyes to the unlocked door, listens for a moment, then, satisfied, resumes.

So, the image to start. The perception of the world as it is, the phantasm, the flare of the visionary idea is flattened to a page by the male intellect. Controlled, categorized, c-a-t-a-l-o-g-u-e-d. The ethereal is quashed. Address, that beautiful oration announcing itself, becomes a dress feebly worn, becomes a picture of a dress in a catalogue.

Yes. She will begin her story like this, with a catalogue, where James — who will stand in part for herself, in part for her younger brother Adrian — the visionary, the dreaming boy with scissors, is cutting out the deflated picture of a man-made thing. A machine, perhaps, is most pointed, she thinks, a refrigerator, a wheelbarrow, a lawnmower, because that is all he is allowed, all that his pedantic, gloating father — their father — will grant him. But all the while the boy's mind, his hope, his lifeblood, is in the sea, just as hers was, and in the waves, the unreachable, the soothing finger of light, silvering each night across the bay.

The stroke of the lighthouse laid its caress.

She does not say this last part aloud, but it hums in her repeatedly, and she feels its hypnotizing hush. Her breath begins to pace itself again, quelling the kindled thoughts.

Caress. The stroke. The lighthouse laid its caress.

Her lips move over the music, making no sound, and a swell fills her chest, warming outward and through her, down her slackened arms and wrists and fingers to the very tips, which are touching now, five to five.

Gratified, she sighs.

Now there is the expected tap on the door, one soft knuckle, meek and respectful, but a touch alarmed in spite of itself. Leonard's voice is kind but firm, treading the balance of care and control.

"Are you there?"

He says this with the accustomed lilt, and she grins accordingly. It is one of their jokes, a relic of his Cambridge days, something the ruggers were meant to have called to each other down the field through cupped hands before kickoff. Where he would have heard this or judged the truth of it is, for them, most of the joke, since at college he, the spindly, bookish Jew of newsprint caricature (another joke), had been an intellectual of the proudest and most rarefied sort, as were all his closest friends. The Apostles, they had called themselves, joining the select and secret group. They had not been grasshoppers hanging about the rugby pitch. They had spent their days arguing about Plato.

She is still smiling fondly at this as she rings the appropriate response to Leonard's greeting, parting the syllables and rounding them with added plum to reassure him.

"Ra-*ther,*" she says.

There is a pause in which she can almost hear his relief, and then his encouragement attempting to displace it. This morning will go on as usual. Pat the head of your feral wife, she thinks, contain her and proceed, or so the regiments of doctors have always advised. He is only doing what they have told him to do, after all, or the few sensible things that he has managed to cull from their nonsense over the years.

Then, more gently than before, if this is possible, he says, "Have all the animals had breakfast?"

"Yeees," she drawls, with only a trace of impatience. "Bath always follows breakfast."

In truth, her breakfast tray lies mostly untouched beside the chair in her room, the bun pecked at as if by a marauding sparrow. The egg is still in its coddling cup, uncracked, the mug of milk has gone cold, its scorched meniscus wrinkled into a skin.

"Splendid," he says, as if replacing a prop stethoscope around his neck. "And the music?" he adds jauntily.

Obediently, she places her fingers on her wrist, counts the beats, which are eager now, but not uproarious.

"Positively funereal," she lies. "A veritable dirge."

"Love?" He prods, knowing he must push her for the fair answer.

She sighs loudly, bustling into the words, so that he will not hear the irritation in her reply.

"Coming down from the climax, dear heart. Not to worry. We are not at full tilt."

He places his right palm and his forehead very gently against the door.

"Promise?" he says.

"Promise," she echoes wearily.

He rests there for a moment, rolling his brow against the grain of the wood, fighting the momentary impulse to kick open the door, rush in, hoist her from the water by her throbbing wrists, drag her dripping and kicking into her room and belt her into

9

her armchair, beside which he knows the breakfast tray has long since been abandoned to the drying air, like the heap of last night's supper.

But the fury passes as quickly as it came, and he feels his sudden burst of will dissolve into the helplessness of his regard for her. Let her be, it counsels for the thousandth time. Let her be. She is where she is, and where she is you cannot follow.

So it is. He knows this is true. He has always known it. He thinks of the way she is in the world, of how her mind separates her from it even as it aids a deeper communion, and this helps him to relax. Let go.

He thinks of how, when they are out walking together in town, people, women, children stare and titter, discomfited by her; something in her slightly shabby, raffish style of dress, perhaps, or her distracted air of always being not quite there, that marks her out as one of the touched, the unlike. Why this makes people laugh he has never quite understood. But there is more of awe than ridicule in it, and he knows that it is really just a shortfall in them, an inability to compass her strangeness. They, too, cannot follow.

Yet, he reminds himself, as he so often must at times like this, when she is on the precipice of breakdown, her strangeness is just that. Other, not wrong. Not mad, or not wholly mad. Verging on it, yes, but she is there, in a real place nonetheless, threading the shadow line of thought where light and darkness meet, a line that is no line to speak of, and has abysses either side.

Yes. He knows all of this. Yet he cannot back away from the door. His palm is still there flat against it, reaching for her. Will you be all right? it pleads. Will we?

Thinking this, he smiles at his own need, his own willing part in the conjugation. He worships her oddity even as he worries it, wringing it through his mind like beads through his fingers. At last, he pulls his head away from the door, straightens himself as if one of the servants has come into the hall, though no one has. It is only her discernment he fears, even through the thick oak planking between them.

Superstition gets the better of him, even as his hand drifts toward the knob, then retreats: She will know what I am thinking. She has that gift. She knows the ciphers of my brain, just as she knows the secret speech of rocks and trees and the language of the light on them. Silliness, he chides himself, to think this way, but there it is.

He remembers her teasing him early in their courtship and in that first teetering year of their marriage, when he did not yet know what she was capable of. Taking his habitually trembling hand in hers, and looking contemplatively into the middle distance, she had simply tossed the atrocious cliché at him, or so he'd thought, as if he wouldn't know what it was.

"You are my rock," she'd said solemnly.

And he, hurt, not getting it, had answered flatly, "Yes, of course, and rocks don't speak or think or feel."

She had started violently at this as soon as he'd said it, turning on him and taking his gaunt face in her cold, searching fingertips. "Oh, but they do," she'd protested. "They do."

Trust her, says the voice of his experience now, and obediently he steps back from the threshold.

Now one of the servants, Nelly, does come halfway into the hall, craning at him to ask what she can do, clear the breakfast tray, perhaps, or expedite an exit from the bath. He shakes his head, and reluctantly she disappears. He waits for the slow weight of her to unburden the stairs and recede.

Satisfied, he addresses himself once more to the door.

"I'll leave you to the slow movement, then, shall I?" he inquires with a solicitude he cannot conceal, and a small smile at the double entendre. She herself has compared the creative act to defecation. He hopes she will hear the levity in his words and his willingness to leave her to it, however *it* transpires.

But she does not reply, and so he waits a moment longer.

Immediately he hears her standing in the tub, the cataract coming down loudly around her. He hears the squeak of one foot pivoting as the other reaches for the floor, and then the soft whiplash of it, too, pulling out of the water. She will not use a bathmat, despite the servants' frequent complaints, preferring instead to watch the runoff darken the slate beneath her, each stain unique as a cloud in which she can discern a recognizable shape.

He turns at last and begins his own slow descent of the stairs, reminding himself not to fret or feel dismissed by her silence: She is engaged elsewhere, he tells himself, not absent, not ignoring. Yet, in the craw of him, there is still the prick of a childish petulance that wants its way, attention paid.

The tyranny of illness, he thinks before he can stop himself. He takes it all. He props her up, he steps away, he ministers, he allows. He maneuvers, always within the confines of this hysteria.

He falters on the shame of the last word, stopping on the stairs and sitting on the warp of a worn step. Tracing the whorls of the wood with his fingertip remorsefully, he cannot believe that this, of all words, has come into his mind. He will not claim it as his own. It is too grotesque. These are the villains speaking in him, saying the worst conceivable thing.

It is their malevolent pull that he feels when he is sitting quietly in Fabian meetings or at some other solemn event. It is their call to mischief he hears goading him to shatter the decorum of his politic life. At such times, he sits, his weak hands wedged beneath his scrawny thighs, his caved torso rigid against the seizure that he fears will make him leap from his chair and begin shouting irrevocable curses that will banish him from the company of all right-thinking men *and women*.

Yes, women, he thinks. Right-thinking women.

Who, after all, is hysterical? It is your hands that are always shaking, he reminds himself bitterly, looking down at them as they lie on the step quivering.

He winces and turns on himself sardonically now, as if in the voice of some hectoring Greek chorus. Shake, you fool, and see to your wife, because she is your *superior* in every way, or have you forgotten? He feels the usual sting of this assessment, which is both his own and everyone else's, though it is never said aloud. He will always grind himself on the wheel of her genius, grappling for purchase against it, and the inadequacy it feeds in him.

Those who can't write, print — is that it? — says the same goading voice in him. He is digging into the step and pulling up a large sliver, which catches on the soft flesh beneath his fingernail and makes him pull back sharply. Was that the truer reason for acquiring the printing press? Not for her but for you? Bury your squelched attempts in a pile of worthier submissions, hers prime among them? But squelched by whom? Not by her, certainly, or not actively by her. By the image of her? Or the shadow it has cast over your — ah, there is that obstetrician's word again — hysterical imagination?

Envy is an opportunist, he knows, and in moments like these, when he has been tossed to the point of senselessness for weeks on the welter of her moods, he is susceptible to petty resentments; the jargon of those Neanderthal practitioners he has consulted over the years.

He can see them now, the innumerable boors of the medical

profession, hunkered behind their monstrous clawfooted mahogany desks. God, had he not heard enough of their smarmy club
talk about "women's troubles"? How little they understood and
how pompously they pronounced, as if it was all simply a matter
of bringing her to bear.

Yet clearly he is no better, carping their carps, and more shame-
fully still, doing so in the confines of his head where no one can
hear or hold him to account.

He stands again and hops angrily down the remainder of the
steps, punching at the sides of his thighs. Within three long, swift
strides he is in his study, with its anodyne fug of pipe smoke, damp
wool and old books. He breathes it, standing there, gazing fondly
round the room, the few prized possessions of his life in letters,
and his mind begins to clear.

He seats himself purposefully at his desk, and with his thumb
begins to strum one of the many reams of manuscript that lie before him in stacks, neatly spaced like city blocks seen from above.
The floorboards above him creak, and he casts his eyes up at the
ceiling, following the swift, light progress of her footsteps and
then the muffled yet firm closing of her door. He waits, but hears
nothing more.

He will not see her till the afternoon, if then, when they will
both abandon their labors for the outdoors, he in the garden,
where the plum trees need pruning and the vegetable plots weed-
ing, she on the downs, where she will stride out her demons and
shout their execrations to the air. He shifts in his chair, pencil in
hand, takes up the nearest pile and begins to read.

From its accustomed place in a wad on the floor, Virginia retrieves
the threadbare floral print dress that she so often wears when she
is working. Gathering it hastily between her thumbs and forefin-

gers, she places it like a wreath around her neck and shoulders, pulls her arms roughly through the sleeves and lets it fall loosely over her narrow hips.

The fabric, seldom washed, is grubby with use, oiled and inked and sweated in, so that it is as flanneled and funked as a beloved toy bear. When they are at each other, Leonard complains about this garment, its shabbiness, its ubiquity, its smell. He has dubbed it the Lambeth laydeez 'ousecoat, but she thinks of it more as an artist's smock, like the one Nessa sometimes wears.

The dress. Distress. The lighthouse lays its caress.

Absently, drifting in the rhythm of the phrase, she scans the breakfast tray. Standing over it, she stiffens, eyeing the delinquent bun as if it were a calling card left by one of those unctuous second-tier society women whom she somehow both needs and loathes.

It must be dealt with. But how?

She stares at it for a moment longer, hating it irrationally, for itself and for all that it represents, the blameless bread placed before her each morning like a reproach. Doctor's orders. The indignity of it, the intrusion. She feels her scalp prickle with indignation. Then, gripped by a sudden fury that some overseeing part of her knows is absurdly disproportionate, she seizes the bun and rips it to bits. Before she can stop herself and think — the lavatory would have been wise — she strides to the open window and hurls the pieces out.

She doesn't bother to see where they have landed, but she will have to check when she goes out this afternoon. It is the kind of thing Leonard will notice and say nothing about, though he will no doubt scratch it into his diary as diligently as he records every other assertion of her ill health.

Ah, well, she allows mockingly, one must do what one feels.

There are many reasons. Not just one, infallible, but varieties of sane response and a host of sensible premises behind them, whatever the logicians might say. But there is only one intimate to receive them, two if she counts Nessa, but lately she does not.

So, then, I count on misinterpretation instead. How, really, could it be otherwise? My food lies decimated in the azaleas, truly one-tenth dispensed, if that, and the remainder is for the birds. She smiles at the pun, hearing some fusty Victorian shrew exclaiming, "This breakfast is for the birds," or one of the servants, clearing away yet another unkempt meal, declaring, "Good lord, ma'am, but you do eat like a bird."

But then her mind snags more hurtfully on the birds, because it is in fact they who speak to her in the voices that no one else can hear. If only the bread would placate them, she yearns, or make their learned shrieking intelligible to someone, anyone, else. There is so much pain in this lack of understanding, so much terrified struggle in these fits that Leonard and the others see as mutinies. But it is concord she wants most, strives for so desperately in everything she writes. There must be a way, she urges herself each time, some way to inscribe the storm of her experience so that she will not have to be alone with it.

She thinks of John Clare's plaintive lines, and feels their same regret:

> . . . *Even those I loved the best*
> *Are strange — nay, they are stranger than the rest.*

She falls with a hollow thump into the worn armchair, which enfolds her like a mouth, the molded cushions tonguing the length of her like an indulgent mother cow. She places the lap desk across her knees, slides the pen into the yellow calloused groove between the first and second fingers, first and second knuckles of her right hand, steadies the paper with her left hand and poises the nib.

She looks up at the facing wall where a lozenge of nacreous light displays the shadow of a breeze-blown branch trembling. She gazes at it for a long moment, entranced, then drops her eyes to where her knobbled fist has already begun to make its slow, mesmeric way across the page. She follows it lovingly, indulgently, tilting her head to the side like a small child drawing her first sun. The trick, the quickness, is in the fingers, hinging tirelessly above the stylus like some huge and bloodless insect spinning out worlds. She loses herself in the motion, the pleasant scratch and whisper of the act, and, relinquishing herself wholly now to the illusion, she disappears.

10:47 A.M.

THEY ARE LYING on the narrow bed side by side, woman and girl, facing each other like mirror images, each propping the side of her head with the heel of one hand against the temple. The supporting arms are bent at the elbows. The opposing arms are stretched the length of each body, the wrists languid on the curve of the hips, the fingers loosely spanning the upper thighs. They are looking intently into each other's eyes, not besottedly, as lovers do, but studiously, as if examining rare stamps under a loupe.

You first, says Adeline, squirming to adjust her pose.

"Patience, little goat," Virginia chides, leaning in to place her lips playfully against the tip of the adolescent's nose. Adeline wriggles delightedly, then goes quite still again, softening her gaze so as not to blink.

"Now then, shall I begin?" says Virginia, bringing her own eyes very close to and even with Adeline's so that she can see all the shapes and shades in the hazel pinwheels of her eyes.

Adeline nods once, gravely.

"Very well. There is the black dot in the bottom half of the iris, exactly in the center."

My second pupil, Adeline says.

"Yes," answers Virginia, "through which you see the first world."

And what is the first world? Adeline asks, knowing the words that Virginia will say but needing to hear them again.

"The one that lies behind this one," Virginia obliges, dreamily.

Adeline sighs at the confirmation, relieved. *Yes.*

These answers, said and heard many times before, are the game between them, the reestablishment of sameness.

Adeline prompts again: *Is it very like?*

"Not at all like," Virginia says. "Quite different." She pauses tenderly to stroke Adeline's cheek. "But you must tell me. What do you see?"

Adeline drops her propping right arm and rests her head on the pillow, hugging it for comfort. She lets her eyes unfocus and glaze.

I see the man sitting at the end of Mother's bed, she begins, very slowly and precisely. *I see the darkened room, the heavy drapes, the bedclothes carefully arranged, the shape of Mother, laid out. I have never seen her lying down. Not ever before. But now she is perfectly still and straight. The composure of her face is . . .* Adeline falters here. She darts her eyes away and back. *Her face is like . . .* She breaks off, unable to go on, and so the other dredges up the description.

"An ecstasy of absence," Virginia says, smoothing the familiar phrase.

Adeline nods, and her cheek makes a soft breathy sound on the pillow. They lie there quietly for a moment, breathing. Virginia reaches over and brushes a loose strand of hair behind Adeline's ear.

"And what do you feel?" she asks.

The answer comes quickly this time, sharply, with the usual stab of self-reproach: *Nothing.*

She waits again, still stroking Adeline's hair, patiently, coaxingly, letting the somnolence of ritual take its effect. "What then?" she says at last.

I stand beside the head of the bed, bend and kiss her cheek.

Another pause for the seeing of it, fractured in their minds' eyes. Then Virginia asks,

"Which is like . . . ?"

Which is like cold iron, says Adeline, frowning. *Like kissing cold iron.* She closes her eyes wearily.

"Yes," Virginia confirms. "Yes."

The recitation is complete, the moment shrined. It casts its pale shadow on them like the watermark of an event too imprinted to erase.

This is where I remain, Adeline says, *and where I come to you.*

"Broken off," the other continues absently to herself, as if this were all written down somewhere word for word. "The seed of me that was then, and grew no further."

Adeline says nothing to this. She has no line. But after a long pause, she lifts her head, newly inspired, and asks brightly,

Do you remember Mr. Wolstenholme? The mathematician who used to come and stay with us every summer at St. Ives?

Virginia thinks for a moment. The name, the image of the man are fixed in her memory, yet the man himself, if there was such a thing, is obscure. He is only as she remembers him, sketched and kept, the placeholder for an idea.

"Of course," she says at last, fondly and only a little dishonestly. "The Woolly One. He sat in his chair and smoked and read and never spoke."

Yes.

Adeline lets herself down again on the pillow. Rolling on her back, she searches the canvas of the ceiling as if descrying there the image of what she is about to say.

But, she resumes, with the lurch of disclosure in her voice, *he did speak once.* She waits for the surprise of this to penetrate, then adds solemnly, *I have never told you this before.*

This falls between them awkwardly, but with the promise of something meaningfully withheld, the recovery of an event that Adeline has clipped out of time and stored in the hollows of her expurgated self.

She begins again dreamily, without prompting.

It was one of those washed late afternoons of late summer when the blue of the sky is so pale it feels as if it is fading away, but the sun is still fierce and small, glaring from its corner.

This is like something she would have written for practice in her diary, though if she did, it is lost, and Virginia has never found it among her things.

I was sitting on the lawn, squinting out at the waves in the bay, watching the whitish blue blossoms of foam spread and dissolve on the swells. I remember I was thinking that it was like watching lichens growing and dying on rocks, but in sped-up time.

"Good," Virginia whispers. "That's very good." She waits for more, but Adeline is snagged on the memory. "Go on," Virginia tells her soothingly. "You can."

Adeline blinks rapidly and sighs. She brings her hand to her throat for comfort, resting it on the birdbeat of the pulse.

It was strange to think this, she resumes hesitantly. *I remember being a bit startled by it, because I had never really had a thought like that before, and never one with such strange feelings attached to it. The world seemed to be speeding up and slowing down, going liquid and solid at the same time, and me with it.*

Virginia considers this. Yes, she thinks, that's right. That's right. I remember it now.

"Yes," she says aloud. "I remember."

And Adeline continues more confidently, the words coming now without hesitation, the memory tumbling through.

I felt as though I had stepped — like Alice — into another world, or a slice of one that was showing through a gap in this one. It was so odd and hypnotizing, and the longer I looked, the odder and more hypnotizing it became, until I began to worry that I might be having some sort of fit or break or collapse. I didn't know what, and it frightened me.

It frightened me only a little at first, but then the fear began to grow, getting larger with every breath, spreading like a cramp inside me and then breaking into a rush all through me. I could feel myself becoming physically weaker and weaker, less and less able to rouse myself or squirm or even go rigid against it. And then, finally, I lost the fight. I was paralyzed. I could not move.

Virginia lies back on the bed, seeming to stare into the same imaginary place and time that are locked in the girl's memory.

I wanted to get up and go inside, she hears Adeline saying. *Go anywhere to get away from this thing, whatever it was, and I tried several times, but I couldn't. I could not even get my little finger or my lips to move so that I could make a sign or cry out for help to whoever might be near.*

I was helpless, cut off by this kind of horrid waking seizure. I was panicking and trapped, as if I was being held down by some huge invisible weight. I began to think that I must be dying, and that this must be what dying was like, the mind going wild, and the body a sack. The horror of it went on in my head for what seemed like a very long time, with all my worst, most frantic thoughts and feelings swirling and swarming inside this corpse that my body had become.

This is all very familiar now, Virginia thinks, her body beginning to display the agony that Adeline describes. She is stiffening on the bed, as if the event is passing through her. Adeline is going on quickly now, without pause.

I could not put these opposites together. I did not want to. I fought with all the strength I had left, even though I knew it was diminishing all the time. Knowing this only made me fight harder with less, and with no relief.

But then, after a terrible struggle that seemed to last forever, though I suppose it must have lasted only a few minutes or even seconds, this awful whirlwind inside me sucked up the last of my resistance, and I was suddenly . . .

She pauses to get this right.

. . . well, I suppose I was suddenly released. I gave up. I went slack under the fear. I stopped trying to push it away or avoid whatever it was bringing me to.

She stops again, not quite believing her own words, her eyes seeking out Virginia's for the necessary contact, but Virginia is too deep now in her mind and in the past to act her part. Adeline must find her there, and by talking.

And so, suppressing the doubt, she goes on.

Then the whole nightmare . . . it somehow turned perfectly tame in an instant. I went numb all over and weightless and the terror became a kind of nothingness that drew me into it and calmed me. All the parts of myself that had fought loosened their hold on me. Questions, worries, beliefs, doubts — all my thoughts — fell away one by one until I was left there floating, limp and colorless and empty.

"But aware," says Virginia, rushing in to finish the thought. "Absolutely aware. Without sense. Without thought. Without will. And happier — more at peace — than you had ever been."

Adeline does not answer. She has broken off, breathlessly, her chest rising and falling, flustered under her hand, which has moved from her neck to her sternum and curled itself into a fist. She has only a little more to say, but it is the most important part. She does not want to leave it for Virginia.

I was in a trance like that, she says, the words coming quickly once more, *drifting blissfully for I don't know how long, when all at once in a kind of mindless but somehow knowing flash I understood.*

She is speaking now in Virginia's language, the adult mind changing with the child's, but the words are still in her mouth, running out.

I knew what was happening. I was not having a fit or a breakdown. I was not even having a vision. I was the vision. I wasn't watching the foam and the waves and the lichen and the rocks change places and repeat. I was not finding their pattern . . . Do you see? . . . I had been woven into it. There was no separation. No girl on the lawn and no sea out there, no world with people and things and spaces and thoughts between. There was just this boundless, flowing sameness beneath everything, and I was part of it.

"Yes," Virginia answers dreamily. Her eyes, like Adeline's, are no longer engaged. They are somewhere else, and she is smiling absently at what she has heard, entranced by the recovery, amazed and not amazed at all, but pleased to find this event perfectly preserved, shelved inside her, and retrieved intact.

They are the same now — almost — the woman and the girl, but Adeline is eager to remain apart, just that little bit separate, and poised to finish her side of the story.

Without my noticing it, she says, animated once more, *Old Woolly had gotten up from his chair, come all the way across the lawn and sat down beside me. I knew he was there only when he put his hand on my arm, his whole heavy hand on my forearm, and then squeezed. I looked at him, still half through the dream, and I thought he must be a ghost. He appeared so suddenly, and he was so pale and startled-looking.*

It was so unlike him, she says, touching Virginia's shoulder, demonstrating what she wants to say. *Well, you know he never got up from his chair except for meals or if the weather was turning, and he never put his hand on anyone's arm, especially not like that, as if he didn't know himself that he was doing it until he was pulling away.*

Virginia nods her agreement and places her own hand on her shoulder, gently covering Adeline's.

And he pulled away so suddenly, Adeline continues, encouraged by the touch. *As if he had been given a shock. But he never took his eyes from my face.*

She turns to look at Virginia full on, adding,

He looked at me almost as you do, searching me, but he was also afraid, so afraid and completely without understanding. He looked for such a long time and in such a panic that I thought perhaps he had been paralyzed or struck just as I had been.

He looked . . . how can I explain this? She searches for the words, scowling down at herself as if the obstruction is in her bowels or some farther reach of the illusion. She lights up triumphantly when she finds them.

He looked as if he was trying ... with the whole ... the whole force of his intellect to reconstruct something ... like an event ... an experience ... no, no a revelation ... yes, a revelation, like mine, that had been made to him whole, all at once, a moment before, but which had shattered against his categories and was now lying in pieces behind my eyes.

She is well satisfied with this description, and slows, warming to it now with the full power of her instinct.

He didn't speak for a long time, but finally, when he did speak, it was in a terrible hoarse whisper that was so dry and far away and scratched with pain that it didn't sound like human speech. "Sadness," he said. "So much sadness." *That was all. Just that. And then streams of tears burst from his eyes and fell into his woolly beard, and he began shuddering with these awful wrenching sobs.*

Adeline's voice dies away here, and the sight of her fades for a moment with it. Virginia, returning to her present self, alone in the sterile room, recites, very slowly,

> *... the waves draw back, and fling ...*
> *With tremulous cadence slow, and bring*
> *The eternal note of sadness in.*

Yes, she remembers sweet Woolly now. His reading of her that day, his consumption of her, as if he had sucked the sadness through her like a liquid meal and been sickened by it. It was the sadness she herself had suckled from the world without diminishing it, had consumed and likewise been sickened by.

It had been there for a long time, this malaise, ebbing and flowing without warning or cause, or none that she had ever discerned. But she had not recognized it, not known that it could be conveyed, not until that day on the lawn with Woolly, when the transmission was unmistakable.

And the poem, too. Matthew Arnold's mesmerizing poem. She had read it so many times as a child, and heard it, those three haunting lines in particular, their hard, insistent wistfulness, ringing in the crash and recession of the tide outside her window in St. Ives as she lay in the dark nursery for hours, listening. It was in the sea, the poet had said, in the waves, the ceaseless, torpid repetition of the waves, which themselves were so much more than waters. It was there beneath and constituting everything, as she now, and she then — as Adeline — had understood.

And so it would be in her rendering. The shadow play of memory and time, etched, as it was in life, in the dream language of light. The past is here now, she asserts, and I, this manifestation, am in the past.

Yes, the past, she repeats, and Adeline, who is the girl that she once was, the bright Victorian girl shut behind dark paneled doors with her thirteen, fifteen, eighteen years of life and a Greek lexicon. She is the girl stopped in time who could not speak or feel at the side of her dead mother's bed. She keeps the cold, clear information of those days, unclouded by revision or the lies of age. She is there still, communicating, conjured by this strange Virginia, who is the woman she did not become.

Here, now, that same Virginia is thinking of those old days again, both fondly and not — of her lessons opened on the desk, and the lexicon, and Father downstairs in a temper curled like a gargoyle, glowering over his own dry books and papers.

She thinks of the word itself, "lexicon," and chops it now to her fancy, though it is not technically correct. LEX/ICON. Word idol.

Idolatry of words. The sacred word, which, of course, she ponders, is John. The Gospel of John.

> *The Word was with God, and the Word was God. In him was life; and the life was the light of men. And the light shineth in darkness; and the darkness comprehended it not.*

There is the expression she is aiming for. This is the book she wants to write about her childhood. The light as language, the language as light, penetrating darkness, and the despair that lies enshrouded in the world, appearing to her. That alone is the revelation. Poor, plodding Woolly, who could not contain it, and she, equally untrue, gaping out at the bay where the lighthouse stood, inconsequent in daylight.

This is the only deity she accepts. God as word as light. This is the only phrase of any gospel that resonates, and it is rightly incongruous to the rest, this strange and surprising rendering of God in the Greek: *logos.*

I was so happy there, Adeline says, appearing again. She is sitting upright now on the bed, bouncing lightly, her arms and legs crossed playfully, like a Red Indian. *I was so happy there by the seaside, with Mother and Father and all the children together.*

"*We* were so happy there," Virginia corrects, smiling into the past.

Were you there? I don't remember.

"I will be," Virginia answers, placing a hushing finger against her own lips.

Adeline smiles and does the same. *I will keep our secret.*

"You do. You have always done. And I will write it down. I will put it into a story, so that we may be free of it."

To the Lighthouse, she thinks. That is the right name for this journey.

Adeline grimaces, as though the idea of putting their secrets on the page discomfits her deeply. But it is not that.

"What is it?" Virginia asks, alarmed.

It hurts, Adeline groans, and presses her hands to her abdomen.

Virginia leans over and puts her hand there, too. "Here?"

Yes, Adeline whimpers, moving her own hands away and allowing Virginia's to rest there instead.

"Is it the pains?" Virginia asks, moving her hand to Adeline's forehead to see if there is a fever. "Like before?"

Adeline nods, still grimacing.

"Does it hurt here, too?" she asks, pressing her palm and the back of her hand by turns against Adeline's brow.

A little, Adeline replies, her face relaxing slightly as the worst of the cramp subsides.

"Better?" Virginia asks, removing her hand.

Yes, says Adeline weakly, taking a deep breath. As she lets it out, she drops her chin to her chest. Virginia moves her hand to the back of Adeline's neck and begins to massage it.

"There now," she whispers, repeating Nessa's healing words. "Breathe, dearest. Breathe. It will go."

Adeline breathes for a few moments, resting there and letting her head bob gently under the pressure of Virginia's touch. Then, with a sudden rush of anger, she sits up again and, glaring at Virginia, says,

Why must it hurt?

At first Virginia does not reply. This is not something she wishes to discuss. They have done so before. And anyway, Adeline is not green. She is very young, but she knows what she is about. She knew well in advance of the event what to expect at the onset, mostly because Nessa, being older and having been through it herself, prepared her. Still, she has been frustrated, upended by this abrupt and unwelcome end to the carefree reign of girlhood. She wants to be soothed.

As Virginia watches her face, reading all the feelings that are passing so transparently across it, Adeline sighs and looks away, as if to deflect the scrutiny. But she looks back again quickly to insist on an answer. She appears more confused now than annoyed, her features wrinkled into a pout around the tense determination of her mouth. She is touchingly unsure and inquisitive, like someone who has had her heart broken for the first time and thinks that if she can only pinpoint the source of this curious discomfort she can make it go away. Virginia is moved by the guilelessness of this and smiles.

"You know why it must hurt, little goat," she answers, kindly but firmly. "So that we might bear a child."

I know that, Adeline exclaims, exasperated. She looks away again, her eyes filling with tears. *But why must it hurt so much?*

"I don't know," Virginia concedes. "That I do not know. But you must endure it all the same, as I do, without knowing or under-standing. You must be strong."

She says this confidently, like a mother, as Nessa said it to her, but she is sensitive to Adeline's complaint. The severity of the af-fliction has always troubled her, and the unfairness of it, too, which had always made her feel resentful of Nessa, and by exten-sion other girls, whose intimate lives she was not acquainted with but whom she assumed, like Nessa, were more the norm, and had monthlies that were far less debilitating than her own.

For Nessa, she remembers, there had been no affliction to speak of. Nessa's monthlies were simply there for a short time, and then they weren't. They were dealt with as swiftly and summarily as all other minor dramas of that time of life. Head colds, pimples, the periodic bleed, they were all one to Nessa, inconvenient, but unremarkable and, most important of all, passing.

Unlike Virginia — very much unlike her — Nessa had seemed to glide effortlessly into womanhood, bearing the burdens of her sex lightly on her shoulders, even flourishing them like a cape, and duly coaxing forth her share of muddled young bulls.

Nessa had found their entrance into society as tiresome as Virginia had — they had done much of it together, sitting alone, wilting in the corners of countless festive and outlandish rooms, longing for rescue — but Nessa had carried it off infinitely better. Nessa was prettier, or had been considered so, and this had made it easier for her to hide in plain sight. She had been steady, patient and unprepossessingly stylish enough for both of them, holding herself straight, as their mother had advised, remaining as quietly decorous and unthreateningly beautiful as a porcelain vase, while Virginia had sat beside her like some lesser appurtenance, dull and lifeless to the eye, but fuming inside, digging her nails into her palms and stifling her cries.

Nessa had done it all so very well: come up, come out, taken on, shrugged off, found art and pursued it, married before she was thirty (and a man of the arts as well as one of her choosing, no less), had children, took lovers, and now lived an open, charmed bohemian life at home and abroad. There were no seams showing in her world, only the unbroken expanse of her fulfillment, stretching effortlessly, endlessly and enviably in every direction.

Has Nessa any children? asks Adeline, tugging at the root of Virginia's thought and squeezing it, with a child's unfailing accuracy and indifference, precisely where it is most inflamed. Virginia can't help chuckling at the cruel, inveterate ways her mind has of tearing at itself.

"Why, yes," Virginia says with sarcastic cheerfulness, "indeed she does. Nessa has three children: Julian, Quentin and Angelica. And — would you believe? — they are all now older than you."

Truly?

"Yes. Truly."

All Stephens?

"No, Bells. Nessa's husband's name is Bell."

Oh . . . And do you like them?

"Indeed, I like them very much. Julian especially. He's the oldest and very clever."

Cleverer than I?

"No, little one." Virginia smiles. "Just different. He's a boy."

Like Thoby?

"Yes, in fact. Julian reminds me very much of Thoby."

Adeline accepts this without comment. She knows that their elder brother, her adored Thoby, died young. They have spoken of it before, and while Adeline seems in some manner to have acknowledged the fact, she has kept it aside and separate. She has not let it in. When they mention Thoby now, they do so like this, briefly and carefully, but his name is always drenched in love. Virginia suspects that for Adeline, halted as she is in the past, Thoby is still there, alive as ever, or nearly so.

Adeline has never asked about the others, not even their youngest brother Adrian, who seems to be more of a figment in her memory than even Mr. Wolstenholme, though Adrian is still very much alive and well. She has certainly never ventured to inquire about their half siblings, George, Stella, Gerald and Laura. Virginia is grateful for this, because she cannot bring herself to think, much less discuss the fate, of Laura in particular, their father's daughter by his first wife. It is simply too awful to contemplate, and too close. Laura had lived with them for several years, and even gone with them to St. Ives, but she had been put away in an asylum several years before their mother died.

With Nessa, of course, it is different. Adeline can feel her fully, and she is still amazed to hear that her playmate sister is really all grown up with children of her own. She is troubled by it, too, and makes the inevitable comparison to herself.

How strange, she murmurs, looking down dolefully for a moment at her empty lap. But then, looking up again, she adds with the same innocent incisiveness as before, *And you?*

Again Virginia smiles, thinking how satisfied her enemies would be to know that she is every bit as cutting with herself as she is with all the unsuspecting greenhorns she humiliates at parties.

"No," she concedes, "I have not been well enough for that."

Oh, Adeline murmurs guiltily, looking down once again at herself, the body that is bewilderingly to blame.

"It's all right," Virginia says, taking up one of Adeline's hands. "Really. It is."

Adeline nods reluctantly, knowing that it is not really all right at all, but that there is nothing she can do.

So, then, there is only me? she offers, meaning to condole, but her voice is pitched greedily like a spoiled only child's, delighted to reaffirm that her mother's affections will not have to be shared.

"Yes. There is only you," Virginia agrees, adding somberly, "and the work."

But I am the work, Adeline cries. This is one of the things she has learned, but still, she needs to hear it said.

"That's true," Virginia obliges. "You are the work."

When I can do it, she thinks. When the pains and the headaches and the episodic flares and despondencies don't keep us down. When we are not racked in this dilapidated body, leaking through a cracked brain, whirling without sleep, fingers picking purposelessly at food. And all the while, these people that I am, we are trapped and talking to ourselves, both as we are now and as we were then, because there is no one else.

So, yes, Virginia sighs, you are the work. But when we are well again. When we are not mad. No, she catches herself here, we are not mad. *I* am not mad. I am not. I will not be that woman out of a novel from the last century, locked away and wailing in the attic. I am now, and I am putting it down as testament. My past, my people, my evidence, my will.

9:54 A.M.

LEONARD IS SITTING at his desk thinking about numbers. Household accounts. The cost of things. Money coming in, going out. This is all quite personal to start, as it must be. What they spend. What they can afford. Down to the shillings and pence. To him, this is not only responsible, but indicative. It tells the story of their life, any life, both as history and moment, however one may dream.

After all, he reaffirms soberly, dreaming is the luxury of order. Art is the beneficiary of businesses well run.

He can make such heretical pronouncements to himself here, straightedge in hand, drawing the table of the year's earnings and expenditures. Yet he wonders how thoroughly it divides him from his peers, if at all, or if, to the properly initiated, this is just the rusty old paradox of political economy, known and politely overlooked, like the flaws in the people one loves.

Well, not by all. Not overlooked by all, but by the shrewder ones, surely, the most learned progressives, like himself, for whom a premise is a premise like it or not, and its conclusion inexorable. Not that this "problem," call it, of how money works in the real world takes the form of a syllogism. Far from it. It is more like the problem of the missing mass, which academic friends of friends in the field have only begun to whisper about in circles, and frown.

It is not at all formulated, this notion, especially in his outsider's understanding — he won't yet write it down — but for his purposes it works. The new physics, the new economics, stymied alike by inconsistency. Mass or the masses, same difficulty, neither the universe nor the populace behaves predictably. They don't compute.

It is just the kind of argument they always had as undergraduates at Cambridge, and still do when they gather, smoking and drinking, shouting over each other and dissolving in fits of affectionate laughter. He has kept them all very close — Strachey, Keynes and Forster in particular — because he has never found anything to equal the pleasure or intelligence of their company, and the reminder they give of how it was to be truly intellectual and young and eager to change the world. Stephen, too — Virginia's brother Thoby — would have remained one of his closest confidants from those days had he not died of typhoid so tragically young.

These college men are all that save Leonard from the drab realities of his agitant life. It irritates him just to think of them, the true believers. These horrid little hobgoblins of the movement are a plague to him, a threat to the viability of the Left, to which he is giving his lifeblood. They are a grim and tedious lot, the Leninist cortege, as he has dubbed them, with their red kerchiefs flying and their manifestos clutched to their breasts, trudging all the way from the Finland Station to Finchley Station, spouting the creed of their dead savior without so much as stumbling over the pitfalls of common sense. They are puritanical idiots to a one, dried up, dreary monomaniacs who don't have the brains among them to see that they have simply substituted one apotheosis for another.

"Your messiah," he so often wants to shout at them, "has simply trimmed his beard."

Humorless, cultureless, imaginationless, they are a breathing contradiction in terms. But then, he supposes, he is hardly different, or has become so, even if, in his case, it has all been whiskeyed and watered down to a kind of acceptable upper-crust socialism. Strachey—or Lytton, as he more often calls him now that Virginia has mostly rid them all of the habit of calling their former school-mates by their surnames (he must remind himself more often with Keynes and Forster to call them Maynard and Morgan)—Lytton calls him the armoire revolutionary.

"There you are, dear liar," he teases, his distinctive castrato voice emanating from deep within the immense russet curtain of his beard, "sitting safe within the walls of your bought privilege, thinking the thoughts, writing the screeds that only the fed, housed, rested and leisured can possibly indulge."

It is all infuriatingly true, but in Lytton's mouth it also manages to be very amusing. He and Lytton, at least, can argue it through the way he likes to, half in earnest, half tongue in cheek, and this is as indispensable to Leonard now as it has always been. His sanity depends on it. Lytton's wonderful feistiness, combined with his penchant for never taking anything too seriously, can encompass it all quite amicably. This helps Leonard to maintain the perspective he needs; the view that so many of his colleagues pointedly lack.

He remembers that he had actually said something along these lines to Lytton not a week ago. They had been in Lytton's study at his newly acquired retreat, Ham Spray, lounging after dinner, just the two of them, a lesson in contrasts. There was Lytton, pale as a statue, bespectacled and languid as ever, reclining with a crumbling mid-nineteenth-century edition of *Julius Caesar* in his hand, from which he had been reading aloud. Then there was Leonard, Sephardic, sharp-featured and irascible, crouching on a footstool like a crow. They had segued jaggedly from the heights of Mark Antony's funeral oration to Leonard's far less lofty political preoccupations.

"The insufferable irony of it has been there from the start," Leonard had wailed, which, as usual, had only made Lytton squirm with glee at the prospect of yet another opportunity to needle his old friend for being such a fussbudget. "Marx in the British Museum library, comfortably immured in the embrace of an empire"—Lytton had raised his eyebrows at this, but Leonard had ignored it—"what a farce. There he was, kicking holes in his sanctuary, which, of course, speak of the bloody devil, profit and exploitative labor had built. Can these Bolsheviks not see this?"

"My dear boy," Lytton had drawled wearily, "once upon a time you could not see it either, or have you forgotten already the errors of your morbid youth?" He cleared his throat archly here, in the Strachey way, to suggest that perhaps not all of these errors were entirely or so far in the past.

"Yes, yes," Leonard had stammered, "but—"

"But," Lytton had interrupted, putting an enragingly pedantic emphasis on the *t* and then leaving the rest of his objection to make itself.

Leonard smiles thinking of it now, how easily Lytton has always been able to rile him, because he knows him too well, and because, as he had always done so effectively among the Apostles,

Lytton could devastate a foolish conceit with a single word and leave them all roaring.

And so, now, with the same damning terseness, there is Lytton's "but"—they would have laughed, too, over this pun—hanging there, posing the question that is too obvious to need asking outright. Marx, it says. Yes him. *But* you? What about *you?* After all, as you yourself have just been so clever as to point out, what could be more bourgeois than scholarship?

"Days and luxurious days of it," he hears Lytton saying, rolling his outstretched hand through the air, "in the quiet of the *cordon sanitaire.*"

In short, Leonard's life. And in Sussex, no less. Social justice. "*Pah,*" Lytton had scoffed by way of conclusion. And, of course, he was right, Leonard thinks now, a little defensively. A fool's errand run by a hypocrite. And yet, he would run it all the same, even as Lytton laughed.

Yes, it is all so useless and absurd, he concedes, and all the more so because he proceeds, knowing this, but refusing, purely for the sake of his Jew's conscience—is that it?—to quit. There, at least, is a guilt he can quantify: "And how like a Jew of you to think so," he can hear some Tory prig griping. But he does not even twist his lips at such remarks anymore. They are too ingrained, as old as the old religion itself, and the mind of Europe, which, he knows from experience, has been jaundiced for almost as long.

He is what he is and will always be, a Hebrew who got in, as the dons at Trinity no doubt used to put it, muttering to each other over tea. The others, his adopted (or was it adopting?) group, the whip-tongued gentiles of the university, are what they essentially are, too—inveterate anti-Semites to the core—and always will be, though they have been made less rudely aware of it. Even Virginia, as well as Thoby, of course, had been tarnished in the same way by their parents', by their whole people's, views on the subject. Lytton, too, carries it still, as so many Englishmen of his class and upbringing do, in the same rear pocket as his misogyny, his pederasty and the remnant sting of the lash on his backside.

"Coins of the realm, I'm afraid," some helpful schoolmaster had once told Leonard when he was just a boy starting out, trying to make his way, an outlander at home, held apart among the main. All these years and a world war later, he knows that this is still the case.

Anglo-Saxons are a tribal people, he thinks sourly, however hyphenated their provenance. No escaping it. They drink, they dine, they remain faintly dismayed by his presence — the nostrils at times give this away. They poke fun as only the English can, relentlessly, good-naturedly, without saying a word — or not one to the purpose. That would be rude, naturally. Not cricket.

But beneath it all, their acid presumption runs. He has no trouble imagining the scene, played out in a thousand drawing rooms across the land, drawing rooms that are exactly like so many of those he has been in and left, with the subtle dusting of racial distaste on his shoulders. He can see it now, the pudding-faced, public-schooled country squire in his quintessential milieu, standing by the fire in his plus fours, leaning on the mantel, riding crop raised in his hand, making it plain, at last, in unmixed company:

"The secular Jew is the ideal revolutionary, always has been. He is, by nature, a money-grubbing, sanctimonious intellectual. He can't help it. But now, with his side locks and his yarmulke thrown off, he must put his obsessions somewhere. In place of his Torah and his dead God, he has put his *Kapital* and his higher cause. And what — can you guess — is this newfangled Shylock's one unshakable belief? What is the great insidious truth and solution that

has squirmed out of this wily bookworm's brain and is now ooz-
ing its way across the civilized world? Why, of course, that wealth
must right the wrongs of history."

Leonard catches himself sharply on the end of this, snapping
the ruler against the desk and groaning to himself: Oh, leave off,
can't you? But he does not have Lytton's gift for levity.

And he can't leave it, of course, because at bottom he is that
same godless Jew who can't help himself. Yet he is also the establishment, or the product of it. He was schooled among these
landed Philistines. No wonder, then, he can neither leave well
enough alone nor break free. He is much too high-winded to shut
up. And so he keeps on, being himself, slipping, ever the wily Jew,
through the loopholes in his contradictions while sidestepping his
abiding self-contempt.

He talks to himself like this half the day, every day, round and
round, full of debate, half abashed, half thrilled by his insights,
which he then scrupulously writes down. How clever, says the
wordy boxer in his brain, patting himself on the back for a stout
showing. But the rest of him is there, too, shamed by the rebutting
punch, bent around the better man's fist.

Even Lytton would not say it quite this way — there is too much
fondness between them — but he implies as much, and Leonard
puts it to himself in the harshest terms in his own voice. Useless,
it says, pathetic, one more sedentary snob lip-serving the cause of
the common man for the sake of his own self-image.

He glares at the mess on his desk, the papers, the paper clips,
the pens, the books, the ashtrays, the pipes, the pale blue stationery, all the twee accoutrements of his class and lifestyle, and observes caustically: This whole ridiculous midden is all just more
rubbish to the rubbish collector in the street, and rightly so. Too
bloody rightly so.

Ah, well, he sighs, stretching his arms above his head and lightening slightly. It doesn't matter. So what if none of these mock-heroic struggles on paper will make the slightest difference? Who cares if none of this will be taken seriously by anyone other than my debate society friends, or remembered by anyone at all? I could play table tennis all my days, I suppose, he thinks, and achieve the same result. Lytton would approve.

He winces a little at the defeatism in this, but then smiles again, remembering, after all, how Lytton did once phrase it.

"You're stuck with it, I'm sorry to say, Woolf, as trying as it can be — and, heavens, don't I know it — but it's simply how you think."

Lytton had paused here wryly, in his typical style, the great bush of his facial hair almost but not quite hiding the smirk that he could never deny himself.

"This is the boring through-line of your mind, alas," he'd said drolly, rubbing his hands along his thighs. "Which is, by the way, boring in both senses — dull and skewering."

This last bit was yet another set piece of Lytton's delivery, the kind of parenthetical aside he always threw in, a grace note to the main dig, because it delighted them both. Leonard had giggled, as usual, at Lytton's flirtatious way, though he had done so, also as usual, with misgivings, because he had known that this was not an attitude or a sound he could reproduce under any other circumstances. Not even with Virginia.

It was theirs alone, his and Lytton's, one of many small but precious vulnerabilities they shared. He'd let these tender intimacies stand, because they had done so for such a long time, and because he needed to maintain in adult life the kind of closeness with another man that he had so enjoyed in his youth. But he did so now less easily than he once had, and against his wiser judgment. Every unguarded portion of himself leaves him more open to the ravages of loss.

His feelings, he thinks, looking down again at his handiwork, are not like all these tables and charts and arguments, subject to his need for control. He can feel himself nearly choking on this reminder of love, as he hears Lytton's jolly, lilting voice summing up "the fierce and lugubrious mind of the Woolf."

"Sorry, old man," he'd said, at last setting aside his *Julius Caesar* with a sly grin. "But there's just no stopping it. It's like some heinous carnival spit, your brain, turning over and over the same charred carrion. Poor fellow. I do sympathize, but there it is."

It has always been a good joke, and a needed one, but it does not change the fact.

Overriding it all, he hears his father chiding with his clarifying mind, as he so often did over supper with his wife and brood of nine sitting awed. It is his father's blood ethic that boils in Leonard's veins, forcing him back always to the same ideal, even while he sees through it.

To concede failure, and so relatively early in life, that is a sin against suffering, surely? This is what he has always said in his own defense, and all teasing aside, it is a view Lytton, Keynes, Forster, Bell and all the others share. It is what defines them as a group, their belief, and their insistence, held over from the Apostles, but perfected in their soirées: Everyone must speak clearly and honestly always, saying precisely what he *or she* means, and only that. They — Bloomsbury, as they are called — have been abused by society's dogs, branded as precious and self-indulgent aesthetes who are not in any way serious about real life. But this is untrue, philosophically and demonstrably untrue, and the lie of it makes him angry. Yes, they have had their sport, their fun-making, down-dressing and hoaxes, but they have never been frivolous or disinterested. They have always cared.

What are people like him for, he has always said, if not for this? The effort, the attempt to work out in the closed room what has gone wrong in the trenches? Is this in no way laudable? He thinks of the many ifs this entails. Even if implementing all this higher good is just a dream, even if whatever paltry sand hill of progress he and his cohorts erect is sure to be swept away with the next war's tide, and finally, even if entropy is the inescapable rule, who can live without illusion?

He can't.

She can't.

For a moment, the thought of Virginia holds him suspended as he conjures up her face, with its looming-browed sleepwalker's eyes, staring at him through the rushing hours of the day. No, she is not Lytton. She is not a man. She does not have a man's conviction, his command, his stoic forbearance. But she has her own amalgamation — inventive, surprising, new — and he loves her for it all the same. It complements and comforts him in ways that Lytton and the others do not and cannot. Those eyes of hers have seen right the way through the kaleidoscope, well into the belly of illusion, but they have also seen too much of this world, which illusion cannot touch.

Thinking this, he comes back to the day's first notion — art as the beneficiary of businesses well run — and he adds to it something far more personal, the fruit of his current thinking. The role he plays in her life, and she in his. This morning, in the bath, he resented her privacy, her shutting him out, but now he asserts it in a different way, seeing that they are doing, each in his or her own idiosyncratic way, the same thing.

Their life, their bond, their work and their circle of closely kept friends are about one thing: maintenance of the necessary illusion.

It is what he does every day, for her and for himself, in order to go on. And she, in turn, does it for him and for herself for the same reason. And that is also why she falls so hard when she falls, because she, too, knows that when the scrim falls away, all of their pondering and their ponderous scribbling is futile. At those times, she knows it better than he. But sometimes, in denial, or in the fury of her dream, she finds the strength to go on with the charade. For how long he cannot say, nor can she.

It is the most tenuous strand between them, as well as the staunchest, the one they cannot break, however tortuously they twist it. It is also the only real argument they have — managing this sustaining falsehood — in a thousand times and forms, the same tug of war where neither stands nor falls, but both are dug in to the waist, resisting. In this, theirs is a marriage like all marriages, he presumes, an embattlement of foxholes. And the tether between? Well, he can't help invoking Lytton again: "That is the free means of torture doled out with the vows. One is given just enough rope to harangue, but not to hang by." That is the sum of it, hilarious and difficult, though his own way of putting it is, as usual, more sedate. Together they uphold a fantasy that upholds them both.

The subject is inexhaustible. Marriage. It is on everyone's mind, even — he smiles fondly — the filthy minds of buggers. He, accordingly, has put a great deal of thought into it. Marriage is a black box. Someone said that once. He cannot remember who. But it is true. So very true. No one else can know what goes on inside a couple's life together, or untwine the cat's cradle of intimacy that weaves between husband and wife. The couple themselves cannot really know, though daily their hands jigger the threads. They can know only in one sense, kinetically, habitually, as hands do, performing expertly and without thought a task they have repeated many times. But there remains the great riddle of personality, and how to domesticate it.

This has always been of particular interest to Virginia in her work. It is the substance of *Dalloway*. How do you make romance into a way of life? Can you? Especially when there is so much confusion in what you feel. At times, thankfully, it can seem clear and singular, as when you are sitting in the parlor of an evening, smoking by the fire and thinking, I am content. But far more often it is mangled and alloyed, or it does not come through at all, because sorting out the junk heap of your heart is more than you can manage most days. So you leave it dark.

Virginia had written as much in *Dalloway*: *What can one know even of the people one lives with every day?*

And the answer is: very little. Only what one knows by rote, and the rest is wisps and guessing, a mist of fogs and foreign atmospheres that may, when you're lucky, burn as bright and enchantingly as the boreal lights, but may as likely stir up a tempest, or cast a gloom, grim and suffocating as a mine.

This is one thing that Lytton will never understand, even knowing Virginia and him as he does. Lytton had chosen not to marry, as so many of his fellow unfortunates had done — using a wife for cover and then keeping on as before, having assignations on the sly in alleyways and cheap hotels, avoiding arrest. Lytton had been honest enough in that. He is living with Carrington, but it is a knowing arrangement. Both of them are having their affairs with other men. They are maintaining their own illusion, perhaps, but it is not the same.

When it had come to magnetizing Virginia and Leonard, way back in the dark days of the Edwardian lacuna, as they had dubbed it — 1901 to 1910 — the marriage question had turned into a very strange ball of wax with Lytton. It had been an odd, odd business all the way round. Leonard does not like to recall it in detail — he finds the melodramatic highs and lows of his youthful confessions, almost all of which were made to Lytton, embarrassing — yet, when he is being honest with himself, he is unsparing.

It had happened while he had been abroad in Ceylon. He had left in 1904 and not returned until 1911, and all that time he had been out of pocket, so to speak, with what was then only the proto-Bloomsbury crowd. He and Lytton had written to each other almost daily throughout. It had been, in many ways, the flowering of their friendship, for they had relied on each other like family, when in truth family was rarely this reliable or close. They had held and bucked each other up through the inevitable comedowns and disappointments of postgraduate life. They were not in Arcadia anymore.

They had poured out their broken hearts to each other on every subject, from the minutiae of Leonard's administrative duties in the jungle, trying to hack a semblance of order out of the underbrush, to Lytton's unrequited passion for his cousin, Bloomsbury's resident Lothario, Duncan Grant. Their correspondence, lengthy, deep and lasting, had got them both through seven long years of alienation and unhappiness.

But then, in February of '09, Lytton had written with the strange news that he had proposed to Virginia Stephen, and what was more, she had accepted him. But in the very next sentence he had gone on to say that it had all dissolved quite quickly, as both of them had realized the folly of such a course.

In Leonard's estimation, the proposal itself had not been altogether out of place. In his letters, Lytton had confessed to feeling lonely, as Leonard had himself, and to being full of anxiety about where his life was going. Marriage had seemed a logical next step and certainly one that would afford him the much-needed warmth and approbation of, as he'd put it, "the phalanx of the norm."

But then, within days — and this, looking back on it now, Leonard sees is the part that had been truly out of place — Lytton had proceeded to extol the virtues of Virginia, and essentially to play the part of the pimp in inducing Leonard to come home and pay his own court to her.

Why not you, if not I? he'd said. If you ask her, she'll be sure to accept. It's a natural fit, practically incestuous, what? And on and on. He'd been a relentless winking eye on the page for months afterward. And, while Leonard had been much more attracted to Vanessa when he had met the Stephen sisters for the first time, on a visit they'd paid to Thoby at Cambridge — she was the more beautiful, everyone agreed — Vanessa had already married Clive Bell. And marrying Thoby's sister was practically like marrying his own sister. The same had been true of Clive's marriage to Vanessa. They were all as close as kittens, first the men, and then the women, too.

He sits up suddenly at this, remembering the day's mail. He looks impatiently around his desk and begins riffling through masses of strewn paper. There is an unanswered letter here somewhere from Tom Eliot. His own form of epistolary coaching, but this time from the midst of the marital experience, one husband to another. He has been advising Tom for several years now, both in writing and in person. It was only natural. Leonard's and Tom's marriages are quite similar in certain respects, and Tom and his wife Vivien have become more or less sucked into Leonard and Virginia's extended brood. Close as kittens.

Tom and Vivien had been married in '15, just three years after he and Virginia had been, and, like them, without fanfare, in a peeling London registry office. They moved in the same circles. They practiced the same trade. Leonard had assumed his current literary editorship of *The Nation,* for example, only after Eliot had been offered it and turned it down. Two years ago, he and Virginia had been the first to publish Tom's abstruse and groundbreaking work *The Waste Land* in book form under their very own Hogarth imprint. It was the poem that had really set Tom on his way to becoming the towering literary figure he had long dreamt of being. Virginia herself had set the type.

Now Tom is joining the Faber & Gwyer publishing firm, a competitor to Hogarth, and that, after Virginia had worked tirelessly, raising funds to free him from the drudgery of his former position at Lloyd's bank. It is a touchy business at times, their various entanglements — that is Bloomsbury now, every bit as much as it was back when — yet the man-to-man correspondence Leonard is sharing with Tom is quite different from the one he had with Lytton. It is more mature, for one. Thus far, it has managed to survive the stranglehold of the pile.

There are other parallels between their marriages, though he does not like to dwell on them. Vivien suffers from a nervous disease whose origin is at best poorly understood. According to Tom, it manifests physically most often during menstruation, and, much like Virginia's disorder, in headaches, which precipitate violent upheavals in her mood. Both couples are childless, and for the same reason. Fearing exacerbation in the mother, as well as the likelihood of passing the defect to the child, the doctors have advised against conception.

But this, as far as Leonard is concerned, is where the likeness ends. Vivien is no Virginia. Not a practiced or established artist, not an intellectual and decidedly not a genius, however Tom might sometimes boast about her brains and her indispensability to his work.

Yet Tom has come to think of Leonard as something of a source, someone who knows all about managing troubled and troublesome wives, and who can advise discreetly on how best to bring about the kind of lasting connubial truce Tom seems convinced that he and Virginia enjoy. Mostly this is true, and Leonard won't shatter the illusion. He's worked too hard for it. Besides, as it happens, he does know quite a lot about balancing in a squall. He has gotten his sea legs by painstaking trial and error over the last thirteen years. Why shouldn't he share what he knows? And why shouldn't he receive the occasional comradely boost from a husband who finds himself at times in similar straits?

He has found Tom's letter at last, and he will answer it now, before lunch, when his thoughts on the subject are focused, if not quite fresh. He has wasted much of the morning in thought. This at least is something to do and to finish. The press of manuscripts and his own research can wait.

4:16 P.M.

THE AFTERNOON SUN is bright and keen on the bricks of the cobble path, and gently warms Leonard's calves and thighs as he kneels, deadheading the sweet peas that he has trained so carefully all season. Lean cane stakes, five feet tall, are posted a foot apart in neat rows up and down the length of the path on both sides. Between them he has threaded four-by-four-inch knotted cross-hatchings of string, an active system of support, both supple and strong, that took him many hours to fashion. By means of it, the plants have thrived through the usual whips and bastings of an in-clement English spring, coiling their tendrils up and through the subtle trelliswork and hanging tightly, even through the worst of it. Now he is having his reward. The flowers are a boisterous pro-fusion of pink and lavender and magenta, which—he repeats this pedantically every year—this pruning will enhance and prolong well through the summer.

Though the sun is out at last, the air is still cool, as it so often is in early June when it has rained this much. The water meadows are swamped and the river Ouse is a milky torrent overflowing its banks. She is standing above him on the path, alert and attentive, her arms wrapped about her in place of a shawl, watching him pinch and discard the errant growths.

He never says so outright, he wouldn't, but he wants this ritual to be observed, daily, she suspects it would be, if he had his way, but weekly will do. He needs her to appreciate his competence in this, to note and acknowledge the details of his craft, and so she does, outwardly, though it is really he, not his gardening, that she is observing so closely.

He does not know it, but he gives himself away when he is like this, alone with her outdoors and thoroughly absorbed in something he enjoys. This is the person she first loved, and the one that no one else has ever known. Some of their set, the closest and of the longest standing, have sensed this part of him and loved it, too, but none has known it, not as she has, nor can they. This is not the man (she conceives this at first regretfully, then with a blush of satisfaction) that history will remember.

So be it, then, and good. It belongs to them alone. She approves, except that she would not have the hacks get hold of the wrong end of him after the fact — he in one claw, she in the other — and set him up against her as something he is not, a scourge, say, or a keeper. She sighs over this, chagrined and guilty. The conjectures of sex will be a war one day, and she will have played her part in starting it. The spoils will fall to the executors: interpreting all, knowing nothing.

For how would anyone see — how could they, through the masks of his political self, and even hers — what she sees kneeling before her in the garden on this fragile blue day in June? Here is this impossibly gentle, nurturing—and yes, she would go so far—this maternal man taking the tender sprigs of plants between his fingers as lovingly and wonderingly as if they were the tiny, perfectly formed toes of his own newborn child.

Down the years, they will be wasted, these treasures of his secret self: the warmth of kindness and trust that gathers about his shoulders and glows in him as he crouches on the grass in the shade, resting, unawares; the fierce protectiveness of life and of all living things that simmers in his eyes as he sits stroking the dog, staring into the middle distance, or as he watches, sometimes for an hour or more, a common sparrow make its way to and from its nest to feed its young.

It is incommunicable, she thinks. It is the very thing she has to say to him today, shown in another way. The same mystery lost because it cannot be adequately expressed.

"I have been thinking about Talland House," she says suddenly.

He has stopped plucking to straighten a listing stake. With the palms of his hands he is tamping the loose soil at the base of one of the plants, firming the sod above the rootstock.

"At St. Ives, you mean?" he says, grunting as he leans more weight onto his arms.

"Yes," she says, "the summers before Mother's death ... You know the anniversary has recently passed."

He stops what he is doing, turns and squints up at her.

"Of course," he says apologetically, "I hadn't thought."

"It doesn't matter," she continues absently. She is not going to tell him about Adeline. "It's just that I was remembering something very specific that I did there."

He is still stopped, looking up at her a little sheepishly for having forgotten the date of her mother's death, but his hands have begun to move again beneath him.

"I haven't thought of it for a long time," she resumes, more dreamily. "It was a small thing, a very small thing, yet important. At first I was not at all sure why. I was quite puzzled by it, in fact. Of all the things that happened there, all the things that I might have held uppermost in my memory about those summers with the family in that house, but haven't, this incident has stuck fast."

"Have you told me about it before?"

"No. I have told no one. It didn't seem significant enough to relate. I've hardly thought of it myself."

He has righted the stake, and stands to face her, brushing his knees.

"Will you tell me now?" he says.

She is lighting a cigarette.

"If I can," she says, drawing on it through pursed lips. Exhaling, she adds, "But there is a lot in it, and it has all just come pouring out together in a rush this morning."

"Go slowly, then," he says, still facing her, "and I will try to help if I can."

He turns back, at full height now, and resumes his plucking.

"In the hall at Talland House," she says, taking another slow drag on the cigarette, "there was a looking glass." She pauses for a moment, picking a piece of loose tobacco from the tip of her tongue. "It was almost too high for me to look into — I must only have been six or seven at the time — but if I strained and stood tottering on my tiptoes, I could just see my face in it. It was a kind of game I played with myself, though it was serious, too, and secret. A strict and careful secret kept with myself. I did it only when I was alone, and only when I felt sure that no one could possibly come into the hall and see me doing it."

His back is to her, but he nods as he shuffles another few steps down the row.

"I was ashamed of it," she says, a little disbelievingly, as though it is something she thinks not even a child would be foolish enough to do. "Terribly ashamed of such a trifling, commonplace thing as looking at myself in the looking glass. Indeed, I remain so to this day. I dislike looking glasses. I dislike looking at myself. And, as you are only too well aware, I detest being looked at by others. Still, as you are also regrettably too aware, this happens everywhere I go."

He smiles ruefully with half of his face, and without looking, reaches back and puts a consoling hand on her. She pats it briefly and he withdraws it.

"I feel people's eyes on me," she continues, more concertedly now, "and immediately there is that shame again, the same childhood shame, welling up and mortifying me. It's worse than you know. Walking in the street or into a room full of staring people is a torture. Really, a torture, like being made to run the gauntlet of the *galerie des glaces* at Versailles. Exactly like, in fact, because to my mind, the eyes are not the windows of the soul but the mirrors of it. They do not reveal — certainly nothing of the observer. Instead, they reflect only the distorted image of what or whom is being observed."

He has finished the row, and she has turned with him and begun ambling toward the orchard. He is holding a large piece of bark that he found lying at the end of the path, probably blown in by the last storm. As they walk, he is turning it over in his fingers, deciding what species he thinks it is, frowning at it as if it were the culprit she is speaking of.

"In any case," she says, watching him, "that is how it has always seemed to me, and each time this kind of dreadful showcasing occurs, even now at middle age, I am transported back, and there I am again, this child, compulsively looking into the looking glass, yet cowering in shame."

"I see," he says, still examining the grains and whorls of the bark.

"And so, as I sat there this morning thinking of the past, going over this strange episode, I tried to make sense of it in all the predictable ways—the shame, I mean, and the curiosity. What conflict was expressing itself? What explained the discord?

"And you can imagine what I came to. It was all very well-trod ground. Was it my and Nessa's tomboyishness, I wondered, asserting itself, instinctively reviling the practice of feminine display? We were well-bred Victorian young ladies, after all, training to be seen and then possessed by our husbands as ornaments. We hated this, of course, and resisted it as vehemently as we dared, even at so young an age. Yet we were drawn to it nonetheless, like Narcissus himself, compelled by the evidence of beauty in ourselves. This was Mother's legacy, naturally, the primary trait for which she had always been—and we, her likenesses, would one day be—famous. Well, you said it often enough yourself. At that age, it was who we were, entirely. It eclipsed everything else."

He is down again on his knees, yanking at a large, recalcitrant weed that has entrenched itself in one of the outlying beds.

"Yes," he agrees, his voice straining with both the effort of uprooting the weed and the archness of intentionally repeating a cliché: "The lovely Stephen girls," he says. "That day you came to Cambridge to visit Thoby. My, who could talk of anything else? I've said it a hundred times, everyone has, and still it jars me. The first time I set eyes on you and Vanessa, sitting there, the two of you side by side, all in white, with your wide-brimmed hats and your white parasols straight as rods in front of you. You were like two Graces, upright and poised and impossibly beautiful."

He sighs again at the memory. "Incredible." He lifts off his gardening hat and scratches his scalp with a slightly pained expression. "Ah, well," he says at last, dropping his arms and swatting the hat lightly against his thigh to shake the grit from it. "Now, of course, I know that I was just one more awed face in the maddening crowd that beset you."

"You couldn't have known. I hardly did, except in the raw discomfort of it. It is only now, looking back, that I have begun to feel its full weight, and possibly its cause."

"Indeed?" he says, placing the hat back on his head and adjusting the brim on his forehead.

"You see," she says, drawing deeply again on her cigarette, "Mother's femininity was not the only influence. There was also Father's puritanism. It had been passed down to him for generations, and it was passed in some form to us. His harshness, his morbid self-absorption and bottomless need for reassurance, his overbearing seriousness and hatred of *shallow idle things*? That was all there, too, in us, roiling behind the mask of Mother's face."

"Yes," Leonard agrees, "your father was a formidable man, and you were absolutely his daughters — not simply the pretty picture of young womanhood that you presented. I could tell that the moment I looked into your eyes."

Virginia nods in recognition of the fact, but it is not at all the main thing, and she rushes past it, explaining, "But, still, none of this is sufficient. Knowing it all, putting it in place, these reasons, these influences, still I come back in my mind to those moments in the past, in front of the looking glass in the hall at Talland House, and I am not satisfied."

"Is that really all?" Leonard asks.

"Well, no. There is that other deeply buried family secret that you have heard something about. George and his *mishandling* of me in that very hall, but —"

"Ah yes," Leonard interrupts sarcastically, "dear brother George."

"Half brother, please," Virginia says. "It makes some difference. In any case, I needn't elaborate. It was fundamental. The violation, the squeamishness and disgust, none of which I could feel properly at the time, but which have done their bitter business down the years."

This is an ugly memory. Not something they talk about. Her misalliance with her half brother George Duckworth is at the root, Leonard believes, of their ongoing nonconsummation. All attempts at sex were abandoned long ago. The honeymoon had been a travesty in this regard, and had they not been the people they are, this would have sunk them.

It is no one's fault. For whatever reasons (they are varied and mostly obscure, no doubt), she is amorously, but not at all carnally, inclined, and truth be told, Leonard is much the same. His apparatus, as they have at times fondly referred to it, is a friendly appendage, far less insistent than most. It has never plagued him as it does so many men, and so he has (mostly happily) gotten on with other things. Still, the subject is inherently delicate. It must be turned between them, as it so often has been in the past, on other ideas, and a bout of careful teasing.

"You sound as if you've been downstairs rummaging through the Freud," he jokes, a little feebly, hoisting the convenient thing. They have acquired the English-language rights to publish Freud's work under the Hogarth imprint, and the papers have just come in.

"Yes. Yes. I realize," she says testily, partly because she has not been able to bring herself to read a word of the Freud. Still, she has heard enough of Sigmund bandied about by Tom and Lytton, and by all the other men with whom she is on intimate terms, to know that she doesn't want to bother with him now. "But I could hardly fail to invoke him," she moans. "His jargon is the lingua franca of our age, and all the more so to us now that we have him wholesale. We are nothing if not publishers of fashion, are we not? The doctor is decidedly in."

She has not taken Leonard's remark as he meant it. She has grown much shriller in the course of her little speech. "Freud, Freud, Freud and his brilliant insights into the female mind, ever dropping—or is it slipping?—into the great elucidating cesspool of male conversation."

He scoffs. "Oh, that's unworthy of you."

"Yes, sacrilege, I know," she says, undeterred, "since we are all so enamored of the great man." She fans herself theatrically, doing her best imitation of posh feminine bewilderment. "All those clever drives and complexes." She drops her hands abruptly and her cigarette brushes against the side of her skirt, leaving a smear of ash. "Yes, isn't it a marvel," she resumes in her own voice. "All those avenues of inquiry and their inexhaustible relevance to our endless fascination with ourselves."

This is deliberately brash as well as contradictory.

"You, of course, see the egregious hypocrisy in this," he grunts. "You've just finished—"

"I have not finished," she shouts over him, chopping the words so harshly that the conversation all but slams shut.

There is a long moment of angry silence. She glares at him all through it, but then her expression softens. With a brief downward glance, and a flickering of his lips that he knows she will recognize, he apologizes for them both.

"I," she resumes, tartly nodding to him, "who am, it would seem, as infected by the Freudian vogue as everyone else, went through the whole rigmarole myself this very morning."

She considers this, seeming to allow his criticism to penetrate, and adds more defensively, "I am, I confess it, very interested in me, and my past in particular — it being mine."

Leonard smiles graciously at her concession, but then turns up one side of his mouth at her need to make it sting.

"So, there I went," she is saying, "taking up each of my tried, true possibilities, the obvious explanations — and, to be fair, I found them half useful to a point. They are valid enough, such as they are, as reasons, and they will do" — she bows here to acknowledge the quotation — "*to swell a progress*. That is, if one is content with small talk."

"Damning with Tom's praise, then," he ventures playfully. Sharing allusions — this time, it is to one of Tom Eliot's poems — is one of their deepest bonds, stronger than any temporary discord.

"But," she says, narrowing her eyes at him a little impishly, "and I know it will shock you to hear it, I have never been content with small talk, and I was not now." More seriously, she adds, "The truer meaning still eluded me."

They have reached the orchard, and she stops beside one of the plum trees to examine the young fruit. It is coming along nicely. Leonard is pulling his shears out of the front pocket of his gardening trousers so that he can carry out the task he has set himself: removing any dead or diseased limbs from the canopy. She sees that he has already brought out a small stepladder for the purpose. It stands propped against the trunk, and he is reaching for it. In one swift motion, he pulls it toward him, rattles it open and sets it on the ground in front of him.

"In fact," she says, watching him ascend, "to be quite serious,

I was in something of a crisis over it. Disturbed and vexed by the limits of my reach."

He is reaching for one of the branches just as she says this, and he smiles down at her.

"I knew I needed a finer instrument," she says, not smiling back, "to scratch this particular itch. I knew I needed a more . . . well, I suppose . . . a more abstract technique, but I couldn't think what that was, or how to go about it. So I sat there for a long time, thwarted and angry."

She takes another long, contemplative drag on her cigarette and stares at the smoldering cherry on the tip, which is bulging now quite close to the butt end that she is holding pinched between the edges of her fingertips. She considers whether to put it out, but decides against it.

"But then, finally, something happened, a shift of some kind in my thinking. And suddenly, oddly, everything was clear. I knew at once what I had to do. Actually, it was quite funny, now I think of it. I sat up, took myself by the scruff and said, 'You must stop this atrocious rationalizing!'"

Leonard looks down and rolls his eyes at her teasingly, as if to say, Not this tiresome anti-man business again. But she is not looking at him.

"I was exhausted, I suppose," she sighs conclusively, her brief comic burst having disappeared, "by the futility of trying so hard to nail a rigid frame around this clouded mental event from the distant past."

She is frowning as she thinks of this, still eyeing the butt between her fingertips, but then her eyes widen excitedly as she asserts, "So I dropped it. I simply dropped it — all my learning and reaching and intellectual pretense — dropped it all, and for the sheer pleasure of watching it shatter like the looking glass itself might once have done had I had the gall to put my little head through it. Except that shattering is not actually what happened. It was a transformation far more subtle and strange, a sort of lique-fying, I would say, as if the glass had dissolved into quicksilver."

"Hmm," Leonard interjects a little breathlessly from his perch, where he is wrestling free a tangled branch. "That *is* strange."

"Yes, I thought so. Anyhow, that is how it came through. It was as if I had stumbled upon an entirely new way of seeing. And when I say seeing, I mean not only the incident in the past, but the whole, the absolute whole of everything. There I was, seeking it without knowing, and then, well — then it simply came."

Leonard makes another murmur of interest, like an accompa-nist punctuating a singer's voice, though this time he seems to be taking the matter in. He has frozen with the shears in the act of making a cut, and lowered his head thoughtfully.

Seeing that he has stopped, she says, "This is where it gets a bit involved."

"All right," he says, snipping off the branch and tossing it to the ground. "Try me, then." Raising his arms again above his head and grasping the tree so that he can lean back and turn himself all the way round on the stepladder to face her, he adds, "I'm listening."

She smiles fondly at him. She has decided to abandon the dy-ing cigarette at last, and snuffs it between her thumb and finger, enjoying the mild sear of it on the stained, toughened skin of her fingertips.

"I saw at once," she says, "in that image of myself as a child, looking at myself in the looking glass, the revised vision of myself as an adult. Do you see?"

Leonard nods, but he is clearly not seeing, and she shakes her head.

"No. I have said this far too simply. It was more than that. Much, much more than that."

Leonard is wise enough to say nothing, but his eyes are fixed expectantly on her.

"How can I explain this properly?" she says. "I saw myself, you understand. I was there. A person of surfaces in the glass. But then, dizzyingly, ecstatically even, I plunged below that surface and saw myself *as a self,* a multiple, layered, simultaneous self that could not be contained in the two dimensions of the looking glass."

She seems more pleased with this rendition, and he nods again, as the rest of her thought tumbles out.

"And then, beyond this even, I saw that this self of mine was — like every other self — almost endlessly myriad and diverse, and as phantasmagoric as the spaces and times through which it flickers and flits."

Glancing at her briefly as she is finishing, he can see that her eyes have turned a little wild. He will encourage her discovery, but he wants this whiff of mania to subside. He is still standing on top of the stepladder, balancing with his hands gripping the branches above, but now he is looking off, over and past the orchard. His mouth is set firmly, the lips pulled tightly, as if he is confronting a problem that has just arisen in the fields.

She has stopped speaking. She, too, can feel that her energy is high. She looks to see how Leonard is taking this. "What?" she asks innocently.

"You have had one of your revelations," he says proudly, but there is a note of caution there, too. "How wonderful."

"An overwhelming revelation," she corrects.

"Yes, yes, I see that."

"*The* breakthrough."

"For the next book?" he asks.

"For everything," she cries. "This is the novel I am to write, *and* this is how I am to write it. It is the subject and the form. Do you see?"

"Yes, quite," he says stiffly.

"Here is the multifoliate self on its journey through the dream of time, in language that shimmers and billows and flows with the narrative of experience."

Her enthusiasm is carrying her right away, just as he feared it might, and the words are coming too fast to control.

"It is what I began somewhat shallowly, imperfectly in *Dalloway*," she says. "It is everything of the world that I wish to convey in a work of art, if it can be conveyed—though I am not at all sure that it can be. Still, I must try. I must keep on from where I began, invent and reinvent a method, a new composition that can communicate this vision."

"You think now that *Dalloway* is incomplete, then?" he asks, a little foolishly. In the past, she has cuffed him for asking these kinds of questions, because she has seen that he was merely using them as drags. But mercifully, this time she accepts it.

"Yes. I do. *Dalloway* was a start, but I didn't carry it off. Lytton said as much when he read it, and I was grateful for his honesty."

"What did he say, exactly? I don't recall."

"He said that it was very beautiful, but that the events and the people, Clarissa in particular, did not quite stand up to the language or to the ideas that I had put into their heads. He thought that perhaps I had not yet mastered my method."

"And you agree?" he asks. This is another patent stall, but again, she seems content enough to answer.

"Yes, though I did not know how much until this morning."

"I think you should bear in mind," he says, "that Lytton can be rather shallow in his tastes. He does not have the stamina he once had to linger in the depths. He prefers high drama to contemplation."

As Leonard comes down from the ladder, he adds, "*Dalloway* is profoundly psychological. I am not surprised that Lytton did not have the patience for it."

This appeal to her vanity has its usual effect. As he lowers himself onto the grass, he can see that she, too, is easing down into the talk.

"Yes, perhaps he didn't," she says, "and on the whole I agree. I am generally disinclined to take his criticisms of my work entirely to heart. But in this case I think he was right, and what's more, it didn't bother me much to hear him say so. Given my usual sensitivities, I think that means something."

"Yes, I suppose it does. You are never this sanguine about reviews."

She has taken out her tobacco — a good sign of the desired shift in her mood — and is rolling herself another cigarette. She concentrates on this, tightly packing the moist shag, frowning as she considers what he has just said. She shoots him a mildly testing look over the top of the roll as she licks and seals the paper, but says nothing. This, too, is an encouraging sign.

"You know," Leonard ventures, more confidently, "it strikes me that you are touching on cosmology here, and that it is Newton, perhaps more than Freud, who is leaving you dissatisfied."

"How do you mean?" she asks. Her tone now is almost demure.

"Well, Newton's is the insufficient universe you have described — the one symbolized by your looking glass — rigid and superficial, the picture of discrete entities obeying laws."

He is still standing on the grass next to the stepladder, but he has put away his shears and taken out his pipe, which he is now packing and preparing to light.

"Yes," she says patiently. "Go on."

"Well," he resumes, putting the pipe in his mouth and striking a match against the tree. "Is that not your objection to Freud as well? The superficiality of his vision? Or did I misunderstand?"

He holds the match to his pipe and begins to puff, his eyebrows rising inquisitively from behind the column of smoke.

"Old astronomy, old art, old medicine," she asserts, driving home the previous point, but with much more control. "They are the same blunt instruments. We are here now, modern man, looking into the enigma of the self, and Freud offers us only egos and ids. We are searching up and out, seeing through, seeking our glimpse of the unfathomable, and this . . . scatological charlatan . . . is telling us to look down, between our legs, where, he assures us, all the truest answers are to be found."

Leonard pulls the pipe from his mouth and smiles at her in spite of himself.

"Yes. Yes," he proceeds more smoothly, "I understand your objection to Freud, though part of it, you must admit, is purely xenophobic —"

She begins to object, but he cuts her off affectionately.

"But Newton was an Englishman, and he was making the same mistakes, albeit centuries before. Still, you call it Germanic imbecility in the mouth of Freud, but I am right about the cosmology, and I'm sorry to say that the modern improvement on Newton that you are so clearly invoking comes from the same Teutonic stock."

"What *are* you babbling about?" she squawks, but there is delight in her voice.

"You said this very thing in passing at one point in *Dalloway*," he says. "Like poor Septimus watching the aeroplane disappear in the sky, it is with the eyes of Herr Professor Einstein that you are seeing your new world."

"Oh, don't tell me about Septimus," she cries. "Or Einstein, for that matter. Yes, it's true, I referred to Einstein in *Dalloway*, and yes, I meant it, but right now, the thing I am talking about right now, well, I am not seeing with anyone's eyes. I am not seeing with eyes at all. That is the point."

Leonard is not remotely convinced, of course, but he is too relieved by the turn in her to do more than puff contentedly at his pipe and wait.

"I am saying merely," she resumes, "that the old ways of thinking will not do when we are trying to capture the mystery of consciousness, the complexity of the human personality or the shifting texture of the world as it really is. Newton, Freud, they are stuck in the same dead nomenclature. Using it in this context is like trying to play a violin with a cudgel, or like conducting a séance — as the devotees of Dr. Freud no doubt would — by defecating on the floor. Only the flies will gather."

He is enjoying this immensely, and grinning. She is whipping herself up again, but harmlessly.

"But it is not just science that has it wrong," she is saying. "Even language as we have used it, the corseted novels, poems, plays we have known, they are all still more of the same. Inadequate to the task. Henry James is the prime example. When in art we attempt to render a person, his concerns, his time and place, we say with Hamlet that we hold the mirror up to nature. And so we do — so I did in the hall in Talland House — but that is precisely what is wrong. We reduce this thing we are reaching for to our limited terms, and in doing so, we are merely aping (and I use this word particularly) what we do vainly every day in the dressing room — what I was doing as a girl in the house in St. Ives.

"We look in the looking glass to see ourselves. But we do so — I say again — *vainly.* For what is vanity but action in vain, ineffectual, a mistake, the primate's blunder of taking the beguiling silver surface for the thing itself. We reduce the wonder of ourselves and the universe to two dimensions, an ape, or a silly little girl, primping before a plane of glass."

Leonard is beaming. The thrill of her mind never loses its power to beguile. Yet he is struck by the predominance of her vanity in all this, though he knows that he should not be struck at all, since vanity is one of the traits in her that is most familiar and entrenched. It played its vital role in the subtext of this exchange.

And yet, he marvels, look how she plays it. For all her flaws and failings, all the hardships of staying by and righting her, there is this: She knows herself. She knows that she is vain. What's more, she has turned the awareness on itself. She is making art of it — and science and metaphysics, too. Talking with her this way ameliorates everything. Without bodies, it is how they make love.

"But surely," he exclaims with uncurbed relish, "you concede that Joyce at least broke through all this primitive realism. *Ulysses* is nothing if not a reinvention of the novel, and a complete break with the past? Even Tom Eliot was awed by it, you remember. He claimed that the book single-handedly destroyed the whole of the nineteenth century. And do you know, just repeating that now, I wonder again if we were perhaps foolish to decline *Ulysses* for the press when we had the chance."

"We had good reasons, you may remember," she chides. "The length, for one. You might also remember that at the time, in response to Tom's fulminating praise of Lord Joyce, I said I thought the man a he-goat and, in the context of the present conversation, I would add, every bit as irritatingly priapic as Dr. Freud."

"Oh, come now," Leonard cries. "You cannot possibly dismiss Joyce so crudely, and you know it. Yielding so utterly to this obsession with the distastefulness of the male sex—well, I can only repeat, it isn't worthy of you. It belies even your own more considered assessments of Joyce's work."

"Yes. Yes. All right," she concedes, chagrined to be caught carping. "Joyce is unquestionably brilliant, has written many gorgeous and deeply satisfying passages, and he has, as you suggest, been reaching into consciousness as I have. But in these bold and flashing forays he is constantly pulled down by—I am sorry to have to say it—his typically male adolescent urges, which have persisted, as they so often do, in the grown man. They show themselves not only in the book's relentless vulgarity, but also in its exhibitionism. He comes across as a clever schoolboy showing off, jumping up and down and waving his arms: Look at me! Look what I can do! And so, sadly, we do look at him, rather than at the cosmic wonder to which he is attempting to point."

"I think he more than attempts," Leonard scoffs, letting himself be drawn in. "As shrewd a critic as you are, Virginia, I don't think that even you can contend that your assessment in this case is quite free of a certain taint."

He regrets this the moment he says it.

"A certain taint of what?" she snaps.

"You know very well of what."

"I'd like to hear you say it."

"Very well, then," he shouts, intending to pounce, but his dread gets the better of him and he merely stammers out the rest. "The taint of—well, of what? Well, shall we say, of professional insecurity?"

There is a tense pause, but this is a much less painful swipe than she had expected, and her answer is surprisingly subdued.

"Now *that* is unworthy of *you*."

"I hardly think so," he replies, too quickly. "I don't say you are wrong in your assessment. In fact, as you are all too aware, I, and many others, consider you to be an extremely astute literary critic."

Virginia has been standing in the same position throughout this exchange, holding her rolled cigarette unlit, as if threatening to stalk off with it in a huff, but now, having procured Leonard's defeat, she lights it.

"I agree wholeheartedly," he continues, hating himself, "with most of what you have ever said about any book, including *Ulysses*. But when you speak of Joyce you cannot possibly pretend to be objective. The matter and the man are too close. It was very much the same not long ago with Katherine Mansfield, and if she were still with us, the conflict would still be with us, too. Joyce is, as Katherine once was, a writer who is both an immediate con- temporary and — you must admit it — a competitor?"

"I don't admit it," she roars, exhaling an avalanche of smoke. "And I forbid you to speak of Katherine. That conflict, as you call it, was as deeply personal — no, more so than it was profes- sional. And regardless, with what I accomplished in *Dalloway*, I left Katherine behind once and for all."

"I'm glad you know it," he says hotly, but with a mollifying in- tent. His tone is almost servile, and his transition is decidedly in- ept, when he finally makes it. "So, then, who now, other than Joyce, is doing what you are doing, or anything close? Tell me that."

"Well, Tom, of course."

"Tom Eliot? It's not the same, and anyway, it's poetry. Apples and oranges."

"Fine," she says, "Proust, then. And I admire *him* immensely."

"Yes, well, that's very generous of you, I'm sure. But again, it is not comparable. Proust is a photographer. You are a painter."

"Not true. Not true. In style perhaps he is, yes, but he is taking pictures inside the mind. And time is the centerpiece. The concept of it, the passage of it, the consciousness and, most of all, the capturing of it."

"Yes, precisely, the capturing. That is documentation, not rendering. It is still a representation of the thing, not the thing itself, enliterated by the narrative."

Finally he is saying what he means, and he is not giving offense. "And this," he concludes, "if I understand you correctly, is both what you propose to do and what you have already done, perhaps, as you say, only primordially, in *Dalloway*."

"Yes," she murmurs. "Perhaps."

She seems to have folded up in a haze of smoke. She is holding her cigarette in front of her face, but she is letting it burn there unsmoked. All desire for it apparently gone.

"My dear," Leonard says, stepping closer, "your vision, your technique, they are your own. You have made that quite clear, and I am rightly astounded by what I have heard. Not least because of the science. I was not being facetious, you know, in my remark about Einstein."

She does not respond.

"It's quite remarkable actually, given what you've said, because he, too, has destroyed the models of the past, revolutionized the entire vocabulary that we use to describe our world. And, strange as this may sound, he is with you all the way to the lighthouse."

Again there is no response.

"If you'll bear with me, I think I can explain, or try to. Of course, you know Einstein's famous theorem is $E=mc^2$?"

He says this as a question, but she merely nods compliantly, still staring.

"Right, then. Now, this equation is not only about light — c being the speed of light, E being energy and m being mass — but also about the difficulty, perhaps impossibility, of the very process you wish to describe. The journey of the self through time. You follow?"

At this, she brings her eyes back into focus and looks at him curiously. Even the faintest implication of an insult to her intelligence will rouse her to reengage.

"According to the equation, an object's mass will always be increasing as it approaches the speed of light. Another way of saying this is that it would take an infinite amount of energy to accelerate an object of any mass to the speed of light, yet this is what time travel would require. So far so good?"

Still looking at him, she smiles wanly and nods again.

"But what I think you are proposing is that the self, or the traveling object in this case, has no mass at all, that it is not in fact an entity as such, but a being that is made entirely of thought, and so is itself a kind of light. Indeed, you seem to be saying that consciousness, selves, spaces and times, the whole of experience, is, in effect, a show of lights, and one, therefore, in which it might just be possible to travel through time."

Now she is openly smirking.

"Yes, yes, all right," she huffs, yielding at last as if she has not been away, "but don't make too much of the symbolism of the lighthouse. It was, after all, really there in St. Ives. I showed it to you once. Godrevy, remember?"

"Yes, of course, of course," he says. "But that is what makes this all so especially wonderful. It is both fanciful and true. And why? Because the truth, the nature of reality — as the physicists are at last coming to learn — is turning out to be quite beyond our wildest dreams. This new work you propose will be science fiction in the most literal sense, both a new science of the art of fiction, a complete reinvention of the novel as a genre, and a demonstration, by means of this new genre, of the newest scientific principles. You will write your story, the story of your childhood by the sea in St. Ives, and through it, by means of it, you will lead us through your quicksilver looking glass and into the Wonderland of space-time."

In the pitch of his final excitement, he seems almost to be parodying her, but he is yielding.

She likes this very much, as always, and as he knew she would. He has been listening much more carefully than she assumed and, seemingly without effort, he has made her notion shine again with its own significance.

She looks up and around. The solstice sun is still high over the steeple of Berwick church. It will be light until nearly ten, but the orchard is full of shadows and is quickly turning cool. She takes his hand, turns him and begins to lead him back to the house, leaving the stepladder and the cut branches to stand in the grass until tomorrow.

"Well then," she says haughtily, pretending to look away across the garden, but sharing the private smile that she knows, without having to look, is playing on Leonard's lips as well. "You have understood."

They take the long way round to the house this time, past the rhododendron bushes, which, having thrived under Leonard's attention, are nearly as tall as the two of them and are covered with gorgeous, fat lavender blooms; past the bowling green, where they may still have time for a game after supper; and once again onto the central brick path.

As she opens the rear door that leads into the mint-green sitting room, and stands back to allow him to pass, she looks at him and smiles. "Are you in your stall, brother?" she says.

As he walks by her into the house, he looks back at her and smiles, too. "Indeed," he says, and she follows him in.

Act II

THE WAVES

❧

1929–30

APRIL 1929

VITA SACKVILLE-WEST may be a noblewoman, but regrettably she is not very bright. On publication day—the anniversary of Virginia's mother's death, 5 May 1927—Virginia had sent Vita a so-called dummy copy of *To the Lighthouse* in which all the pages were blank. She'd meant it literally, as a slight, but she'd barely taken the trouble to disguise the fact, thinking that the dummy would be too dumb to suspect the joke. She'd attached a self-effacing note to it by way of excuse, quipping that it was the best thing she had ever written, but by Vita's testy response, she'd known that the crueler hint had been taken, and taken amiss. Ah, well. She cannot help herself. She must tease, and she must, at times, be cruel, especially to those, like Vita, who suffer from an excess of self-esteem. They must be taken down in her company, if nowhere else.

English history, particularly the history of highborn English families with long and distinguished ancestries, has always interested her. The Sackvilles fit the bill. They can trace their line all the way back to William the Conqueror, and their sprawling ancestral home at Knole is the largest country house in England. It comprises three hundred and sixty-five rooms, fifty-two staircases and seven courtyards. The building alone occupies four acres of ground, has a twenty-four-acre walled garden and stands in a thousand-acre deer park. The estate was bequeathed to the Sackvilles in the early 1600s by Elizabeth I, and it has been the family's home ever since.

But as Virginia has so often found with such families, steeped in the lore and fascination of the past though they may be, the family members themselves are often a bore. She considers this the downside of heredity: The less desirable traits also pass down, even when — as is true in Vita's case, because she is a woman — the property does not.

Oh, these aristocrats. They cannot help being caricatures. For a time, she finds this deeply amusing as spectacle, but they, alas — as the late queen had remarked — are not similarly amused. And, of course, the diversion wears off all too quickly in real life. It can only be sustained in stories. People remain interesting when they can be made to speak in her voice and to act out her fantasies, to propel. They rarely do so on their own.

Not that Vita has been entirely a bore since they began whatever it is that they began in the winter of 1925. On the contrary, Vita has been a more willing and more sustainably engaging puppet than most. But in the end, in her own mind, she is still a person, and a person of high birth, no less. As such, she entertains more than her fair share of the common delusion that she matters, and that she exists, neither of which, of course, is true.

But how can one say this in bed? Or, just before and afterward, at Knole, when the two of them are lounging like courtesans on red velvet cushions in front of the columned marble fireplace and the imposing polished brass andirons. How could she even think to speak of such things when she is dwarfed so completely by those high ornate walls and ceilings (they must be forty feet), with their cornices and friezes decorated with mermaids and mermen and seahorses, and the huge gilt-framed paintings (one of Gloriana herself) staring down? No. This is when the fiction is especially rich, when it is most charged with the intoxicating frisson of her imagination.

But oh, if only she could say what she means. If only she could explain. But explaining would mean exposing the brute truth to the brutes who most assuredly do not want to hear it. And so she must rely on satire and irony and parody, as Swift did, to say the harshest things. Yet these poor figures of fun—her material—will always insist on taking her seriously, on being flattered or offended, and on making it about themselves, when that is the last thing it is about.

How simply it is all laid out. She grows weary of the pretense. Even the challenges, the lauded causes of this brave new twentieth century: socialism, feminism, censorship, Sapphism, buggery. Their proponents make it all deadly serious, and she has played her part in their charade, because still, after all this stubborn time, so few have grasped the obvious: that of course these freedoms should be enjoyed; fairness should prevail. Yet it did not. This had made her angry, and so she had stood up.

But she has done so with her tongue firmly in her cheek and with the most abiding, most encoded sense of skepticism imaginable. Predictably, this is often missed, because all the while, all the time that she has been giving lectures—such serious lectures—"Women and Fiction"—at such serious institutions—Cambridge *Yoni*versity (as Lytton calls it, invoking the Sanskrit dirty word) — and agitating for the cause — in such serious journals of opinion and courts of law — she has always and inescapably been thinking what she has always thought, and what she had said to Leonard years ago: We are apes. I am addressing, I am cajoling, I am rousing a decidedly unshrewd shrewdness of apes.

Look around, she would shout, if only she dared. Look at yourselves, you organ grinder's monkeys. Listen to yourselves, beating your hairy breasts and hooting your crude arguments, none of which should need to be made. We are animals, you fools, she would rail, spitting all the way up to the gallery, and we are possessed of only three qualities that might in any true sense be said to separate us from the beasts: We have the hubris to call ourselves men; we have the ambition to make ourselves gods; and we have the voluminous capacity for denial required to sustain the former two pretenses.

Who, she wonders, would pay her to say that? And would her fee include or be in addition to the cost of paying someone to clear up all the rotten fruit and vegetables that she would no doubt leave behind, bespattering the venue? She would have to lecture wearing an oilskin and a sou'wester.

And what, after all, of her? The speaker. Is she an ape? Well, naturally, there's the rub (there must always be one), as well as the extension of the joke, for like all apes, she believes that she is not one. Deep, deep down in her hominid brain, she, too, believes that she is special, rising above. Her politics and culture *will* make some difference, or perhaps just the smallest of ripples in the still-extant primordial ooze.

But — and here is the whole bilious point that so few of even the enlightened few ever seem to quite get — this is why she is so in love with Shakespeare. This is why she lifts him off the shelf almost daily when the work or the world becomes too much, and drinks him in like a cool, purifying draught of cynical moonlight.

He is never serious, and he is full of hate, and though he is rightly said to have invented humankind, he is no friend or lover of his creation. Even his comedies are strong medicine, sugared to help them go down, and the histories and tragedies are unmitigated, bitter as wormwood taken neat.

All his people, with all their overweening self-importance and clamorous life, he creates, he encompasses them so effortlessly, and with a sneer. And, most important for her purposes, all these newfangled bugaboos, these gender troubles in particular; the Bard had dashed them off like so much deadline copy, done and dusted, hands washed. There you are, he'd said in the blithe consigning voice of Pontius Pilate, handing over his folio, I give you the primer, your despicable mankind: *Ecce homo.*

About sex and sexuality in particular, there is not a thing in Freud that was not already in Shakespeare, and infinitely better said. (She still has not read Freud, but . . .) What's more, all of it, all this trickery of men and women, the Bard had debunked and dispensed with properly, in the context of the human travesty, not ululated it from the rooftops.

This is her way — to make her comedy duck and bite — and she has made it do so. *Orlando* — Vita had been flattered by it, of course — is not a serious book. It is not even a flattering one, and certainly no hagiography of Vita, or some Sapphic fantasia clothed in the hoary verdigris of the peerage. Good God, what a thought. The morons have made her into a poster, and her most careless daubs, her palate cleansers, into shrines. She can only laugh, for *Orlando* is already her most popular book by far, though her least well written. But — fate be praised! — it has made her famous, which, of course, only makes her want to climb to the top of the nearest bell tower and bellow to all the riffraff below: I was teasing, you imbeciles. I was clearing my throat.

Well, let them slurp and moan. She will not shave her head and play Joan of Arc to their sideshow—especially not on behalf of that spitcurled invert Radclyffe Hall, who had, it was true, been unjustly tried and convicted of obscenity in November for daring to write (talentlessly) of women in love. But that did not make her a saint, or Virginia her paladin.

No. Shaw is for canonizing, if that's your sport. Take his Joan and his tone, and let him orate as he would. The people's playwright had been given (by his rankled compatriot Joyce, no less) his appropriate title, the Right Honorable Ulster Polonius. Wonderful, and perfect. Let him bask in his plastic laurels. She has no use for them.

Yes, she had done her duty by Hall the previous fall, but *against* the abomination of censorship, not *for* the red herring of inversion. She had signed her worthy name to the sonorous letter of protestation penned by Morgan Forster and published in *The Nation*. She had even trudged to court to testify, if required. But, alas, she had been dismissed uncalled. The book had been banned with a single sweep of the berobed arm and a single indignant toss of the periwigged head. And the presiding buffoon? Ah, well, he had, no doubt, gone to school with Leonard and Lytton.

Does this honestly make no one else laugh?

In *Orlando* she had simply squibbed her own version of what Shakespeare had done. The more direct reference had been, of course, to Ariosto's and Boiardo's epic romances *Orlando Furioso* and *Orlando Innamorato*, but *As You Like It* was indubitably there in the fun, in the fungibility of sex and most of all in the mockery. She had shown, with the lightest of touches, much as the Bard had done, that all the obscenity in the world could be slipped past the groundlings with balderdash, and fall unnoticed into what Lytton called the "great chasm of sar" that forever yawned between the wit and the twit. She had parried their censorship.

Could she make it any plainer? Not aloud.

And then, of course, there is this, which is quite the funniest thing of all—and again, patent to all, but ignored, naturally. In England, the only mannishness is in women, and always has been, while all the most weedy, weak and wheedling of the lot are men, who are either fairies outright—the prettiest of them far outpouting and outrougeing the English rose—or are physically unfit in the soldier's sense for much of anything but billiards and cards.

If Queen Victoria was not a man, who was? And Elizabeth? Was it any wonder such strata of costume and makeup were required? And even then, she hardly outdid her attendant lords. When a smattering of the far-flung native peoples of the Americas were brought before the painted queen's court to be ogled and probed, it must have been quite difficult for them to tell the sexes of these strange ornamented creatures apart. No doubt they resorted to their noses.

And so it is with Vita, true to the aristocratic line, where it seemed that the titanic mustachioed women so often towered above their milquetoast men and outweighed them by fifty pounds. Surely this must have been the reason for the invention of the top hat, and come to think of it, the Victorian gentleman's muttonchops—one could not, after all, be quite so outfaced by one's queen.

Oh, yes, yes, Vita's retiring spouse Harold Nicolson is all right, the diplomat through and through, amenable, sensible, but with Vita, as meek and incumbent as his own mustache. Looking him over, one felt that one could take him in a scrap if it came to it. She laughs aloud thinking of it now: Vita in her breeches and high-laced boots, astride him on his back, pinning him with her knees and gagging him with a pendulous mouthful of her pearls until he gurgles his assent and agrees to let her ride him round the manor like a Shetland.

That is Vita's appeal. The size of her, the bones, the breasts, the breath of her, all outsized and smotheringly maternal in a faintly ursine way: She is powerful and blundering and all paws. And that, Virginia supposes, is what she needs from her. Vita will never be the originals, Julia and Nessa, or even come close. She is their overgrown and allowable imitation, fundamentally *faute de mieux*. Sleeping with Vita is as close as Virginia will ever come to sleeping with her mother and sister, or indeed with herself, all of which, she is not afraid to admit to herself, have been abiding fantasies, laid low and channeled elsewise all her life.

Adeline is only her projection, little goat, and that is not the same. They cannot truly make love. Nessa, meanwhile, is all that is left of their mother. She is her blood, beautiful, adored, and inextricably grafted to Virginia's soul, psychically Siamese. If she, Virginia, could have shot herself into Nessa's veins, she would have done so long ago. But it is one of the things that is forbidden, and one of the very few such things about which she never jests.

This, of course, is well, well beyond Sapphism and feminism. It is abomination indeed, that lowliest of loves that truly dare not speak its name, especially in a court of law. It has no proponents averring in the dock, as Wilde had done, or marching in the street with the suffragists. It has no one to rouse on its behalf, least of all her, yet it matters awfully. It *is* serious, but in it, as in all the best and most important things, she must be discontented with substitutes.

Still, with Vita, the comparisons are not always so pale, for despite her outward mannishness, there is something saturatedly female about her, too. Not feminine, like Nessa, not in the least, but female, with all its attendant odors and flows which act on the brain as nature intended, by instinct. Vita smells and tastes of the sea and the soil. In Vita's arms, Virginia inhales the musk and tidal essences of Earth, and she feels incarnate for the first time. She has only ever felt disembodied before.

She had touched on this abstrusely in her lecture "Women and Fiction," which like so much else had been the tamest version of her thoughts on the subject. She had written and spoken as expected, the advocate for her sex, by turns wry and flinty, but never strident per se. Oh, yes, it would be read and heard as such by the overstuffed boobs of the establishment. They would be provoked, but they would miss the subtext, as, in fact, would the bluestocking disciples she would, and had already, similarly inflamed. They were like an abjection of pilgrims (now there was a collective noun she could endorse) rushing up to the lectern to shake her hand, or barreling into teashops, to behold the blessed face of their paragon and touch the holy hem of her garment. Absurd.

Yet, in one way, they were righter than they knew, for there was that inescapable resurrected quality about this Vita(l)ized Virginia Woolf, the original *noli mi tangere*, which, as of old, had always provoked its opposite. Do not touch, the risen Christ had warned, yet to Thomas he had said: Put your hand inside my wound and believe.

It was the same, what she was doing with Vita, and indeed what all the Sapphists did, most of them unknowingly, reenacting this ritual whose significance they did not wholly understand: the wound where the doubter puts her hand. If that was not sex, what was?

But there is more to it than that, and this she had said in her speech. The lack of identity was prime. She had said it was the anonymity of women who wrote, the authoresses, Elizabethans and before, who had signed their poetry "Anon" because they did not have names. They did not exist. And yet their verses did exist. They themselves disappeared, however, as she did, in the very act of putting words on the page.

A book is a fold of paper and thread, in itself inert, yet in the right hands, it transmits. In the mind of the reader, the hearer, the writing lives. The transference occurs, leaping from one mind to another over time and space and even death. Hence the anonymity of the authorial feat.

And the sex. That is a kind of telepathy as well, achieved in the mind, between minds, and again, by means of primitive instruments. But only with women. A woman. Vita.

With men, even Leonard, dear man, she had never been able to escape her paralytic horror of penetration, the awful sense of being impaled. This was rather the silly bit, though also the ineradicable — she cannot disembarrass the idiom — sticking point. Just at the critical moment, a gruesome image out of *Ivanhoe* (courtesy of Father's library, no doubt, and the hours she had spent there as a child unsupervised, reading unsuitable material at far too young an age) — the sweat-streaked, torch-lit face of an infidel in his death agony ahoist on the crusader's spear — would overtake her mind and obfuscate her senses such that she would undergo a kind of breathing rigor mortis that could not fail to repel even the most ardent of suitors.

Try as she might, and she had tried mightily on her honeymoon, she could not help it. It was what she had done with her half brother George, of course, and after a time, even he had desisted, crying in despair, "Damn you, Ginia, you would make me a necrophile." She had come across this root in her Greek, and noted it in her diary, preferring it thus, *nekro,* the *k* being rightly harsher than the *c.*

But with Vita the act of love had changed, both in posture and, of course, anatomy, from one of penetration to one of reaching out, reaching in for the infusion of belief. They have reclined together for hours, Vita cradling, Virginia nestling in the supple comfort of Vita's bosom. There is no mystery in this. Vita is mother, Virginia child. These roles are also inherent in Sapphism, she feels, and the substance of its appeal.

And so they are incestuous in a sense, after all. Often, as they lie there, Vita reaching ever so tenderly and holding her inside, the pleasure and the sadness overtake, and Virginia weeps. Adeline weeps. And Vita soothes. And then they walk out into the world again separately with no trace of this strange communion on their faces.

In January, she and Leonard, as well as Nessa (who is — can it be? — soon to be fifty years of age), Duncan Grant and Nessa's middle son Quentin, had spent a week with Vita and Harold in Berlin, where Harold has been posted at the British embassy. It had been an awkward ménage, and in the end, the strain of it had made her ill. Upon returning home, she had been in a state of near-cataleptic infirmity for weeks. But while they had been there — what a saturnalia the city had become! — seeking refuge from the boysblush of buggers who had overtaken all the louchest Weimar bars and nightclubs, delirious with their sex and truffling every groin in sight, she and Nessa had had an abundance of time to themselves. They had spent a good deal of it walking in the city's botanical gardens, thinking of home and talking of Vita, or, as they'd called it for lack of a more generous term, the ongoing *liaison dangereuse* that Virginia was having with *La Sackville.*

"She is not your equal," Nessa had said, meaning not what most Englishwomen would have meant by such a remark, that Vita is of blue blood and Virginia is not, but rather what the snobs of Bloomsbury meant, that Vita is qualitatively not up to snuff. That is to say, in magnitude of mind, soul and sensibility, she is deficient; she lacks gravitas.

But Nessa is not one of Bloomsbury's snobs. She is not normally so judgmental, or not at least when it comes to what are arguably extra-moral flaws in a person's character. She requires people to be good, but she does not require them to excel. Virginia has never known Nessa to dash a person for being insufficient. And so, the fact that she had dashed Vita in precisely this way revealed everything about the threat that Vita represented to her, and to her umbilical bond with Virginia, which had never been encroached upon in the least, even by Leonard.

"Need she be?" Virginia had replied archly, leaving aside for the moment the import of what had been said.

"I will not have her trifling with you," Nessa had carped, again, with an unusual flare of temper.

"And what if I am trifling with her?"

"You *are* trifling with her — that is obvious — and she with you, but you will be hurt in the end all the same. You always are, and it is not good for you."

"Oh, you! Always the sentinel. So strict. Yet you know as well as I that every contact has its price. Would you have nothing touch me?"

"Yes, every contact does have its price, but you are more vulnerable than most, and some contacts carry much higher prices than others." Nessa had paused here to groan irritably, then added, "Always, always, these are the ones you seek out. Really, must I remind you?"

"I do not need reminding."

"You do."

"Let it be, will you, dearest?" Virginia had pleaded. "This once."

"Not when the threat to you is so great. Vita has the power to destroy you."

"Come now, don't be sensational. You have just said that she is not my equal."

"Yes, which is what makes her all the more dangerous. She acts according to her whims and without a care for consequence. She is a great lady, after all. She was brought up to do as she likes, and to consign whatever results to the realm of common things that are not her business."

Turning on Nessa, Virginia had asserted, "You are jealous of Vita."

"Nonsense."

"You are."

After a pause, Nessa had meekly replied, "And what if I were? Would that discount what I have just said?"

"No," Virginia had sighed in defeat.

"Well then," Nessa had concluded, throwing her hands out in front of her and opening them wide, palms up, in the gesture of someone who has won her point. After a strained pause she had added, "You think that you love her, of course."

"Oh, Nessa, love is not the word. The Greeks had so many words for love, and yet they could not exhaust its meaning. We have only one, and so much the poorer we. But in the language of love we are all poor. Even if we had as many words for love as the Inuit are reputed to have for snow, or indeed"—here, she had looked up at the overcast sky—"the Englishman has for rain, they would all still be inadequate."

"We are not in England," Nessa had teased.

"No," Virginia had replied. "Alas, we are in Gomorrah."

This had made them both giggle.

"Were the Cities of the Plain so full of flowers as this, do you suppose?" Nessa had said, looking around.

"Undoubtedly. The real paradise lost. Narcissi, narcissi everywhere, and the bee-besotting orchid spread a thousandfold."

Here they had fallen down in another fit of the giggles on a plot of open grass beside a carp pond. Recovering themselves in little gasps of spent laughter, they had lapsed into a dream state and sat for some time without speaking, watching the cream-and-gold-colored creatures dart back and forth in the murky water, and surface occasionally to part their puffed and greedy lips in the hope of some reward.

At last, Virginia had broken the silence. "I cannot say it any better. I'm sorry. But I do *so* love you, Nessa."

Nessa had fixed her then with her powerful grey eyes, which the grey day had made shine dully—like drops of pewter—and glow with unbearable solidity and warmth.

"I know, my love," she'd said. "I know."

JUNE 1929

IT IS SUMMER again, and there is nowhere else to be but in the garden at Monk's House, communing with the sun and the flowers and the air and a dear friend whom one must now begin to criticize. Lytton is sitting beside Virginia on the wooden bench at the edge of the bowling green. He could not be induced to play a game. He is too feeble, never much one for games, and they laugh about this as they sit, content, as they have always been, to talk instead.

Lytton is his usual gentle, drape-bearded, bespectacled self, with his long strands of thin hair parted far to the side, creamed flat across the top of his head and around his ears. He is wearing a beige lambswool cardigan vest under a brown tweed jacket, a perfectly knotted and dimpled cornflower-blue tie and white flannel trousers with a pair of white buckskin shoes. For him, he is dressed for summer, on the bottom half at least.

He has always had what they have in recent years come to refer to as a Proustian constitution: always susceptible to chills and maladies and even loud noises. He has lived much of his life reading in a supine position. It is not at all unusual for him to wear such heavy clothing in the warm months of the year, or to see him sitting outdoors when the weather is fine with a blanket thrown over his lap. But today, Virginia notes, he does seem a touch thinner and frailer than usual.

Virginia is draped for the weather in a long white cotton frock with a wide band of delicate sky-blue striping along the hem. She has a light linen shawl thrown loosely over her shoulders, and she is wearing a wide-brimmed black straw sun hat, topped on one side with a jaunty white spray of tulle.

They have been sitting this way in silence for several minutes, basking in the smell of fresh cut grass and fecund soil and the haven of the shade, when Lytton breaks in, as only he can, with the softest yet most sparing of assertions.

"So, I suppose we must have it out, then?" he says.

"Out?" Virginia coyly demurs. "About what, dearest?"

"*Elizabeth and Essex,* of course. You didn't like it."

"Nonsense," she says. "I have criticisms. That's all. I'd say my feelings are much the same as yours were about *Dalloway.* One can take issue with the particulars of a work, or the bringing off of it, but one can do so within the context of a broader recognition of the overall achievement, don't you agree?"

Ignoring this, he says tartly, "Well, Ottoline thinks it's brilliant."

"Oh, well, if Lady Ottoline Morrell thinks it, then it must be so. Honestly, Lytton, she practically suckled you from infancy. Of course she's going to fawn over it." She pauses briefly and looks away, then adds tauntingly, "*To you.*"

"Oh, you're horrible," Lytton gasps, turning to her with a look of alarm. "Has she said something?"

"No, no." Virginia laughs, cuffing his arm. "You needn't worry. As far as I know, she has been an unswerving advertisement, as usual."

Lytton sits back, appeased, and resumes gazing across the garden.

"That's a relief, anyway," he says, crossing his legs and bouncing the upper foot impatiently, as if he is waiting for a bus. "Still, I resent your putting that picture in my head. Ottoline suckling me. Witch's tit indeed. Good Lord."

"Oh, hardly," Virginia scoffs. "Ottoline is perfectly exotic, I grant, and an acquired taste, I'm quite sure, but not repulsive. She's simply a very brightly colored, somewhat screechy giantess who's developed an unfortunate talent for repeating everything she's overheard. I should think making love to her would be rather like making love to a macaw."

Lytton makes a startled face. "Perhaps, when one is the size of a bunting."

"She can't help it." Virginia sniggers. "She must be six feet tall if she's an inch, and however one may try to robe and swathe and mitigate, a woman of that height is always disturbing."

"And that orange hair to top it. Was she born with it, do you think?"

"Presumably." Virginia sighs. "Oh, and those eyes, like the Sargasso Sea, violent green and churning like little whirlpools of intrigue. It does all seem almost preternaturally cruel."

"No," Lytton chirps disagreeably, briefly stilling his bouncing foot. "Witchy. As I said. Just imagine those sour, cold and wrinkled dugs." He shudders theatrically and goes back to bouncing his foot.

"And you are the viper nursing in Rome's bosom," Virginia says archly. "Though when in Rome, is it not the she-wolf's tit that is suckled?"

"Yes, well." He casts her a knowing glance. "Speak of the she-devil in wolf's clothing. But you were not yet a Woolf when I was of suckling age. In any case, you are mixing your myths. That was Romulus and Remus who were said to have suckled the she-wolf at the founding of Rome, whereas you have just made me Caligula — don't think I missed that — and it was Tiberius who said it about him."

Lytton pauses here to take full advantage of his cue. Dramatically clearing his throat in the practiced Strachey style, he resumes: "Repulsive old disease-ridden Tiberius, looking down and beholding for the first time the full hideousness of his psychopathic heir apparent — the terrible Gaius Caligula — snarled happily and muttered, 'I am nursing a viper in Rome's bosom.' Or so it is written. And so therefore it is Tiberius's tit I must suck — which, by the way, I consider to be a vast improvement over the proposed alternatives." He pauses again, stroking his beard with satisfaction, and adds, "I rather like the sound of that, actually. Tiberius's tit. Perhaps it should be the title of my next book. What do you think?"

"It might be just the thing for you," Virginia teases. "Our very own Suetonius for Bloomsbury."

"And what precisely do you mean by that?" Lytton says, pretending to be very engaged in flicking something off the front of his trousers.

"Only that it would suit your flair for the dramatic," Virginia goads. "I think everyone can agree that *Twelve Caesars* was one of the great potboilers of its time, and a group biography, no less, blurring the line, shall we say, between fact and fiction." She turns to him in mock surprise. "And here we all were thinking that you'd invented the genre. Or was it revolutionized?"

Smiling, he crosses his arms peevishly over his chest. "I detest you."

"And how I love you for it," she says, playfully pulling his ear. "You do it so awfully well."

"Speaking of doing it, I can't help wondering if by 'flair for the dramatic' you are taking what is, if I may say so, a rather shabby swipe at my vice."

"Mmm. And which one could that be, I wonder?"

"Yes," Lytton drawls wearily, "I wonder."

"Oh, I see," Virginia pipes. "You are perhaps referring to vices of *The Faerie Queene* variety? Elizabeth? Gloriana? What have you? Your topic of choice, yes?" She puts a finger to her lips and adds, "It is true that you may have been a trifle transparent in that respect. Or did you not intend to put yourself in the queen's role?"

Lytton makes a cry of exasperated delight.

"How can you be so sure," he says, "that I did not, at least in part, intend the more obvious parallel — *Virginia?*"

"What?" Virginia squeals, clapping a scandalized hand to her breast. "*Moi*, the Virgin Queen? And you, my Essex? Why Lytton, I had no idea you were so engrossed."

"I was your Essex briefly, was I not?" he says, smiling devilishly. "Many moons ago."

"Hardly," she says, an unexpected sharpness getting the better of her good humor. "You were half in love with Thoby, if anyone, and I was merely the next best thing — your last stab at normalcy, I should say? But alas, your dirk wasn't quite up to the job." She stops herself here, embarrassed by the sudden sourness of her tone. "I'm sorry, Lytton," she says. "That was cruel. You were won-derful to me after Thoby died, and I know you loved him nearly as much as I did."

Chastened, Lytton says soberly, "Well, you know, you *have* al-ways cast something of a shadow over me."

She is genuinely surprised. "I'm not sure I understand."

"I have always admired your talent, resented it even. And I sup-pose there is something of you — well, perhaps quite a lot of you — in my Elizabeth."

She considers this for a moment, sifting through what she re-members of what she has read and what she can bear to admit that she recognized. She takes out and lights one of her cheroots.

"You mean her fickleness," she says at last. "Ever dancing for-ward and back, never to be caught?" But she cannot bear to remain so exposed, and adds teasingly, "Or do you mean the sex? Were you making your own rather shabby swipe at *my* vice?"

"All of it, in a way," Lytton says, still serious. "Though not a shabby swipe." He pauses then, as she did, to adjust. He, too, will not give too much away. "Or not entirely that — except insofar as my nature, my bugger's flair for the dramatic, as you call it, com-pels me to make some kind of swipe at . . ."

"Frigidity?" Virginia finishes.

He hesitates, as if deciding again just how vulnerable or cutting he wants to be.

"If we are using all the crassest terms, yes," he says. "But you must see that it is far more complicated than that. You said it your-self. The dance. Elizabeth's entire life was a pavane. A long, elabo-rate pavane that she could never stop dancing, and in which she could never cede herself to anyone. Her power depended on it."

Virginia is listening closely, holding the cheroot very close to her mouth and squinting through the smoke.

"A lifetime of unconsummated sex," he continues, "enacted in every way but in the act itself, performed incessantly between a man and a woman who cannot have each other, or, in our case, who cannot want each other. And yet."

"Yes," she says. "And yet."

Now Lytton is the one turning reflective. His hands are folded in his lap, and he is turning his head slowly left and right, scanning the garden.

"But, you see," Virginia says, filling the space, "I have always insisted that sex is in the mind. These bodies of ours are donkeys, and merely doing it is . . . well . . . merely doing what donkeys do. It's utterly ridiculous when you think of it. Aristophanes showed as much — and we laugh right along with him. But we don't really get the joke, because we *are* the joke."

She pauses, narrowing her eyes still more behind the smoke from the cheroot.

"What a pagan act of worship copulation is. Two animals praying their hearts out to the graven images of each other. We're only one burnt offering short of the good old days."

Lytton laughs. "I suppose self-immolation after coitus would have defeated the purpose — decidedly not adaptive for the survival of the species."

"And so, to wit," Virginia says, taking a long drag on the cheroot and blowing the smoke into a wide fan in front of them, "we have the ceremonial cigar instead."

They are playful again.

"Or," Lytton says, reverting to his pedantry, "we join at the spine, as Plato had us. The beasts with no backs. We are the third sex, you and I," he chirps invitingly, turning and bending his knees to his chest so that he can put his feet on the bench and lean back against Virginia. "Half male, half female, fused but facing away.

Children of the moon, he called us, Mrs. Woolf." He howls and smiles back at her.

She laughs heartily, and following his lead, turns aside, puts her knees to her chest and leans against him, so that they are sitting back to back like bookends.

"I do think, in any case," she resumes, "that you were a bit heavy-handed in the book."

"Dramatically, you mean?"

"Well, yes, that. It's all a little breathless, you must admit."

"Potboilerish?"

"Not quite," she says, nudging him. "But one does have the feeling at times that one is being played to, or that the words are being worked into a lather for one's . . . how can I put this delicately . . . titillation."

"Then we are back to Tiberius, are we?"

"No, no. And that isn't primarily what I meant to say. I meant that you are heavy-handed not just in tone, and in the way you set your scenes, but in your use of sexual symbolism."

"Too many pricks?"

"Or their stand-ins, yes, if you must."

"Of course I must. We buggers are compulsive about such things, don't you know?"

"Oh, stop. You know perfectly well what I mean."

"Well, it may horrify you to know this, but I received a very thoughtful and complimentary letter from Dr. Freud on the subject."

"I'm not in the least surprised or horrified, actually. The master loves to be stroked, and you have shown yourself to be an apt pupil."

"Now that is a horrifying thought. Stroked? First Ottoline, now

Sigmund. You would have me assuming the position with every last troll of our acquaintance."

"Hardly. But it does prove my point. It's simply your tendency to overinterpret when it comes to matters of sex."

"Yes, well, who are we to talk, I suppose, you and I? We are hardly Rhine maidens."

"Ha! Speak for yourself, Nibelung." Slapping her thighs in delight, Virginia adds, "God, but you know that brings me right back to the old days in Gordon Square when Leonard was just back from Ceylon and we used to go to the opera or the ballet or the theater every night. I'll never forget introducing Leonard to the Ring Cycle at Covent Garden. Poor thing. What he did for art in the name of love. We'd start in the afternoon and we wouldn't finish until after eleven. By the end of it, he was as miserable as a wet cat. I can still hear him saying, in his wonderfully correct but cantankerous way, 'Well, now that's done, I'm glad I've seen it, but I have neither the desire nor the courage ever to do it again.'"

Lytton laughs. "Oh yes, yes, you're right, I do remember that, conscientious Leonard sternly doing his duty and grimacing all through it. I had such fun watching him squirm. Well, I suppose to the unenamored, Wagner is rather the cough syrup of high culture."

"Leonard says we were members of the Wagner cult."

Lytton laughs again. "Didn't you and your brother Adrian go almost ritually to Bayreuth for the festival every year?"

"Yes, yes. It's true. It was all very en vogue in those days, and you were playing the procurer, so I suppose lonely Leonard, coming as he was, all parched and primed out of the jungle, was left with very little choice."

"Procurer indeed!" Lytton cries. "And primed? What can you mean?"

"You know precisely what I mean, you awful little man. You'd been working him up to me for months, courtesy of the Royal Mail."

"Well, it hasn't turned out so badly, has it?"

"On the contrary, I owe you a great debt of gratitude for giving me away." She casts a reproachful look in his direction. "At the altar, I mean, of course. You were the best possible substitute for Father."

Lytton is pleased with this formulation, but, charged as it still is, he knows not to let it lie there undiverted for long.

"Which, incidentally, brings us nicely round again to Dr. Freud. You may find this interesting," he says, pulling a letter from his breast pocket and lovingly unfolding it.

"No," she cries, wheeling around out of her bookend, seeing that he has produced the actual letter. "You haven't!"

Lytton nearly falls over backward without her support, but grasps the bench's arm just in time. Recovering himself and putting his feet back on the ground, he says, "I have, as it happens."

"Unbelievable," Virginia says, dropping her arms to her sides and letting her legs fall wide out in front of her under the folds of her long skirt, as if she cannot be bothered with posture at a time like this.

"I'm quite proud of this artifact," Lytton says, not looking at her. He holds the letter out in front of him as if he is a clerk in a courtroom verifying evidence. "And so I quote," he continues. "'You'"—he turns to Virginia—"and by 'you,' he means, of course, me, Lytton Strachey, the author." Peering over the top of his spectacles, he lets his eyes rest on her for a moment, then turns back to the letter.

"'You are aware of what other historians so easily overlook'"—
he raises his finger and slows his reading for emphasis—"'that it
is impossible to understand the past with certainty, because we
cannot divine men's motives and the essence of their minds and
so cannot interpret their actions. Our psychological analysis does
not suffice even with those who are near us in space and time.'"

He pauses, poking the upraised finger at the air. "'So that
with regard to the people of past times we are in the same position as with dreams . . . As a historian, then, you show that you are
steeped in the spirit of psychoanalysis . . . you have approached
one of the most remarkable figures in your country's history, you
have known how to trace back her character to the impressions of
childhood, you have touched upon her most hidden motives with
equal boldness and discretion . . . and it is very possible that you
have succeeded in making a correct reconstruction of what actually occurred.'"

He puts the finger down, and beginning slowly once again to
fold the letter along its creases, he adds crisply, "End quote."

"Oh, God," Virginia sighs. "Not again. Do you know I had this
same argument with Leonard years ago when we first acquired the
rights to publish Freud's papers?"

Lytton does not indicate that he has heard. He is still putting
the letter back in his breast pocket, and with absurd care, as if it is
a papyrus.

"You are right in one respect, however," Virginia continues. "I
do find it interesting that he admits to the impossibility of knowing the motives of other minds, even those that are nearest to
us. But then he proceeds nonetheless, and by means of his own
clumsy methods, to presume to analyze those very motives, or at
least to praise you for doing so in his stead. The man's arrogance is
quite breathtaking."

"Clumsy methods—thank you. That's very kind," Lytton says absently, looking out again over the garden.

"Well, I'm sorry, Lytton, but you have rather co-opted him whole hog," Virginia says harshly. "And that business about Essex's execution being an expression of Elizabeth's hatred for her father. The Electra Complex, is it? . . . Let me see if I have this right. Her father, that most virile man of men, Henry VIII, who executed her mother, Anne Boleyn, thereby committing a crime, which, though she secretly wished for it, naturally gave rise in our little fiery red-headed queen-to-be a seething hatred not just for papa, but for all men. Kill mommy, marry daddy, and cover your guilt in hatred. That's just about it, yes? And that's already too much, but you don't stop there. Yet another Complex—capital C—must come into it. And so the beheading of Essex is also the great standing metaphor for castration. The woman's abiding desire to do it, and the man's abiding fear of having it done. Bravo and presto. There you have it. Your first-class degree in Viennese twaddle."

Lytton is looking at her in genuine disbelief, as if he has just been deliberately scratched across the cheeks by a passing squirrel.

"My, my. *Quelle harangue, ma chérie*," he says, falling back against the bench with his legs still firmly crossed. "But hark!" he shouts in his stage voice, thrusting his arm out in front of him. "Our Vestal Virgin speaks the truth. And woe betide those who hear it, for her tongue is mightier than the sword."

Virginia makes a sour face and righteously stubs out her cheroot on the arm of the bench.

"Forgive me for saying so, my dear," Lytton adds sarcastically, "but I believe it may be you who has just won the award for dramatic performance."

"Oh, damn it," she says, throwing the butt of her cheroot into the grass. "Freud makes me mad. Always has done. It's not you."

"Maybe a little bit me," Lytton gently suggests. She does not reply to this, and so he goes a bit further. "Perhaps my Essex has feared de-pronging at his virgin's hands." He looks at her submissively, adding, "Do you think?"

She smiles. "Perhaps." Looking out at the afternoon light, she puts her hand on his and adds, "Perhaps the complex, if not the prong, has been on both sides."

He smiles down at her hand as she withdraws it, and murmurs, "Yes."

They sit in contented silence for several minutes, listening to the bees coming and going at their business in the flower beds, and to the innumerable sparrows and finches gossiping away. Then a thrush alights nearby, and its insistent airy cry spears the chatter of the common throng as if someone is at the piano in the corner of a cocktail party, fiddling with the farthest treble keys.

"Are you happy with Carrington?" Virginia asks finally.

Lytton takes a moment to reply. He wants to say this well and simply.

"She brings me tea and biscuits as I work," he begins, pausing respectfully between each phrase so that he can pare the next. "She looks after my feebleness. She is enthralled by my every bon mot. And you are right, I do need an audience. I always have. She is like some gentle creature of the forest who has wandered into my ruin and made the poppies grow there, and the daisies and the clover, too, in all the cracks and empty spaces where the wind had whistled through."

Virginia sighs. "And the boys?"

"They are the wind still whistling through," he says with regret, "in all the rooms where I have not let her enter."

"And are there so many?"

"Boys, or rooms?"

"Rooms."

"No. Not so very many. But they remain. And they remain empty. The company is always temporary, and the emptiness always hurts, but I cannot do otherwise."

"And Carrington?"

"She, too, has vacancies, and guests."

"But it works?"

"Yes. Strange—but it seems to." He turns to her. "And what of you and Leonard?"

She does not hesitate.

"We have a phrase we use for it. It sums up the pattern of our lives. We spend our mornings in contemplation and literary toil. We spend our afternoons walking and gardening. In the late afternoon or early evening we sometimes have a game of bowls. We have supper, and then we sit in the sitting room across from each other by the fire and smoke and talk and read. And every now and then, one of us will look up and say, 'Are you in your stall, brother?'"

Lytton grins, and they lapse again into the tributary silence for which both their recitations have seemed to call. This is yet another precarious place in both of them where they cannot linger too long.

"And what do you hear of your young nephew up at Cambridge?" Lytton says finally, changing course.

"Julian? Oh, all the best and the usual. He's joined the Apostles, of course."

"Of course." Lytton nods. "And good."

"He's having the ripe loving time: the Greeks, the greens, the punts and the pederasty. I don't know if that last bit is really his inclination, or if he's just doing what you all did when it was the time to do it, but whatever the case, he claims to be sleeping with one of his fellow students, Anthony Blunt."

"Interesting."

"I suppose," Virginia says. "Or par for the course. But he does seem to be getting all the benefit of his time there. He's writing poetry. He's growing. He seems happy."

"Then he is indeed doing what he should, and when," Lytton replies, a bit sadly. "He will never be so happy again."

"That does seem true of you all," Virginia says. "I've seen that. Leonard is happy in his own way now, I know that, but I think he still looks back on those days as blessed, and their particular bliss as irretrievable. He tries to keep it kindled with you and the others when you assemble, but it's not the same."

"No, it is not the same. Life goes on, as they say, but something of us does not go with it. It gets left behind somehow, and the separation always gapes."

"I know precisely what you mean," Virginia says. "I don't mean about being at school, of course, or the pleasure young men take in all-male company, but about leaving parts of you behind as you go through life. I have done so, too, and it's painful, like a fracture in the bone that never heals, and always aches when it's going to rain."

She considers this. Coming back to the book, and wanting to say something critical that is not personal, but still important and true, she adds, "I wonder if this isn't the limitation of biography."

"Hmm?"

"This splintering, I mean." This breakage in the self. It means in the end that we cannot know ourselves. In which case, how can we ever know anyone, as Freud said, near or far? Moreover, how can we write a life when the self is beyond our grasp? His formulation there was quite beautiful, actually. When we set out to interpret our own minds, much less the minds of our fellow human beings, whether here and now or there and then, it makes little difference; we are in the liquid landscape of dreams."

Lytton sighs in agreement, then turns to her with a small child's pout. "Was there a compliment for me in there somewhere, dearest?"

She throws herself against him, roughly kissing the side of his face. "Oh, yes, my love, yes. Truly. I only meant that it is a very interesting difficulty, and I am struggling with it myself. How does one tell the truth in biography or in autobiography when the truth is not to be had? Which is to say that if one finds fault with your interpretation of Elizabeth or Essex, perhaps it is because it is inherent to the genre. Someone else's life of these same two people would suffer from the same fault. Misinterpretation."

"So the general fault is my accomplishment," Lytton says, taking a wry delight in the sheer legerdemain of her compliment, which only she could give in just this way. But he is slightly wounded all the same.

"Or the general fault is mine as well," she says, a little stiffly, skirting past whatever nick she has given him. "Which I suppose is most of why I have taken refuge in fiction when telling the stories of real people's lives. Fiction is all there is, and all of my fiction has been, more or less, the stories of real people's lives."

"Yes, I see," he says stolidly, though inside he is straining on the leap from his need, momentarily exposed, to the cold discourse she is insisting on. But she cannot give him anything more. He knows the technique. He has used it many times himself to deny the inconvenient emotion. But he will not indulge her on her fiction, even so. Dropping back is the most he can manage.

She can feel this, too, of course, and he feels her feeling it, but neither of them will own it. They are too much alike, too trained in the gambits of their class and conversation, but they are also far, far too sensitive, by birth or nature or constitution, to ignore what is so potently relayed in all that cannot be said. It is the caughtness of their being, the innermost clash in them repeating. It is the very thing that has drawn them close, yet always held them at arm's length, both from each other and themselves. He would say it is their Englishness doing battle with their ungovernable souls. She would say it is the flashpoint of life where the overflow of knowing crashes headlong against the intractability of the will — again and again and again — like breakers against a seawall.

Leonard has just appeared on the path at the far end of the green, waving and smiling and squinting in the sun. She must give the two of them their time together. Rising from her seat, but without looking down at him, she puts her hand on Lytton's shoulder. He gently takes it in his own hand, like a courtier, and kisses it. Slowly she lets it slide from his fingers, and she drifts away across the green toward Leonard.

NOVEMBER 1930

AT LAST SHE has met the great Yeats. She had met him briefly once before, in 1907, but he hadn't remembered. Well, why should he have, she supposes. She had been an unknown girl of twenty-five, and he, a man of forty-some, had simply been himself, his name, the revered established poet with his seat saved for him in the pantheon.

But this time, at one of the flamboyant Lady Ottoline's Thursday teas at Gower Street, she had met him properly, and this time she had done so as a lauded novelist, critic and essayist in her own right, the now famous author of—it is a list she often repeats, if only to herself—*Mrs. Dalloway, To the Lighthouse, Orlando, The Common Reader* and *A Room of One's Own*. She says it all through this way, like an announcement, because she likes the sound of her titles just so, all in a row, and the mental view they present of her, standing proudly pinned and glowing with awards. Her bibliography precedes her wherever she goes. She has no need of foot-men's introductions, bellowed at the ballroom door. No need except here in her room, alone, where she sometimes fails to exist.

But Yeats. Now *there* is someone who exists. At sixty-five — she puts it about there — he is still a figure, but human, after all. He has lost some of his blood. His mind is still vivacious, quite so, but his flesh, his body, well, alas, it has done what bodies do, and he is now a leached and chalky version of himself — truly dusted white, like a baker.

Meanwhile, she is now the one in her forties, and flying high on the *viewless wings,* as she'd told him right off. Not thrown for a moment, he'd sighed pleasantly at the familiar words, as if tasting them again for the first time, and peering at her through the thick lenses of his lunettes, he'd replied, "Ah, *the dull brain perplexes and retards . . .* but *haply the Queen-Moon is on her throne.*"

Yes, he is still all there all right, and despite his visible decline, he'd still looked every inch the romantic man of letters, perhaps more so, with his brooding brow and his penetrating gaze, his set mouth with its pouting lower lip and the shadowed circum-flex above the chin. And then, of course, because it must be so in this sort of picture, there was the most expected detail, his tou-sled mop of grey hair, which had streamed back from his forehead in set, yet somehow perfectly disheveled waves, as if still bearing the imprint of the anguished hand that had no doubt been clasped there throughout some long and stormy act of contemplation.

Only the softer indications of his demeanor and dress — his general fadedness, the earnestness of his suit with its endear-ing bow tie drooping and half undone on one side, and his thick woolen socks bunching around his ankles — had kept him from seeming both laughable and tragic at once, like something Byro-nic that had been left out in the rain.

He'd seemed to be aware of or bothered by none of this, however, and this, she thinks, is what had given him his air of somehow existing more fully than she and those around him. Other people's eyes did not give him his place. They did not affect him, and this had made her like and envy him immensely.

Then, too, there was his talk, which had been nothing like what she'd expected, not at all the kind of oracular claptrap that one presumed would issue from the mouth of a Nobel laureate presiding at one of Ottoline's teas.

From Keats he'd launched directly into an admittedly overwhelming peroration on his mystical philosophy. This had emphasized, among many, many other things, his belief in the importance of lunar power; the necessity in creative endeavor of asserting what he'd called the anti-self through turning away from or shattering a mirror; and finally his description of the symbolism of the tower — the title of his latest collection of poems — which, when its turret was struck by lightning, became a representation of the human soul galvanized by spiritual force.

"And there," he'd said of this last image, as if it all should have been perfectly plain, "we have your lighthouse."

Listening to him, she had been dazzled by the rush of his ideas and by the seeming completeness and lucidity of his transcendental vision. She had said little. She'd absorbed only a fraction of what he'd said, but thinking of it now, she is amazed again and almost haunted by his imagery, and how closely it bears on her own experience, her own creative, hallucinatory — and yes, perhaps, also transcendental — vision.

She might have liked to tell him about Adeline, about her own transformative encounter with the looking glass in the hall at Talland House, and the revelation it, too, had contained about the nature of the self and the unseen universe. But she could not have done so, not with all those society barnacles clinging.

Even if they had been alone, she feels sure that she would have said nothing, for as she had sat there watching him holding forth on the sofa — strangely excerpted from, yet concealed within, the pomp and puppetry of Ottoline's salon, and reeling off the secrets of her inner world to her as if they'd been written on the palm of his hand — she had become conscious of feeling heavily and almost terrifyingly tongue-tied.

She remembers now that during their conference there had actually been long moments when she had wanted to speak to him, when she had wanted — quite desperately, in fact, she realizes — to tell him everything, yet she had found herself strangely and confoundingly unable to make the words come out of her mouth. What a sudden and powerful feeling it had been. Thinking of it, she can almost feel it again now, that sense of being rendered forcibly mute, as if her tongue had turned to lead or been magically excised.

How odd, yet how wonderful. How stymied. How full.

The anti-self, she thinks, recalling his term. And the mirror. The shattered self, the sharded self, the self that does not walk in this world. This was the very substance of her new work.

And what of his moon? She smiles at the thought of his lunettes, then smiling more, she recalls Lytton howling her married name in the garden that day as he'd talked of Plato's third sex, the androgynous children of the moon.

She might have told Yeats of all these things, of her work now on *The Waves,* whose tides are governed by the moon, or of Arnold's iterating waves breaking in her mind and on the *moon-blanched land.* She might have told him of how she'd first called this book *The Moths,* to invoke these creatures of the dark, emerging under the moon, drawn to the light. Yes, there was the light of the lighthouse — as he'd said — but through time, all the way back to the Alexandrian Pharos itself, there too was his symbol, towering above the basin of the ancient world, its signal fire burning at its tip.

What would he have made of all this? Or had he known it already, and that was how he'd said it all so quickly, picking all the points of contact and stunning her so completely into silence? And then, at the end, the most stunning part of all, as if he had known, too, that in her silence she'd been dying to verify her secrets, he'd said, patting her kindly: "There will be time. Don't worry."

But when? she'd thought. You are sixty-five, and who knows?

"We will meet again," he'd said consolingly. "Wait and see."

And so she is waiting and seeing, sitting in her chair with her board on her lap and listening to the faint crepitation of the fallen leaves as they blow across the cobble path and catch in the close-set brushwork of the hedge that surrounds the churchyard just beyond their gate.

She is reminding herself of what she has already done, because when she is sitting like this before a scratch-ridden page, full of sentences with lines through them, and the blots and bleeds of a stifled pen, she needs reminding. She needs to tell herself again that it is in fact she who wrote — and more so, conceived — *To the Lighthouse.* Sometimes she will even take down the book, as now — it is lying spined on the arm of her chair — and read in it, flipping at random, stopping in unknown places so that she might be helpfully surprised by what she finds there.

It is indeed the story of her family life, just as she promised it to Adeline, but in a dream. As in a dream.

There is Mother, saintly and retiring, gliding like an apparition, swiftly and soundlessly, attending all at once to the whelps and wheedles of her eight children, the pressing idiosyncrasies of guests and the preening of her needy husband spouting Cowper, over and over, so as to be heard: *We perished each alone.*

Or there she is in the next village, suddenly appearing, kneeling at the bedsides of the sick and dying with her basket full of ribboned hopes and consolations. And, look now, there she is again in all her beauty, sitting on the front porch knitting, her portrait being painted by yet another admirer, looking over all her mates and charges and making all her matches between them for life.

Father is ubiquitous, too, frowning and pacing and versifying, banging on the table at dinner. My need, he says. My need. There are the tides and the whitecaps and the little boat, and Adrian's yearning for the lighthouse. And there are all the other siblings, too—half and full—all themselves and all her: Stella, George and Gerald, Thoby, Nessa and herself, and even waifish Laura, ghostliest of all.

It is all there. Read it—she says to herself, as if she is saying it to someone down the years—and dream.

But I must go on now, she reminds herself, crafting the new dream, starting again from nothing. She marvels at this, the way the mind makes a story for itself each night in dreams, scripts it and peoples it, and places it, and puts it out of time, yet in its own time, as if even then, when we are resting, as we must, we must still be entertained, we must have our stories.

What monumental energy it must take, she thinks, how powerful the subconscious must be, to satisfy this endless craving for experience, which though virtual and not our own, will do nonetheless, because we like so much to peep. No, it is more pathological than that. We love—we need to peep through the pinhole in the wall, and not just at anything or anyone, but ourselves. Our species, how thoroughly neurotic it is. Is there any other creature so in need of this as we are, this anodyne of voyeurism? Any being that needs it so constantly like a drug, so addictively, that it will break itself in the trying?

For that is what I do, she thinks. I break myself each time in the trying, because I can do nothing else. I want nothing else. And these are my people. I and Adeline, the selves that I am and those that I have been, my family as it was then and my family as it is now.

She is thinking back to Lytton and this question of the nature of biography, or really of autobiography. They are the same, for we are other people even to ourselves, and other people are our proxy selves, as little known to us as we are. And so—the heady doctor will not let go—we, they, are as interpreted as dreams. Biography is fiction, and group biography, well, that is as old as time, all the cavemen gathered round the fire telling tales. Lytton had made his mark of sorts with *Eminent Victorians,* telling his tales out of school, slighting all the giants of the age. *Elizabeth and Essex* was more so, a kind of gossip as biography. And she had found it superficial and insincere, though attractive to the eye of the common reader, no doubt. They had amused their eyes with it.

Well, this—*The Waves*—would be much the same, but hers. Her elevation of the same, and more honestly put forth as fiction. Or *The Moths,* as she sometimes still thinks of it, those who gather and dance about the flame, never alighting. That is her family now, the people about her, the giants—this is not too grandiose to apply—of her age: Bloomsbury.

This will be, in part, her group biography of Bloomsbury, but, as such, it will be primarily of Bloomsbury as a group, as a collec*tive,* not as a collec*tion* of its members, individually sketched.

There will be some of that, as always, pieces of the people she has known, but they will also, in Yeats's sense, all be one, all her, all the pieces of her split self shattered in the looking glass.

There will be, of course, some of Lytton. She will call him Neville, she thinks, perhaps after Lady Anne Neville, another queen and consort to a misshapen king, Richard III. As with Elizabeth and Essex, he fits nicely both ways, as queen and man, the freak of nature, self-despising, who, because he was not made — or so says the Bard — *to court an amorous looking glass,* he *descant[s] on [his] own deformity* instead. This captures something of the treachery in Lytton, she thinks, and certainly the crookedness of soul, racked on the body. And then again, even there, in those six searing words given to King Richard in act five, thrown into the uproar of the last lost battle at Bosworth Field — *There is no creature loves me* — there is Lytton, entire.

And then there must be some of Tom as well. Goodman Tom Eliot, like some upright rogue out of Hawthorne, black-eyed and guilty as he is chaste. She will call him Louis, because that is the name of a saint who was also a king, and it is the name of that city in the bland American hinterlands where he is inescapably from. He will be the outsider looking in, longing to belong, and stirring in his loins, like all the other boys, for boys, but clinging to his God as a Spartan to his shield, which he will either carry or be carried on to sanctuary. She will make him not American but Australian, and she will make him the son of a banker, who in turn, when he is grown, works stiff and stately in an office, kept tight by his appointments and his desk of drawers. It will be obvious enough, and not.

The third man will be Bernard, who is the suggestion of her male self. But, as the third man, he is also the embodiment of her theme, as it was suggested by Plato and Aristotle: How can man be both a man, unique and singular, and at the same time also be mankind — that is, partake of the form of Manhood, the universal? These are two, not one, and according to the great men of thought, it required a third entity, or hypothetical third man, who could somehow explain the other two. She thinks this same difficulty was transposed into religion as the Trinity: Father, Son and Holy Spirit. The third was needed to explain or link the other two; God the Father and Jesus, God the man, must have an intercessor, and so the Paraclete, subsisting in both and in itself, triune.

So her book will have six narrators, two pairs of three. Three men, three women, but in three dimensions, so that they will be, not triangles, but pyramids, symbolizing another of those wonders of the ancient world that still stand along the banks of the Nile in the shadow of the great Pharos of Alexandria.

She knows that her Greek philosophy is muddled — infernal Greeks! — but it is what she can do. She does not understand it. It is one of the problems of philosophy that show up the shortcomings of her intellect, and this has always pained her. It had pained her father, too. She had had him, as Mr. Ramsay, say as much in *Lighthouse,* railing at his own limitations. If the alphabet from A to Z represents the entirety of what can be known, he had gotten only so far down the way — to Q, as he says. In her case, she thinks perhaps she has only really gotten to H.

No matter. She does not deal in strictures. But the others did. This was exactly the kind of abstruseness that Lytton and Leonard and Morgan Forster and the other Apostles still debated, just as they had done so ardently at Cambridge. In one sense, Bernard will be all of them, these young men, who are not so young anymore, and this aspect of what became Bloomsbury, growing out of the society of intellectuals that had formed half of the group's core—the other half being, of course, the artists, such as Nessa and Clive and Duncan.

She smiles. The oneness of her is many, and the many one.

Thoby must be the centerpiece, the point where the apexes of the two pyramids meet, like the knot in Yeats's bow tie. Thoby must be there, because Thoby is never gone, and because no matter how many times she writes him, he is never written out. He will be called Percival, the knight, the hero, the god who dies young, and Neville-Lytton will be in love with him, because that was true. The others will all meet in him adoringly, too, because the others are also all her, all the points of the geometry pointing to, uniting in, one point.

As for the three women, first there must be Nessa, who will be called Susan because it is nearly an anagram of her name, and because it is the ancient name for the lily or the lotus flower. The still life, the painted object that paints the world. The artist, the mother, the sister whose soul she wishes she could fuse with, and almost has.

The second woman, Jinny, will be a straight shot. Vain Virginia herself, unhidden as her public face, gossiping and flirting and demanding to be admired.

And finally there will be Rhoda, who is the rose, the rhododendron in the garden and that island of the same name, Rhodes—the third of the seven wonders—with its colossus bestriding its shores, hailing across the breaking waves of the rounded Mediterranean Sea to its fellows, the Pharos and the pyramids, grounded by the great river in Egypt. This will be her weak, quavering, despondent self, the one who can be terrified by puddles. Adeline, of course.

Nessa is the only one who will know all of this when she reads it. Only she will see Thoby in his accustomed place, elegized perpetually. Only she will see the shades of herself in Susan, living in the countryside and bearing children and seeing the world in colors and shapes; or the traces of Lytton and Tom in Neville and Louis; or the traces of all their learned men in Bernard; and the two faces of herself in Jinny and Rhoda, by turns cowering and coruscating in the crowd. Only Nessa will see all of this. She may even in part descry this mystic union and dispersal of the self, these triumphs of consciousness that are dreamt of in Yeats's philosophies.

And that will be enough. Any portion of this will be enough when it is lying, held in the comforts of Nessa's understanding, just as she knows that it will rest in the shelter of Leonard's intellect, because Nessa and Leonard are the only ones. They are the only true receptacles for whatever rended thing in her can be called by the name of love.

She has been working some, and making all of these notes, but she has been doing so, much to her frustration and annoyance, between — there is no other word for it — waves of the old afflictions. The same barrage: headaches, racing heart, copious and brutal menstruation, nausea and, in a new twist, a holocaust of the flux. In a sardonic tip of her hat to this last unpleasantness, she is now referring to her diary by the Latin variation of its name, because it is where she is reduced to doing most of her scrawling when she is most afflicted by these runs.

This word "holocaust" reminds her again of talking with Lytton in the garden about Plato and Freud and sex as an act of pagan worship, the burnt offerings of the ancient Greeks — *holokaustos* — reenacted, but only symbolically now, by Darwinian restriction, in the postcoital smoke. She has taken to smoking on the toilet, too, because there is nothing else to do while she waits for the tide to recede.

Well, at least she can laugh about it sometimes. Laugh or die, Lytton used to say. So for now she will laugh at her outputs, upper and nether, which she has always said are not unconnected. If it was good enough for the omnipotent Joyce to have his hero greet the morning *asquat on the cuckstool,* then it was good enough for her. And, if it was good enough for the Bard, whose scatology was far more encyclopedic than Freud's — well then, she would say it again — it was bloody well good enough for her. On the commode she sits, *like patience on a monument smiling at grief,* and over the page she is Rodin's *Thinker,* posed just the same.

Adeline is made queasy by the mention of stools, but that is because, for her, the sensation has so often presaged the act, and mingled disagreeably with all her other cramps and complications below the waist. Still, their talks of late have been different. They have not followed the pattern of her mother's deathbed scene, with its iron-cold kiss of death. They have changed. She would even say they have progressed.

I hated his hands on me in the dark, she had said recently, and of course Virginia had known immediately whom she'd meant. George. Her half brother George Duckworth sneaking into her room late at night and fumbling over her like a bucketful of crabs.

But this had happened later, when she and Nessa had been coming out, thrust out the door and into the limelight of fin-de-siècle London society by George, who had wanted to use them as bait for his own social ambitions. They had gone along, but with extreme reluctance and mortification, because George had insisted — he had done so nearly every night — and because there had been no escape. They had all been living under the same roof with Father at 22 Hyde Park Gate.

And so they had allowed themselves to be dragged, all primped and powdered — to George's taste, of course — into the ballrooms and great rooms of countless millionaires. They had sat there sullen as limpets for as long as George had required, and then, finally, limped home to bed, too exhausted to undress. Not to worry: George had seen to that.

She would have been eighteen or nineteen at the time, and it surprises her that Adeline can remember this far past their mother's death. It is as if she has chipped off another piece, or sundered herself, so that part of her is still stopped at thirteen, but part of her is older, too, and caught again in the dark bedroom with George, the incubus, where she — Virginia or Adeline or both — had come unpunningly of age.

Adeline will say very little else about what happened with George, which suggests both that her memory of it is poor — this is not her time — and that it is poor for a reason — neither of them wishes to remember the details. The shadowed forms of it, the scattered scuttling sensations, the nausea left behind; they are enough.

Adeline would much rather talk about Rhoda, her costarring role, and so they do, though at present Rhoda is an outline. She has no substance to speak of, but then, by design, like the other six, she never will have solid form. She will be, as she once described it to Leonard, a creature written in light, a photographic negative if such a thing could be painted, for in that Leonard was also correct. Virginia is, like Nessa, a painter, not a photographer, and her method is, like the divine Caravaggio's, perhaps, chiaroscuro — *chiar,* light, and *oscuro,* dark. The words on the page, so-called black and white, will paint her scene in the world of light and shadow through which her disembodied souls will flicker and flit. She had also said this last bit to Leonard that day in the garden, and so it would come true. She *had* written *Lighthouse* — she tells this to herself again — and now her vision would reach its fullest, most abstract expression in *Moths,* in *Waves.* She is still uncertain which title is best. But she will know. When it is time, she will know.

Act III

BETWEEN THE ACTS

1932

EARLY MARCH 1932

THE NEWS, WHEN it had finally come, had been too crushing to accept: Lytton was dead. Mercifully, after such a long and terrible decline—it had been months of suffering—he had succumbed. An autopsy had revealed the cause of death to be a large tumor in the stomach, which had blocked the whole of the lower intestine, but no one had known this at the time, and he had had no treatment.

It had been a blessing to hear that he suffered no more, yet she had been unable to feel anything but—she did not quite know what. Even these, the natural effects when the news was fresh six weeks ago, had been beyond her power or willingness to describe on paper, probably because she had not wished to contemplate them too closely. They are plural and unnatural in the extreme, that much she knows by now, a nightmarish commingling, like a slimy, bloody knot of jeweled necklaces and snakes in some wretched painting by Blake: the unsightly image of her Gordian heart.

She had actually loved him once, hadn't she? So, so long ago. Or had she merely convinced herself of this at the time because it had seemed the thing to do, to love the man who proposed to you? Again, it was how they had all been raised, the men as well as the women. And anyway, hadn't he been the closest a man could come to being a woman? An Elizabeth after all? Had that been in her mind as well — the lure of Sapphism even then — unacknowledged quite as such, but incipient and feared? How better, after all, to ward off error and convention with one blow than to marry an un- repentant bugger? Or, as she had once suggested to him so rudely, had proposing to her been his moment of greatest repentance, his dodge in the other direction, regretted and withdrawn immedi- ately?

They had laughed about it afterward, as if it had all just been more persiflage between chums. She had not let it show, but she, or her vanity — which amounted to the same thing — had been wounded by it, and had remained so for years. Perhaps — she can consider this more clearly now — the hurt and the subsequent jeal- ousy over his companionship with Carrington is still there. No, not perhaps. It *is* — laced into the knot with the rest — one of the snakes.

In absolute quiescence let me rest.

It was a line from his deathbed poems that Carrington had shared with her in one of her recent letters. They had been cor- responding since Lytton's death. She had cried when she'd read it, yet now that his death has been accomplished, she cannot grant this last request. She cannot let him rest. He belongs to me, she thinks stubbornly, though in truth he had belonged to no one, not even to Carrington. But Carrington, like her, like everyone he had seduced with the seven veils of his affections, believed that Lytton had been hers.

It is an infuriating position to be in, Virginia thinks, competing for the lion's share of his memory, and after all those years of knowing him, knowing the slipperiness of his appeal and the shabby contents of his character. She knows better than to enshrine him, even if Carrington does not. She perfected her defenses long ago. She had secreted away sweet awkward Adeline behind a dazzle of skill. Yet Adeline remained, whereas — she marvels that this has not occurred to her before — perhaps Carrington has no such avatar inside her, and never did.

She, Virginia, like almost everyone else, had always taken Carrington for a sort of fuddled doll who, with her absurdly wide round blue-ribbon-blue eyes, her bouncing crop of yellow hair and her odd flouncing moodiness, had seemed rather unreal, like the spitting image in miniature of a real girl who had once owned her, grown tired of her and cast her off to make her hapless way in the cruel world. The cruel world she had landed in had been theirs, of course, and she had done so, or so it had seemed then, spectacularly unprepared, her head stuffed with rags, her wooden heart ripe for the plucking.

But perhaps they had all been wrong — all, that is, but the grand impresario herself, Ottoline, who, the gossip was, had had one of her bizarre short-lived affairs with Carrington once upon a time. But the rest of them at least — had they all been fooled by a façade, and the truth was far more sinister?

Perhaps the Carrington of those years had been no innocent abroad, no inert plaything waiting to be picked up, but rather a person of spectacular emptiness and cunning who had hid the horrifying vacuum of herself within a carapace of lies. Then along had come Lytton, with more than enough personality for two, and filled her with his overflow. It — their eunuch union, she calls it now, chortling cruelly — had been an act of true asexual reproduction after all. Lytton had simply replicated, made Carrington into more of himself.

Well, there is consolation in that, at least.

But Carrington. What is to become of her now that her substance is dead? Virginia has tried dutifully to console her in her letters, but her words have rung false even to herself, like the doggerel of a bought condolence. She supposes that Carrington cannot possibly know the depth and entanglement of Virginia's feelings for Lytton and, by extension, her speculations about Carrington herself. Yet surely she is shrewd enough to sense the half-heartedness, if not the clouded hostility, of Virginia's prose.

Carrington had already tried to kill herself once, apparently, a day or so before Lytton's death, when it had become clear to everyone that there was no longer any hope and that the end was very near. Her husband, Ralph Partridge (he had been dragged into her arrangement with Lytton years before, poor lug, and was her husband only in name), had told Virginia and Leonard that he'd found Carrington unconscious in the garage with the motor running and had saved her just in time. Later, when she had come to consciousness, Ralph said that she had raged at him viciously for bringing her back, and he had cried miserably, asking her over and over, "How could you do it?"

He'd said he felt sure that she would try to kill herself again. It was only a question of when. She was being watched closely and cajoled out of her intentions (or so it was hoped) by everyone intimate who could be induced to come and stay at Ham Spray.

Virginia and Leonard are due to make their trip for the day on Thursday, and she is dreading it, more because she will have to invade the place that Lytton has left, the actual place where he departed, and she will have to stand there with his ghost. But his ghost will not be the Lytton she knew, nor will it be some beautified version of him glimmering in the corners of the rooms. It will be Carrington herself, his widow in all but name. It is too macabre.

Carrington has always been Virginia's rival in some unchallenged way, unchallenged because Virginia has never thought Carrington worthy enough to combat; not an equal, as Nessa had once said of Vita. It would have been like playing chess with a goat, she thinks, and immediately regrets the unkindness, for the thought of an animal in pain has always been as intolerable to her as it has been to Leonard, and that is what Carrington is like now, a senseless, keening animal in pain.

The sight of that, the experience of it, will waste me, she thinks, send me right over, and that is not something I can afford. She does not have the resources just now, perhaps never will, to comfort her great friend and companion's surrogate wife, or persuade her not to go ahead with what she intends when Virginia herself has tried to end her life twice. Oddly, she reflects, though one might consider experience to be an indispensable qualification for a psychiatric nurse, she feels sure that hers will be of no help whatsoever to Carrington.

The despair of those days seems so far away now, unreachable, in fact, as despair always is when she is not in it. Despair, she thinks, tacitly thanking whatever quirk of consciousness has made this true, is blessedly unknowable in memory, except as an abstraction, or as a list of the physical symptoms that characterized it: weeping, torpor, headache, inability to eat, concentrate or sleep, the constant awareness of being cold, the hands and feet like ice, then sudden fevers and heats, a racing pulse and hallucinations. This — she can only say so in the past tense — is what it was like — "like" being the apposite word, because one could only ever say what it resembled, or how it appeared, not what it was.

"Oh, Lytton," she cries suddenly, the empty name roving through her brain, seeking its subject, echoing both meaninglessly and momentously, like the byline of a famous writer uttered by someone who never knew him. But, of course, she *had* known him, perhaps not as Leonard had, but she had known a version of him. Was there aught else?

Leonard has always maintained that Lytton had been different with him, especially when they were at Cambridge with Thoby, and shortly thereafter, less vain, less small, less slavish to the tinseled pleasures of the world. And this may well have been true. Lytton had been Leonard's friend first, but she had known him in her own right for years, too, and as someone not yet so wholly enamored of transgression or indulgence for its own sake.

She had known him in the early days at Gordon Square, when Bloomsbury was not yet Bloomsbury but a mere gathering of lively and like-minded students of life, learning, loving and sharing as they grew. She and Lytton had spent hours together in those days, walking in Kew Gardens, talking of the strangeness of reality and human experience as they knew it. And at times like those, when they were luxuriously alone, deep in the heady distraction of ideas, Lytton had been a wonderful private sparkling man and a companion like no other.

He had been, as she had always said, a female friend in spirit, and almost in body, but with the tutored, well-ordered mind of a man. He had been — she remembers him saying this very thing the last time they spoke — like her, a true androgyne, a harmless and half-fanciful yet highly civilized creature out of Milne or Barrie or Carroll that was somehow not indigenous to the stifling culture into which he had been born, and was therefore destined to lead the vanguard out.

She tries to visualize him now, to feel and even smell him as he was then, in all his untidy gentlemanliness, looking mostly the part, but always and endearingly a little off.

Smiling, she recollects her conception of him as Tinker Bell or the March Hare, but she decides that this is not quite right. Perhaps something out of Kenneth Grahame is more apt, the Water Rat or the Mole. Yes, better, she concludes, her smile broadening. She likes this immensely: Lytton the domesticated beast. For, in truth, he had always seemed to resemble most some sort of exotic pet who had become a member of the family, and who, despite being truly dirty deep down in the pores of his skin, overabundantly hairy, greasy and faintly malodorous, had been allowed into the house to play and sleep with the children.

Perhaps, she thinks with a great deal more pettiness than she knows she ought, perhaps that is what he and Carrington had had in common all along, animal magnetism of the uncopulating kind, the goat thrown in with the racehorse to keep him company in his stall. Except, of course, Lytton had never been a racehorse, certainly not so far as his writing was concerned. She had never thought his books at all technically impressive, or even very good. He had written them simply to be able to say that he had written them, and they were full of his cattiness.

Yes, if he was to be a horsy kind of domesticated beast, after all, then he should be more of a dray horse who could speak, she tells herself, smiling again at the naughty picture of it, the two of them a prize pair of livestock, Lytton pulling the wagon, mordantly quipping all the while, and Carrington riding in it, the mum ungulate going to market. I should put that into a story, she thinks, but then immediately she feels ashamed of having shown such disrespect to her dead friend, and to his "friend" who in turn is dying of her grief.

Virginia is swerving wildly now, she knows, between jealousy and remorse, cherry-picking images and memories, but she cannot stop herself. She thinks again of Lytton's proposal—in the winter of '09, was it?—while Leonard was in Ceylon, and to her was still only a peripheral figure, not yet even remotely conceived of as a potential mate. Or, not by her. Lytton had had other ideas, but of course she had not known this at the time, nor had she known how frequently and intimately he and Leonard had been writing to each other all during her travesty with Lytton.

But, she considers more pointedly, what really would it have been like to have been Mrs. Strachey? A marriage of convenience, to be sure, limber no doubt and lecherous on Lytton's part, and perhaps somewhat more adventurous on hers as well. But, she recalls—then stops herself, because she is thinking, with a sudden shock of fear, of the upholding strength of her bond with Leonard, and how abject she would have been in her fits if it, if *he*, had not been there to catch her. Lytton's hammock, by comparison, would have been a very loose-knit and tenuous support, she concludes soberly, that much is sure.

Would she have grown with him? Would she have gone on writing by his side? Or would she have been swallowed whole just as Carrington had been? Tossed, like a dollop of spun sugar, mindlessly down his gullet. She would never be sure of herself in this, of course, of what might have happened, but she knows at least that this is exactly the right way of putting it about Carrington, because Carrington had never been whole. She was hollow, and on Lytton's palate she had deflated and dissolved on contact, like a confection.

Yet the question remains: Would she have done likewise? She, Virginia. It seems impossible, given the rigors of her mind, Lytton's respect and their exchanges, yet she doubts nonetheless. She doubts because, for all her output and showmanship, and even now, with a modicum of fame buttressing her, she feels somehow that she is also hollow, as hollow as Carrington. Or fragile, at the least, as friable as meringue, and as deceptively insubstantial. Goat, she reminds herself, had been her own nickname as a child. "Hold yourself straight, my little goat," her dying mother had said. They had been her last words.

Hold yourself straight. It is still every bit as applicable. Adeline is the proof. Leonard had found her this way, for all intents and purposes a child, for though she had been a near spinster of thirty when they married, she had come to him as a maid. Nessa, having already married and started her own family, and wearying no doubt of the continued burden of her sister's keeping, had passed Virginia on—almost eagerly, and certainly with confidence—to the dependable Leonard.

And Nessa's trust in him had not been misplaced. Leonard has kept her—no, much more than that—he has saved her from all that might have happened to her had she been let go, turned loose or—the most dreaded outcome of all—locked up, as poor Laura had been. There is no question. Lytton could not have faced it, and she feels certain that he knew as much the moment he proposed. Taking her would have been like taking a position. And being in Lytton's care, she concedes, would have been like being the magician's assistant, lying there passively, smiling sideways at the public, being cut to pieces for their amusement.

Yes, she thinks, newly horrified and clear, as if she has just woken from a mortifying trance: Thank God I did not marry Lytton.

Thank God *that* is not what happened. Instead, I am here now, at fifty years of age, safe in the nest that Leonard and I have built over the past twenty years. She says this word again to herself — safe — and sighs with new gratitude and relief.

Fifty is a landmark for certain, she thinks, but she has not been able to celebrate it as such. Her birthday had come this year a mere three days after Lytton's death. She cannot help thinking that this is indicative, but she does not know — or care to consider — of what.

It is an insultingly bright and unseasonably gorgeous spring morning when they set out for Ham Spray in the Singer. Virginia is fresh and curious, as she always is at the start of a journey, though today her excitement is dampened somewhat by the task at hand. Leonard is silent and focused on the driving, still sifting, she intuits, through the jumble of his own feelings about Lytton.

How monstrously indifferent the weather is, she thinks, as she turns and looks out at the morning sun glowing orange on the new green of the trees, to shine so brazenly upon people's suffering.

Their drive takes them due west into some of the most breathtaking country in all of southern England, meandering over the familiar downs of West Sussex, through the scrubby heaths and woodlands of Jane Austen's Hampshire, with the slim jagged spires of Winchester Cathedral rising over it, and on into the lush plains of Wiltshire. Her eyes roam happily, gorging themselves on the scenery, which acts on her like a tincture of absinthe; floats her in the shallows of its emerald dream but never quite puts her to sleep.

They have been driving for at least an hour this way when Leonard breaks the silence.

"I think it was histrionic of her to have tried it," he says.

Virginia knows whom he means, of course, but she reaffirms it nonetheless, as though the name is part of the spell that has been cast over them, and repeating it will help them to break free.

"Carrington?" she says.

"Yes, Carrington," he repeats angrily. The name is a curse for him, too.

He has been brooding about Carrington's suicide attempt for some time. Out of the corner of her eye, Virginia has been watching the conflict in his thoughts cramp across the peaks and hollows of his face. She knows exactly what is troubling him. He resents being thrown in like this to mop up after a family disaster. Carrington is not family, or even a particularly close friend, but her connection to Lytton, especially now that he is dead, has placed her firmly among the array of Leonard's other self-imposed responsibilities to the people he loves, and his conscience is at him as usual to do right by his friend.

The specter of self-inflicted death is something he and Virginia have lived with all their married life. When Virginia took an overdose of veronal one month to the day after they celebrated their first wedding anniversary, it was Leonard's quick thinking and decisive action that had saved her. Since then, nothing they have ever said or thought on the subject has been untainted by this past, and it cannot be now. It is always there, she knows, and it is best to declare it outright.

"Did you think it histrionic of me?" she asks.

"No," he says defensively. "You were ill. It's different."

"Perhaps *she* is ill."

"No, she's upset."

"Yes, well, that goes without saying under the circumstances."

"Precisely," he exclaims, thumping the steering wheel. "She is feeling what any person in her position would feel, what we are all feeling in our own ways."

"You disapprove, then, of her way of feeling."

"I simply think she has behaved badly. Inconsiderately." He pauses here, seeming to consider other, ruder adverbs that he might use, but he loses his temper instead and shouts, "For pity's sake, there is her husband to think of!"

"Oh, come now," Virginia says. "You know as well as I do that Ralph has his own life with Frances, and has done so for a very long time. Carrington only married him at Lytton's behest, to preserve their tawdry little ménage."

"I don't care," Leonard crows. "A marriage is a marriage, and she owes him that consideration."

"The consideration of what, exactly?" she asks, a touch combatively.

"Of not doing him harm. He was clearly devastated by the incident. He said as much to her repeatedly."

"So he claims."

"Well, I don't doubt it. He may be living happily with another woman, but he still cares very deeply for Carrington. She had no right."

"We all of us have that right, Leonard," Virginia asserts, looking righteously away.

"Nonsense," he says, turning toward her. "We have obligations to other people."

She is still staring out the window, and everything about her says that, like it or not, the case is closed. She does not care to contest the obligations of marriage just now.

"Well, in any case," she says at last, turning back to him with a glassy expression, "approaching Carrington with an attitude of disapproval will not be of the slightest use to anyone today, and may in fact make things worse. What's more, since I know you to be incapable of disguising your thoughts, I'd suggest that you let me do the talking, or perhaps find some other employment while we are there."

"May I remind you," he says, matching her tone of cool reproof, "that your attitude toward Carrington is hardly unmixed."

"You needn't worry. I am, after all, expert at dissembling when required."

There is a heavy pause.

"So you are," he mutters, glaring at the road. "So you are."

Neither of them says another word.

By the time they reach Ham Spray, emerging from the dappled nave of elms that shelters the long avenue of approach, the house is awash in midday sunshine. The glare off the white clapboards is nearly blinding, and both Virginia and Leonard are squinting like moles as they get out of the car. Carrington is not there to meet them, nor is there any sign of her when they knock as loudly as their knuckles will bear on the splintered oak door. But they find that it has been left open, as it swings ajar with the last of Leonard's arduous raps.

Still no Carrington. Calling to her, they step into the hall, but there is no response, no sign even that anyone is at home. They look warily at each other for a moment, wondering if Carrington may have tried something again, but decide that panic is premature and continue making their cautious way through the house.

Stealing through it this way, tentatively, their light footsteps echoing faintly through the lofty Georgian rooms, is like sneaking into a museum after hours, or — the decor is so fantastical, yet so familiar — like walking around inside someone's mind. The walls, the fireplaces, even the furniture are painted and tessellated with Carrington's work, and hung with pictures by Duncan Grant,

Henry Lamb and many more of their gifted mutual friends. The house is alive with boldness and the signature blur of color and line that made this place unmistakably their home.

Leonard and Virginia have seen this before, of course. Indeed, it resembles the interiors of their own homes, which have been decorated by many of the same artists. But now, in all its undiminished beauty, the work seems to jump out at them with a kind of garish irony, bearing unrepentant witness to the death it has overseen and the mourning it still contains.

They proceed to the sitting room where Carrington is crouched in the armchair nearest the hearth, though the fire has not been lit. With one glance, Leonard knows enough to retreat. He tries waving meekly and saying hello, but Carrington gives no indication that she has heard, and so making a sign to Virginia that he will wander and wait for her in the drive, Leonard bows out.

Moving slowly and haltingly — she is not sure whether Carrington quite knows that she is there, and she does not want to frighten her — Virginia eases herself into the armchair opposite. It is more sunken and worn than the one Carrington has chosen. It must have been Lytton's perch, but Carrington will not presume to occupy it, or some such nonsense. Carrington will have to be the one to start this. The protocols of grief are obscure at the best of times, and the lady of the house is looking decidedly unhinged.

Her famous bob of flyaway fair hair is now the color of dried mustard seed and thickly molded in a mass around her skull, like a boxer's headgear. It looks as though she hasn't washed it since Lytton died, perhaps since he fell ill, both of which are distinct possibilities. She is as pale and expressionless as lard, not a speck of color or emotion on her face, except in her eyes. They are startling as ever, though they look almost violet against the whites of her eyes, which have turned a semipermanent shade of coral pink from the crying. She is wearing a large, rumpled grey pullover and a grimy pair of old riding breeches. Her feet are bare.

There is nothing to say. Everything is painfully explicit. Everything, from Carrington's urchin-like appearance, to the rows and rows of Lytton's books, slotted like soldiers into the narrow shelves that line each wall, to the soot-blackened maw of the empty grate, it has all become so physically evident, so conspicuous an expression of loss, that Virginia is too daunted to speak.

Carrington is no help. She has no interest in overtures. Every grace has been consumed by the vortex of this place.

"I have been reading Lytton's copy of Hume," she says finally, abruptly and far too loudly, as if she is deaf, or has not spoken to another human in years and does not remember how to do it.

Virginia makes a strangled noise of assent — mm, or hmm — but it's no good. Even that sounds vulgar to her now, like a gourmand tasting the soup.

"He is very good on the subject of suicide," Carrington resumes. "He says that 'a man who retires from life does no harm to society. He only ceases to do good.'"

She has clearly memorized the passage, Virginia observes. This must be the kind of thing she has been doing these past few weeks, holed up here in Lytton's mausoleum for days at a stretch, veiled like an odalisque, with redolent old kerchiefs of Lytton's tied around her face, trying to breathe him back to life.

Hume is not someone Carrington would have read while Lytton was alive, much less understood — or not without the help of Lytton's constant tutelage. He was always one to prattle and instruct, whenever, wherever, garrulously holding forth as if the whole world and everything in it were his entourage by right of birth, and he was bound to share the gift of his erudition. In lieu of his seed, Virginia thinks, he no doubt sprinkled their pillow talk with such pearls — the learned sayings of great men — and Carrington surely swallowed them as eagerly as if they were pearls of those other ejaculations she so vainly desired him to emit.

Virginia is trying so very hard to be good, and outwardly she has been good, or passive, at least, but she cannot stop this cruel soliloquy from banging on inside her head. For every word she thinks to say, this voice has a dozen unsayable ones threatening to interrupt.

"Should we be talking of Hume?" she says finally. She knows it is inane, but it is the only neutral thing she can think of to say.

"Why not? We have no God," says Carrington, as if she is in fact some self-styled student of Lytton's who has crashed a legitimate tutorial and is damn well going to show the boys that she has read the material.

"No," Virginia agrees. "We have no God."

"So, then," Carrington says, "there is no morality. Ethics is all we have left ... Hume argues" — she is quoting again — "that 'no man ever threw away a life while it was worth keeping.'"

It is becoming downright eerie listening to this, Virginia thinks, like talking to a haywire machine or a ventriloquist's dummy that has animated itself. Carrington is gone.

"Worth keeping," Virginia repeats, stalling. A mumbled yes is Carrington's only response.

"That is the question," Virginia continues solemnly, some part of her having decided that playing at pap philosophy is as good a way as any to placate an automaton.

"What makes a life worth keeping?" she ventures, a bit absently now, as if she is indeed talking to herself.

Carrington does not say anything to this, and so Virginia adds, more assertively, "The answer is different for everyone."

"My answer was Lytton," Carrington declares, and Virginia can feel her annoyance welling up.

"That is no answer, Carrington. No one person can give entire meaning to another person's life. You are not Lytton, and he was not you, and he was certainly no answer to anything."

"You did not know him as I did," Carrington says, and Virginia nearly has to cover her mouth to stop herself from blurting: You did not know him at all, you gibbering sycophant. You couldn't have. You do not have the capacity. But with a sudden strength of determination that she manages to drag up and out of her abiding love for Lytton, she is able to control herself, and instead she merely sighs and takes Carrington's hand.

"No, of course," she says quietly, "each of us knew him quite differently. Leonard could tell you things about Lytton that might surprise you. They have me."

"I doubt it," Carrington says petulantly, staring into the nonexistent fire.

Deluded fool, Virginia thinks. As she tries stroking Carrington's hand, the putrid thoughts go on inside her head. Carrington, how pathetically little you knew of your master. What a mirage you made of your life. Virginia knows that she will have to seize on the superficial pity that these thoughts inspire if she is to avoid the stew of ill feeling that lies beneath.

"There is much more to you," she lies, "more value in your life than whatever Lytton gave it. You must see that."

"No. I do not see it. I see only death. That is my answer now."

I cannot keep this up, Virginia thinks, exasperated. The horrid brat is determined to fight. Is she deliberately trying to provoke me because I am who I am, or would she do this with any-one? Well, Leonard was right to call her histrionic. She sounds like a penny dreadful. Oh, but damn Lytton. He really has taken every-thing out of her, and now there is nothing left.

This is the last clear thought Virginia has.

For some reason that she will never understand no matter how many times she goes over it in the days and weeks and years to come, this last thought shakes her violently as she thinks again of the personal vacuity that she had been pondering at Monk's House just a few days before, the hollowness, both Carrington's and her own. And then somehow, suddenly, very suddenly—and a little frighteningly, because this has never happened this way before—she feels this hollowness become itself and expand inside her like an obliterating gas. She knows then that she will not stand apart from this scene any longer.

There is the familiar collapse that happens in her chest, a com-plete dusting of the construct, all the jealousy and pettiness and disdain for the lesser creature—what lesser creature?—all the structure of a lifetime's defense implodes in a moment, as it has done so many times before when she has been so desperately shortsighted and alone, as Carrington is now.

It is all over very quickly, the sham, the highhandedness, the handholding, the bleary-eyed attempt at objectivity, none of which she had pulled off in the slightest. And then, looking about at the fallen fabrication of herself, at the rubble of all this mental scen-ery, at the mote-strewn air and the light hazing through it, she sees only Adeline intact, standing there looking like the smirking after-math of a very old practical joke. Really? her expression seems to say. We got you again?

"Then I will talk to you about death," Virginia says, breaking out of her daze and sounding mechanical herself, or insane. But she does not feel insane. Not in the least. She feels relief, and the elation of at last being able to speak with brutal honesty to another living soul about this one thing. Can it be true? Finally, she sighs, someone I can really talk to about it, and not correctly, not consolingly, not to save or salvage—because that is just the folly of propping up a life that is sliding to its end—but truthfully, morbidly, because sickness is the only path we are on, any of us. Death the only possible outcome. So say it, she urges herself. Just say it. Out loud. To someone. For once.

Virginia's icy use of the word "death" has roused Carrington for the first time, and convulsively so, as if she has been given a shock or an injection. She turns her whole body round in the chair and fixes Virginia with her pink and violet eyes, and the expression on her face is one of hunger, a ravenous hunger that has at last, after a long and dejected search, found its proper food.

This should startle Virginia. It would have done so a few minutes before, but now it does not. Not anymore. Because it is not Carrington she sees, but Adeline, hovering behind her like some wrongheaded guide to the underworld who is yet somehow just right.

And Carrington can see this recognition in Virginia's eyes, or see at least that something vital has changed, the decisive switch thrown.

"Tell me," Carrington says, so eagerly that anyone who was not caught up in this, anyone still in the real world—Leonard, say, who is walking the grounds or tinkering with the car like a normal person—would simply pick up the telephone and call for help.

But for them—how many of them are there now exactly, Virginia wonders, lurking behind and beside?—this is one of those rare psychic dislocations that can be shared.

"I see myself as a girl," Virginia says, not knowing until the words are out that she is going to talk about Adeline. She has never done so with anyone. Not Leonard, not Nessa, not Vita. "She is thirteen, the age I was when my mother died."

Carrington's eyes are gaping like bloodied mouths, gruesome with fascination.

"She is stuck in the past," Virginia continues, "with the first pain, the original pain that was my initiation into unbearable loss. She never recovered, and her only real wish, her only release, will be in death. She is waiting for me to die."

Now who sounds like a penny dreadful? The thought flits across Virginia's mind, but does not stick. These sentiments are Adeline's, and they come without oversight; they have no valuation attached. She pauses here and looks blandly at Carrington as if to say, Does that satisfy you? But she knows that this is a long way from being finished.

"Does she ask you?" Carrington says, her mouth flopping open like an imbecile's. The old Virginia wonders, Will she now begin to drool?

"Ask me what?" she says testily.

"Does she ask you to die?"

"She has no need to. That is why she is there."

"And do you listen?"

Virginia sighs, more than half regretting that she has brought this into the open, and with someone — she sees this now, and should have seen it before — who is so poorly able to withstand it. She thought this would be like sliding into a warm bath with a doppelgänger, but it is like slashing a cutlass through butter. She feels like a criminal.

Carrington, meanwhile, knows that she has failed. She is looking down at her fingers, which are spread out on the tops of her thighs, displaying the variety of sores that are clustered around each cuticle. Some of them are infected, others are calloused and yellow-scabbed from having been picked and bitten so many times, still others are new and strawberry red, each with its own pale pink halo.

The body says everything, Virginia thinks, looking at the hands, recalling her first impressions of this place, and Carrington in it, and her own sense of the redundancy of saying anything when the objects had said it all already. She is feeling the same incompetence now, the writer who has nothing to say, because she has chosen the wrong medium.

As before, Virginia is torn from the temptation to distinguish herself from Carrington, and from what is so clearly happening to them both, the same inarticulacy, the same impotence in the grip of the same distress.

"You know where I am," Carrington says gravely, still looking at her hands. "I knew that you would."

"Because Lytton told you about my past," Virginia says.

"No," Carrington says with a strange assurance. "I would have known just by looking at you. I did know. It was I who told Lytton."

This shocks Virginia. "Told Lytton what?"

"That you were a liar like me, and that your lying would . . ."

But she will not finish, and Virginia cannot decide why. Carrington looks oddly afraid and cowed suddenly, as if her own version of Adeline, or someone else more domineering, is actually standing there with a hand on Carrington's shoulder, warning her that she has said too much. But, Virginia wonders, too much of what? More than is proper? Or more than is *allowed?*

Does Carrington believe that the rest of what she had to say would have offended me too deeply? No. It cannot be that. She is beyond manners. So then it must be the other. She knows that she has said more than she ought. Virginia shudders a little at this no-

tion, remembering Tom's line from *The Waste Land*, the clairvoy-
ant stymied by the blind spot — *and this card, / Which is blank, is
something he carries on his back, / Which I am forbidden to see.*

She smiles slightly at her own fear. Silliness, she chides. Such
infantile silliness. Let her die if she wants to die, but leave my
horoscope out of it. I cannot save her, nor do I much want to. But
this is not fair or altogether true, and she knows it. She is on her
usual merry-go-round with herself. It has nothing to do with Carrington.

"Carrington," she says, again surprising herself. She waits for
Carrington to look up. When she does, Virginia adds haltingly,
pausing between the words, because she does not know herself
what she is going to say. "Think . . . Ask yourself what is true . . . Be
sure . . . Then tell me . . . directly . . . Do you . . . want . . . to die?"

Carrington hesitates much longer than Virginia expected she
would, and this, she thinks, could be either a very good or a very
bad indication. Now she is the one who has said too much, and
she feels again as if she has committed a crime. Either that or she
has taken the calculated risk of going too far, because doing so is
the only way of bringing the patient back.

Carrington is still sitting there so strangely massive in her silence, and once again Virginia thinks of something inanimate. She
fixates on the idea, perhaps because she does not really believe in
fixity. Yet here is Carrington seemingly just that, fixed, occupying
space like a thing, insensate, obvious, sure, not indecisive in the
least. Not a fool in temptation, succumbing, but an essence, pure
and unwavering and simply, immitigably there. She is the stillest
living thing I have ever seen, Virginia marvels enviously; what the
will must look like before it moves the soul to act.

She wonders what Father's philosophizing would have made of
this, or the Apostles': the will as a Platonic form, inert, still and

solid as a bloody rock, but showing itself like this, as a woman, as a monument, like some bronze rendering of Justice herself, welded to her pedestal.

Almost smiling at the thought of Carrington plunked in Trafalgar Square beside Admiral Nelson, Virginia comes back to herself, unsure of how long she has been lost in thought. She is almost convinced that she is going to get away with what she has just said, or that her question has been somehow magically voided by its own impertinence, when Carrington finally speaks.

"Is there any reason not to," she declares. It is not a question. She is not asking, nor is she looking to Virginia for an answer. If she is expecting anything, it is only one syllable, if there is one, that proves what she has said is patently false or mad. Yet it is not Virginia, but Adeline who answers.

"I can think of none," she says dully, and as soon as she has said them, Virginia can feel herself scrabbling to take the words back, but the struggle is horribly inept and futile, like drowning in a dream. Carrington merely nods once, stiffly, in recognition, as if Virginia is in fact a physician delivering the fatal news.

Then, unexpectedly, either because she senses that Virginia is in turmoil or because she simply feels that their grim business together is done, Carrington stands and motions Virginia out.

Her motivation is opaque to Virginia now. She is unreadable once more, expressionless, shut off, but whether from resolution or reproach it is impossible to tell. An aftertaste of blame is clearly there, but whether it is coming from Carrington or herself she does not know. This is not a familiar misgiving. She always knows. She always knows too much, but now there is nothing but static, and as they walk swiftly and wordlessly down the passageway to the stairs, Virginia first and Carrington behind, the feeling worsens to the point that she must stop and turn so that she can look once more into Carrington's blankened face. But by the time she manages to do so, they are at the bottom of the stairs and Carrington is pushing her, politely but firmly, backward out the front door, to where Leonard is loitering at the car. The conclusion has flown by, the moment gone.

Something unnamable is between them. Carrington knows it, too — that much Virginia has discerned — but is it the compact of co-conspirators, the imputation of a supplicant wronged or simply the cold dismissal of a cat's paw used?

She hates it that she cannot decide, but, finding herself outdoors again, breathing the clarifying air and blinking in the sunshine, she begins to sense that the black enchantment of Ham Spray has lost its hold on her. She can feel her social self returning, gloves on, armor up, and as she looks one last time at the waxen changeling that Carrington has become, she resolves not to let confusion show. Never again. She is Virginia. Adeline is the lie, the liar that Carrington sniffed out.

"Goodbye," Carrington says, throwing her arms loosely around Leonard and then more loosely still around Virginia. But Virginia will have none of it, and with a slight but definite shove, she frees herself from Carrington's embrace and turns away.

"Come and see us next week," she calls, her hand on the car. "Or not. Just as you wish?"

"Yes," Carrington says, "I will come . . . or not."

EARLY SEPTEMBER 1932

IT IS THE same now every summer. Guests. An endless parade of unwanted guests at Rodmell. The idea of entertaining always appeals, but then, when the people come, and they stay, and they stay, and they draw on her greedily like leeches, extracting all the best material that she has been saving for her work, well then, it is no fun at all. Then it is like enduring some quack treatment, ordered but clearly daft, and possibly harmful into the bargain. Then she can feel herself desiccating like clay, her face aching under another forced smile, and she finds herself sitting for the last half of the engagement like some melancholy recluse longing for the fullness of solitude.

Is this what it means to be famous, she wonders, or to preside over a famous group? Though infamous is more the judgment now, she hears. Among the up-and-coming set of standouts, the Bloomsberries are right out of fashion: a bunch of self-indulgent, pseudo-socialist, bed-hopping prudes — and yes, the last is a real epithet, apparently, *the* received contradiction in terms, used and endorsed by all who are anybody, intellectually and artistically on the rise.

And, oddly — this is a very new feeling — in the right mood, she finds that she cannot disagree. She hasn't yet said this in company, but it has been on her mind. In fact, privately, when she doesn't have her fists up for debate, she thinks it rather a deft summation of their disease. They really are a willfully ignorant contradiction in terms in almost every way, a pack of cross-dressing Quakers, a gaggle of loose-limbed pacifists dancing atop the cenotaphs. They had been virgins — most of them, well into their primes — who had thought, mistakenly as it turned out, that you could root out a century of squeamishness by playing at sexual excess.

The hubris of the young. It never fails to amaze, she thinks, even retrospectively, in oneself. They, every last one of them, from herself to Leonard to Lytton to Ottoline and on and on, are Victorians — period, full stop — no matter what they pretend. Yes, they have had the nerve to call themselves Georgians, but nerve is all it has been. And Lytton, who had so famously and pricklingly purported to dress down the great era of the Empire once and for all in '19, had done nothing of the sort. He'd merely pulled off an elaborate stunt that the public had mistaken for a serious treatment. No. They had all been raised at the knee of the Dour One, buttoned up in black, and there they remained, in id if not in fact.

Tom Eliot is the exemplar of their type. He embodies what he isn't. Or — to put it more accurately, and for the sake of the enemy's argument, more irrefutably — he emblazons what he isn't all over his skin in every detail, like some savage's tattoo, because he can't, in fact, embody it. That is Tom. That is all of them. All over.

Tom is coming to tea this afternoon, as it happens, and with his awful raving wife Vivien, too, of course. Virginia has made this mistake before — allowing that unruly woman through the door — and, after the last time, she'd sworn never to repeat it. Tom could come to tea alone, she'd said. He could come to breakfast, lunch and dinner, or to stay as long as he liked, so long as he left this creature at home. She is not housebroken. Sorry to all and sundry, but there it is. Vivien has become a nuisance beyond enduring, and she is ruining Tom to boot.

Well, at least he is going to Harvard in a few weeks. That will be a year out of Vivien's clutches, at least. She wonders if Vivien knows of this yet, or if Tom is planning to cable her from America with the fait accompli. Tom is hopeless at confrontations. It will not be a surprising move on his part if he keeps his nervy polecat in the dark until he's put an ocean between them.

Virginia only hopes, for the sake of their afternoon, that this has been his chosen tack. Otherwise, they are liable to end up fishing wifey out of the pond, or — and this is all too likely — having to wrestle the bowls from her as she heaves them one by one onto the dining table, gleefully shattering all the china and glass. That kind of outrage would be just up her street. Her type always seems to find catharsis in the sound of fragile objects breaking, the outward expression, no doubt, of her internal state.

Ah, well, Virginia's own state is fragile enough these days, having come through the tempest of *The Waves,* intellectually, artistically, bodily, emotionally spent. Now she is writing a biography of Elizabeth Barrett Browning's dog, of all things, to cleanse her palate and rest in levity for a change.

But she has come through, having fulfilled the promise of her vision, the bold creative mission that she had conceived in this very house seven years before and hammered out with Leonard in this garden on a summer's day not unlike this one. She has done it.

Leonard has called it her best, and though he often feels obliged to say this about new material, she cannot always agree or maintain her satisfaction with finished work. Often, after the thing is done, published and reviewed, and especially after it has been out in the world for a spell, suffering the slings, she finds it difficult to feel sure of it or to love it as she had when it was fresh. This time, however, she does. She knows *The Waves* for what it is and holds it to her as her own, beyond the reach of recklessness.

She is having arguments over poetry with the disapproving young set out of Oxbridge, especially her nephew Julian, who, having followed in his father's — and Leonard's and Lytton's — footsteps and gone to Cambridge, and joined the Apostles, is now fresh out of school and bearing down on the world like a Turk. With his first book of published poems under his arm, and his pen sharpened and unsheathed, he is spoiling for a fight.

What is the art form of the decade?

To him and his cabal it is poetry, of course, or so all the cockiest pansies are insisting. But what kind? That had been her main point of attack in "A Letter to a Young Poet," an essay that Julian's friend and fellow Cambridgeite John Lehmann had proposed she write for publication at the press. Lehmann, like Julian, has literary plans for himself, and so after having helped Leonard to run Hogarth for the past two years, he has given his notice. Still, he has put them in touch with Auden, Spender, Isherwood and other combatants of their generation. Whether it is for good or ill, she remains unsure.

She enjoys a good scrap, and she had given it to them in the "Letter," arguing that the topical preoccupations of the young — the plight of the working class; the Manichaean conflict they saw shaping up between communism and fascism in Europe, which they seemed convinced presaged nothing short of Armageddon;

and their insistence that even the most grubby and abject details of real life, as they called it, must be made to sing—none of this had served their poetry well.

Art that is made to serve politics—or worse, civics—is, she feels, bad art. A glorification of the gas works is not a poem. It is as simple as that. She had not written it quite this way, but it was what she had meant. They have great big brains, all of them, and, like Lehmann, great big plans to match, but they are simply too young, too arrogant and—she had not, of course, been able to say this in print either—too single-mindedly and shortsightedly entrenched in their buggery to know, to have lived widely enough or to have developed their craft enough to write what needed to be written.

What did need to be written? Well, that is the bigger question, and not one to which she had provided specific answers in the essay, mostly because there are none. Abstraction and theory are all you have before the words have been written, before the work of art itself has arrived. Art, she thinks, is ontological in this sense. It must exist first, and by existing, both assert and demonstrate its necessity. Analysis can only follow. It cannot create, or envision the spirit of the age *avant la lettre*.

Yet that is the game now, and in many ways it is good fun, even if it is just a bunch of overripe intellectuals pelting each other with wind. It is thrilling to be caught up in the blowdown, especially with Julian. Had it not been for him, she doubts she would have bothered with the other children, as she likes to think of them. But Julian has always been a special child, and these critical skirmishes with him have been, well, rather Greek, actually, like taking your student, or your brother, or indeed your son as your lover. Symbolically, Julian is all three, and though he is—obviously—not her lover, there has been something unmistakably flirtatious in their private exchanges, even, or perhaps especially, in her harsh criticism of his work, which he had shown her early on, asking for comment.

Such passion is not really to be found in her generation anymore, and she misses it. She is, in fact, rather hoping to rouse crusty old Tom to a scrimmage this afternoon. But that will depend on Vivien.

Tom and Vivien arrive promptly at four, when the garden is at its warmest and loveliest, heavy with scent and magicked by the first inklings of the long evening to come. Virginia and Leonard greet them there, sitting in the pair of four assembled cane chairs that face the back of the house. The other pair of chairs — strategically placed — face the two of them and give a view of the garden. They have been tactfully reserved for the guests. Virginia had urged, and Leonard had agreed, that this was the most prophylactic course to take for the containment of the lunatic — set the proper scene, bucolic, serene, hosts benignly in repose, and hope for the best.

Tom has on his customary three-piece suit, funereal grey, with a sad white kerchief crumpled in the breast pocket like a failed flag of truce. Virginia can't recall seeing Tom in anything else, always the most formal of suits, though this one is so uncharacteristically rumpled and careworn that she wonders if he has taken to sleeping in it. The stress of seventeen years chained to Vivien is showing more than ever, she thinks, as she looks at Tom's shoes, which are so scuffed and in need of polish that they look as though he's walked the length of the country in them pondering how to throw off his shackles.

He is thin and very pale, his face preternaturally so. Vaguely slimed and sickly white, he seems to be sweating milk, though his nose, especially its trademark pointy tip, is quite red and faintly spider-veined. These are the effects of the drink, she presumes, which he has taken to like a Catholic in recent years. His hair is parted severely, as usual, just off center, which gives him the slightly clownish appearance of a man whose grooming habits were harshly imposed long ago — as his were — to create an impression, and have not been revised since. Naturally, to anyone with half an eye for these things, this style is painfully out of date and, aside perhaps from the ersatz Anglo-Brahmin accent he affects, is the strongest evidence of Tom's overall constructedness.

Vivien, by contrast, is in white, head to toe — lacy summer frock, dainty low-heeled shoes and stockings. She is almost pulling off the picture of wounded innocence that she is trying to project, except for the narrow-brimmed bucket-style sun hat that she has pulled down so lank and low on her lolling head that it looks as if it was filled with water when she put it on.

He looks like an undertaker. She looks like a misfit figurine torn from the top of a botched wedding cake. They both seem to be slightly drunk or — surely in her case — sedated, which makes their entrance that much more ominous. Clearly, Vivien knows about Harvard, and she and Tom are in the throes of detachment. This is not going to go well, and Virginia sinks deeper into her seat as she watches the toxic couple cross to the quartet of chairs.

"So, Tom," Leonard blurts, leaping from his chair and thrusting himself awkwardly forward to shake Tom's hand, "how are things at Faber and the *Criterion*?"

Obviously, she thinks, feeling vindicated, the mere sight of these two has worried him as much as it has her. Normally this would be a question for an hour hence, but panic has taken hold, and Leonard is running roughshod over the introductions, attempting to steer past catastrophe. There is a pall looming, one that even the newcomers have sensed.

"Oh, very well, very well, thank you," Tom replies, taking Leonard's hand in a firm grip and sitting down gingerly on the edge of the chair opposite him. "Been enjoying bringing the young ones along," he adds, unbuttoning his jacket and sitting back. "Auden, Spender, what have you. But then, you know. You have been doing the same. Really promising stuff — exciting."

He says this last word a touch nervously, perhaps concerned that his enthusiasm might sound proprietary and dismissive, but Virginia, at least, appears not to have heard, and Leonard doesn't seem inclined to start anything.

Still, Leonard has noticed, and can't help thinking what he will not say. As Tom is aware, that spring, Hogarth had come out with a collection of new verse that included work by Auden and Spender, as well as a selection of pieces by other promising young poets out of Oxbridge, but Tom had already poached Auden's and Spender's first individual books of poems and, in essence, claimed them as his own. Poaching was a sore point between them, though somewhat less of one than it had been back in '25, when Eliot had first defected to Faber.

Leonard takes silent pride in knowing that this has been Hogarth's best year yet, and their best overall financially as a working literary couple. Virginia's books are selling well. He has just published the first volume of his own intensive historical study of warfare, *After the Deluge,* which he plans to extend to at least two more volumes. Life is good. Besides, seeing the condition that Tom and Vivien are in, sore points of publishing are the least of his concerns. It's true; he isn't going to start anything.

"Yes, it is very exciting, isn't it?" he agrees emptily, dropping the subject.

Virginia, meanwhile, has not even risen from her chair. Instead, she has remained seated in the same posture that she has been in for the past half hour, with her legs twisted round each other. She looks as if she has been unwelcomely disturbed alone with a good book, and she has not bothered to remedy this impression. Vivien sits unbidden, pretending not to notice the slight, and sighs rhetorically at the beauty of the day. "Isn't it lovely here."

Now that Vivien has taken her chair, Leonard sits as well and vigorously rubs the palms of his hands together, trying to summon an air of excitement that no one feels.

"We think so," Virginia says with a shade of condescension in her voice. But, sensing that she has perhaps been too cutting too quickly, she adds brightly, "The garden is Leonard's baby. He's worked quite hard on it. And I simply couldn't live without it."

Despite the effort, this last part comes off sounding like a mockery of polite conversation, and Leonard is obliged to rescue at least the appearance of sincerity, if not the fact.

"It's true. Virginia wasn't much for it at the start, but now she practically lives out here whenever the weather allows."

They all nod and smile appreciatively at this, relieved to be ignoring their discomfort, at least for the moment, but the smiles are visibly forced on all sides, as if the four of them have been surprised by a photographer and asked to pose for a snap.

They had called it tea, but Tom and Vivien both hastily ask for drinks instead. Naturally, Virginia thinks — must keep up the derangement. When the servant, Nelly, comes for the order, Leonard asks her to bring Martinis for their guests, though by the way he asks, Virginia can tell that he is urging her to go light, light, light, please God, on the gin. To keep their composure, Leonard and Virginia opt for a lesser poison, sherry, and come off looking like a pair of vicars. Tom doesn't fail to make this point, though it is a feeble one, for it is he who has become almost intolerably sanctimonious since he became an Anglo-Catholic five years ago.

Virginia is tempted to chaff him over this, but decides that it is too complicated. Their balance is too weak. And anyway, now she thinks of it, he is really only sanctimonious these days in public, or for public consumption. In private, gossip has it that Tom and his coworkers at Faber spend a good portion of their weekly editorial meetings boozing, passing gas and telling off-color jokes.

Part of her finds this impossible to believe, because she has always known Tom to be such a prude about bodily functions. Once, years back, when he had visited them alone at Rodmell, the three of them had been walking on the downs and Leonard had fallen behind to relieve himself. Tom had made a point of saying that he disapproved of such behavior, adding, in a shocked tone, that he could never bring himself to urinate in front of other people, much less outdoors. She and Leonard still laugh over this when it comes to mind.

But Tom's drinking and his years doing battle with Vivien have changed him, that's clear. He still presents a pious face to the world, but behind closed doors, at parties mostly, she has seen him misbehave under the influence, and, seeing him like this today, soused in the middle of a Friday afternoon, she is coming to think it probable that his manicured front hides a truly twisted disposition. How could it not, really? He had always been a battened soul, latched watertight. Now, with the wear of time and conflict, the man is like a coiled spring, and alcohol, true to form, has proved a treacherous lubricant.

When the drinks come, he and Vivien scramble for theirs as if they have been bitten by venomous snakes and these are the anti-dotes. Raising his glass immediately, Tom offers a cheerful toast: "It keeps you young. That's what De Quincey says."

"Does he say that?" Virginia inquires skeptically, taking a very small sip of her sherry and thinking that the drink has certainly preserved Tom, but like a corpse. "I've just been reading De Quincey, as it happens," she adds, "and I don't recall."

"Really? Imagine De Quinceydence," Vivien drawls, and pulls a face. She downs her drink in one and pours herself another from the shaker, which Nelly has been either heedless or mischievous enough to bring with the drinks.

"Easy," says Leonard, trying to tease, but his worry is all that comes out.

"Yes. Never you fear," mumbles Vivien over the rim of her glass, her eyes rolling. "It goes down so easy."

"He and Baudelaire," continues Tom, ignoring this exchange. "They understood what the sages of the East have always taught, that paradise is a state of mind."

"Yes, but induced," Virginia says, "which is not quite the same thing."

"On the contrary," Tom asserts. "All higher states of consciousness are induced, and psychotropes, whether ingested or endogenously produced — by fasting, flagellation, what have you — have been a part of religious ritual since the advent of man. For Baudelaire and De Quincey, confined as they were by the strictures of their time and place, it was simply a question of expedience, the means that were to hand, and the fervent desire to explore. Opium, hashish, absinthe, wine. The trappings of the Western mind, you know, are deeply entrenched and harder to disengage." He raises his glass again. "They require a stronger solvent."

Yes, Virginia thinks — glancing over at Vivien, who has wandered to the rhododendrons nearby and is staring at them as if they have faces — just look to your wife. She is a veritable pharmacopoeia on stilts, and the Dharma Body of the Buddha is apparently in the hedge at the bottom of the garden, after all.

But despite her annoyance, Virginia identifies with what Tom is saying. It is, of course, her mindscape he is describing, and the essence of what she has been trying to convey in her work. The same is true of him, and this is what has always drawn her closest to him in spirit, his deep understanding and expression of this shared experience, the profound mysticism of everyday life. Thinking this, she feels snubbed by his pedantry, which seems artificial and intentionally insulting. He has never taken this tone with her. She dearly wishes that he had seen fit to say something about *The Waves,* or would now, but today he seems determined not to acknowledge her as a peer or as the confidante that she has often been to him.

Well then, she resolves, taking an emboldening sip of her drink, I can give as good as I get. Raising her now half-empty glass, she says, "I should like to make a toast." Over her shoulder, she calls in the direction of the rhododendrons, "Vivien?"

"What?" gasps Vivien, startled from her reverie. Turning suddenly with a bracing hand over her heart, and surveying the group with huge, accusing eyes as if the three of them are fiends who have just materialized to torment her, she says angrily, "What's the matter?"

"Nothing, dear," Virginia says as if she is speaking to a cretin. "Only we're having a toast. Come join us."

Warily approaching them, Vivien looks over the low table where the drinks tray is set. Gesturing nonsensically at it, she cries, "Why have you taken these? Are you trying to confuse me?"

"No one has taken anything," Tom says. "Now sit down."

Leonard is more consoling. "Yes, Vivien. Please do sit down. We should so like your company."

"Oh, you should," Vivien mutters. "You *should,* if it weren't for . . ." But she trails off without finishing and decides instead to smile at Leonard. She does so almost pleadingly, as if she is asking for his forgiveness, or thanking him in a backhand way for his persistent gentleness in what even she knows is quickly becoming a debacle.

"Now," Virginia says, to break the spell of Vivien's appeal. Turning to her husband, she announces, "Leonard and I have just celebrated our twentieth wedding anniversary."

In the awful pause that follows, this jab does its dirty work, and Virginia smiles, adding, "So, a toast, then. To marriage, and death do us part."

Tom gamely raises his glass, but with a noticeable sneer, and says the obligatory "Here, here." He cannot bring himself to say the words "marriage" or "death," however, and he sets down his glass without taking a drink.

Leonard is balancing his glass on his knees, with both hands wrapped protectively around the stem as if he intends to plant it. "To marriage," he says dolefully, casting a reproachful glance in Virginia's direction, but he does not move.

Vivien has lit up at the challenge. Seizing the Martini shaker and popping the top off, she salutes Virginia with it, nodding to acknowledge her opponent. She then downs the contents like a Viking, so violently that half of it streams out the sides, down her cheeks and onto the front of her dress. Her thick coating of face powder has washed away in stripes from the corners of her mouth like a tragedian's frown. The sight of her is so distressing that Virginia has to look away.

Vivien swipes at her chin with the short sleeves of her frock, sighing contentedly at her achievement; another conflict success-fully provoked. She is very clever — at her best really — in the heat of a good row, and so she is now. She loses no time in cutting to the quick.

"*What you get married for,*" she squawks in a perfect cockney, modifying her husband's famous line just slightly for the occasion, "if you didn't want children?"

This is almost unanswerable, and it hangs there over the four of them, dangerously pregnant and inadvisable, like some depraved piñata that has been filled with nails and nitroglycerin.

We should have expected this, Virginia thinks, determined, at least for the moment, to deflect the palpable bull's-eye of this taunt. Vivien has always claimed this line as her own, her indelible contribution to the greatest poem of the twentieth century, a mere five hundred lines, give or take — she remembers the drudgery of setting the type — that had arguably grown more iconic in its first decade of existence than even Tom himself.

But it had been they — Tom, Leonard and Virginia and their forward-thinking press, not Vivien Haigh-Wood cum Eliot — who had brought this monumental work of art into the world. Who was this harridan to think she could turn it on them like this? It is unconscionable cheek.

But she knows she should not allow herself to be drawn into a brawl. It is, of course, what Vivien has intended all along, and that is among the best reasons to avoid it. Deny her her scene.

And yet, children. Children, damn her. It is *the* incontestable absence that has always bound the two couples together. How ter-ribly and precisely it has touched all the maladies of sex and cre-ation that Leonard and Virginia have stubbornly refused to ac-knowledge they have in common with Tom and Vivien, but which, just as stubbornly, some part of them has always known they have in common all the same.

And the poem. It was devilish quoting the poem to this end, for it was the poem, and the very autobiographical pain of it that Vivien was pointing to in that line, that had once brought them so close to Tom, and in some ways to Vivien, too. It was the poetry, the life and life-giving force of letters that they had all seen living on as their legacy in place of children. Subliminally, but no less passionately for being so, this was what had inspired them to collaborate in the first place. But since then it has only torn them fretfully, fitfully, yet never quite fully apart.

The moods, the troubles, the sicknesses. They are at the root of it all, writing, not writing, surviving, not surviving, marrying—how? And staying that way or not. And, most of all, or worst of all, not having children. The chafe of it never goes away. No matter how they write it—question it, dismiss it, defer to it, going over and over it with their pens, as if scratching it obsessively on the page can desensitize the nerve—nothing has changed.

It is why they are here having "tea" at this late date, and with so much festering displeasure between them. Tom and Vivien are on the verge of what is likely to be a permanent separation. Virginia and Leonard are more together than ever. And yet. Yes, and yet, here they are, at each other like badgers in a sack. All except Leonard, who is trying, as always in his quiet way, to make peace.

They are as combustible as the times, these four, and lining up on opposite sides. She has heard rumblings about Tom's growing fascist sympathies as well as his anti-Semitism. The Jew-baiting has always been there, often in muted form, but now, from what she's heard, it is beginning to leak out. Meanwhile, Vivien reputedly worships Oswald Mosley and the Blackshirts and skulks about London with a knife. Not that her behavior at present can count for much, yet even so, Virginia wonders, how much of this viciousness — and it *is* coming from both of them, she feels sure of that — is bound up in a politics that, of late, has become all too personal to everyone?

Here, after all, is Leonard, the socialist, pacifist Jew who has just come out with his own book on the prevention of war — Tom has made no mention of that either — arguing that the roots of armed conflict lie in the very jingoism that the lovely couple before them would seem to endorse and embody.

No one says any of this, of course. No one will. But it is there, suppurating.

They are opposites who have been stranded, by fate or biology or sheer bad luck, in the same shameful fix: Barren and squirming on the razor's edge of matrimony and madness, for better and for worse, in sickness and in health, they are too alike to bear it and too disparate to come to terms.

Children, as everyone is so fond of reminding them, are the future. So, they have always consoled themselves, are ideas and works of art. But, as Vivien has so cruelly conveyed with that single, vilely chosen snippet of verse, they have none of the former, precious few of the latter, and nothing in the end that has any real power to avert teatime spats, much less world wars.

If anyone has bothered to dispute Vivien's last words, Virginia has been off spiraling too ponderously to have heard, but she doubts it. They are all as listless and dejected as prisoners. By the look of him, Leonard is too drained or despondent to try to shepherd them back to neutral. He is looking longingly at one of the apple trees as if he is thinking of hanging himself from it. Tom has lit a cigarette, and is smoking it like it is his last. He is holding it so still in front of his mouth, merely opening and closing his lips to drag and exhale, that the ash on it is nearly an inch long. Even Vivien seems mollified by her joust and its deadening effect. She knows that it has hit home and doesn't seem to require a retort. Virginia's torpor has told her as much, though she would have known anyway. She knew the instant she opened her mouth that there would be no going back.

Despite her better judgment of only a few moments before, Virginia cannot bring herself to leave this comment or its mouth-piece unquashed. But before she can summon the killing words, Vivien erupts again, responding as she has been doing all along, not to Virginia herself or this situation, but to the years of unac-cepted likeness and dislike that are between them.

"You are a wicked, wicked woman, Mrs. Woolf," she cries. "The White Devil indeed."

"I beg your pardon?" Virginia scoffs.

"Or didn't you know? Since we are talking of the poem," replies Vivien. "We emended those lines for your sake."

"We?" cries Virginia. "Hah! I doubt that very much. But re-mind me, since you clearly fancy yourself the coauthor, which lines were those?"

Not to be outsparred, Vivien focuses her eyes fiercely for the first time all afternoon and raises her voice to a volume that even the servants must be able to hear inside the house. "Remind you," she shouts, "must I?" She shoots Virginia a withering look. "Well, of course, having never been formally schooled, you could be for-given for not knowing your Webster."

This is too absurd to acknowledge, one of Vivien's character-istic flights of delusion, for as everyone has always lamented on Tom's behalf, one of Vivien's chief faults has always been her scho-lastic deficiency.

"My dear Vivien, you forget. We knew you back when. We

know you now." Virginia casts her eyes across Leonard and Tom, to reinforce the suggestion that they are sharing a private barb. "And you are nothing more than what you have always been: a dull-witted and failed arriviste clinging to the coattails of your betters."

But Vivien will not relinquish so easily what she knows she has gained. Pretending not to hear, she picks up her glass, which still has some liquor left, sweeps it instructively over the company and, ignoring the splash that falls across the front of her frock, goes on with her lesson.

"The original lines, as they appear in Webster's play, are as follows," she slurs pompously: "*But keep the wolf far thence, that's foe to men, for with his nails he'll dig them up again.*"

She pauses dramatically here, the remainder of her face powder seeming to puff off of its own accord, as if from a barrister's wig in the heat of a summation.

"In *The Waste Land*," she continues, as if anyone needed reminding of the poem's title, "we rendered them thus: *Oh keep the Dog far hence, that's friend to men, or with his nails he'll dig it up again.*"

She pauses again to suppress a burp, and draws herself up, as if she is addressing a group of feckless students rather than the author and publishers of the work in question. "An interesting change, don't you think?" she says, adding triumphantly, "Especially in light of the latest discovery at Ham Spray."

At first no one can take this in. The unexpected affront to Lytton's and Carrington's deaths is so much more of an outrage than anyone had expected even Vivien to commit, that for a solid thirty seconds no one reacts. Vivien sits patiently upright, beaming with the success of this strike, sipping demurely at the dregs of her drink. The other three are slumped more lifelessly than they were before, like novelty toys that have been unceremoniously un-plugged.

Virginia turns wordlessly to Tom, not for confirmation of the truth of what has just been said, for she does not for one instant believe that there is any truth in it, but for some acknowledgment of the sheer magnitude of the treachery that his wife has managed to unleash, and he to tolerate. But Tom is frozen with his eyes fixed firmly on the ground, terrified, mortified or both. She sees immediately that he will be of no use.

She looks at Leonard. He, too, is a wreck of disbelief, the Englishman still clinging to his raft of good manners, stunned into mute passivity. Seeing that she is the only one willing to or capable of defending herself, Virginia turns at last to address Vivien, who, this time, has been attentively awaiting her reply. The look of venomous anticipation in her eyes provokes a frenzy.

"You witch!" Virginia shrieks, lurching forward as if she means to strike Vivien, but drawing back at the last moment. "How dare you mention that accursed place? You can have no idea what it was like in that house. What we went through. We were there the day before Carrington shot herself."

She stands, white with rage, overturning her chair behind her onto the grass and swiveling on her heel to march into the house, but Vivien is too quick for her.

"Oh yes," she says exultantly, "I know you were there, and that you spoke with Carrington alone." She takes a short mocking breath and turns her head on its side. "One can only wonder what you said to her."

She keeps her head on its side. Her smeared face is now gashed by a vile, gummy grin, and her eyes are so maliciously bright that she looks possessed.

"Among Carrington's papers," she continues with taunting

surety, "was found a note with those very same lines from Webster — can you imagine? The very same lines, written out in Carrington's hand, and the word 'wolf' underlined."

Vivien jerkily rights her head, crosses her legs and settles back in her chair. "That cannot be a coincidence, do you think?" she says.

Yet another astonished silence engulfs the other three, who are once again utterly at a loss, like characters from a different genre, thrown in with this harpy. Virginia had been almost halfway to the house by the time the words "'wolf' underlined," had registered. She stops cold at the sound of them. She is standing with her back to the others, shaking, as before, with rage, but also tottering with the jolt of this new insult.

Leonard stands and goes to her. He puts his arms around her and she collapses against him. But then, flushed with a fresh resolve not to be beaten by this bromided nobody, she rights herself again, takes her husband by the shoulders and swings him aside. She turns and makes her way toward Tom. She stumbles slightly when she reaches him, and leans over to grip the arms of his chair for support. "Is this true, Tom?" she gasps, glaring into his eyes. She is close enough to kiss him. "You must tell me if it is."

Very slowly and reluctantly, he nods, but he cannot bring himself to say anything.

"Of course it's true," shouts Vivien triumphantly. "We heard it directly from our mutual friend Ottoline, and, well, you know how close *they* were."

Vivien is like a crocodile clamped on its prey. She will not let go. She will roll right to the bottom of the bog with her victim and thrash it until it is dead. There is no graceful way out, and Virginia is too sideswiped to try. Leonard will have to euthanize this fiasco.

Without looking at Tom again, Virginia pushes herself back from his chair and, without another word, makes her way across the lawn toward the house. Leonard is still standing where she left him, and she meets him on her way in.

"I'm so sorry," he whispers as she passes. She will not look at him either, though he sees that this is because her eyes are no longer functioning as they should. They will guide her to her room, where she is likely to spend the next several days incommunicado, but that is all. She is locking down into her most isolated self. Once there, she will be gone for as long as it takes, all the doors and windows shut tight. He can only wait for her to come back.

Leonard's eyes are on her all the way to the house. When he sees her reach it, open, then shut the door behind her with a brisk and terrible click, he shifts his gaze to Tom, who is already up and handling Vivien. Grasping her by the shoulders, he hauls her to her feet, which she is clearly unable to keep beneath her on her own, roughly grapples her to him by the waist and marches her toward the front gate. Vivien is one of those petite women who look immediately ridiculous when they attempt a show of force. And so it is now. Her feet are no longer touching the ground, and she is repeatedly attempting to kick Tom in the shins. Meanwhile, she is pummeling his chest quite uselessly with weak and uncoordinated fists, and spitting unintelligible insults into his face. He, however, looks only faintly annoyed and oddly focused on his task, as if she is not a human being, but an unwieldy object that he has been hired to transport. It will be no great tragedy if he drops her; just more time on the job.

Over the top of Vivien's head, Tom is slurring his apologies to Leonard, and Leonard is waving him off, saying some insincere variation on "It's all right" or "It's all over now," but Vivien is screaming too loudly for him to hear. The gist of a formulaic send-off is all he can get, which is undoubtedly for the best. He can't apologize enough, and Leonard can't pretend enough to make this parting anything but a farcical dumb show. Tom will have to make this up to Leonard over time, if he can. Virginia will require more finesse. And Vivien? Well, before today, she was on her way out. Now she has stamped her ticket.

Act IV

THE YEARS

❧

1934–1938

October 1934

WHY DOES THIS not get easier? Honestly, why? It makes no sense. Other labors improve with repetition; streamline, accrue, accelerate. Not this one. The novel, it seems, is definitively always just that, new. Damned thing. And she is damned along with it, again and again and again. Bloody hell.

Except that hell is not the outer darkness. Hell is writing novels.

What else can she think? She has done this seven times already, and the last was her best. But it is coming on five years since she touched *The Waves*, five long, terrible years since she wrote those final resounding words: *Against you I will fling myself, unvanquished and unyielding, O Death!* Had it been a malediction? A valediction? In retrospect it sounds as if it was both. Seal your lips with a curse. She is working harder than a dung beetle, yet she has nothing to show for it but dung.

The startling skirl of the telephone ringing fills her with a sense of childish liberation; class dismissed. And indeed there is a reprieve on the other end, for it is Ottoline calling to absolutely beg her to come over to Gower Street at once and salvage one of her teas, which she swears is falling so mortifyingly flat that she will be shining bald the next time they meet if Virginia does not fly to her rescue immediately.

Virginia laughs. "But what can possibly have gone so wrong?"

"I've deliberately kept it scarce," Ottoline huffs in a scratching whisper—she has clearly got her hand cupped round the mouthpiece—"because blessed Yeats has graced us again. But Stephen Spender is in there with him now, and I would swear to you it is *not* a happy meeting of two poets. It's like some forced détente between diplomats, neither of whom speaks a word of the other's language. It's simply ghastly. You must come. You are the only person I know who can possibly resuscitate this conversation."

She drawls the word "conversation" as if it is stretched to the breaking point between quotation marks. Virginia is loving the picture: the poets, old and new, stuck and writhing, and, of course, the sound of the grand Lady Ottoline on her knees, flustered and beseeching her to—only she can possibly—save the "conversation."

And why not? It is certainly better than being a dung beetle. What's more, how can she pass up another chance at dear, mystifying Yeats, of all the prophets, who foretold that they would meet again? And so, here they are. Again.

She must go.

She throws on her shawl, careers down the stairs and out the door to fetch a taxi. It is only several blocks to Gower Street from Tavistock Square, but she must do as asked and fly.

Coming into Ottoline's flat is like coming into a funeral home for atheists who grew up going to church. It is not dour, but it is not dapper either. It bears the morbid legacy of the prior age: the damask, the chintz, the paneling and the long, dark, polished dining table, which looks as if it might have been a bier for Gulliver. And then there is the portrait of Lady Ottoline herself, by Augustus John, hanging above it like a vaguely macabre portrait of the deceased, who is every strand of pearl and Ascot chapeau the great lady, except that she appears to be feasting on a leech or biting off the end of her tongue. It is hard to know with Ottoline whether she has hung the portrait in spite of or because of this unflattering detail, or simply because it is by John, but one does feel inclined to give her credit for brashness in this, as in all things.

There are other paintings throughout the flat, by Walter Sickert and Henry Lamb, which are part of the modern flair and liveliness of hue that mitigates the funereal fust of these rooms. Still, the faint odor of airless parlors and sickrooms out of the last century lingers in the pomander bowls that are spread about the room. Again, one never knows with Ottoline whether this is a provocation or a compulsory nod to tradition.

When Virginia makes her way through the sensory assault and busybody battery of the anterooms and arrives at last in the sanctum, she sees that for once Ottoline has not been exaggerating. Yeats and Spender are indeed as forked and twisted as mandrakes in their chairs, and seemingly afflicted with encephalitis lethargica.

Spender is lean and fine-boned, with a Cupid's-bow mouth that seems to slip a contradictory come-hither into his otherwise tense and serious face. Those lips, with the lapidary jaw and the winning cleft in his chin, make him almost handsome, but not quite. His thin mousy hair is a roguish swirl that he will lose in middle age, and which, Virginia observes, only gives him a more rending boyish appeal. Like many English princes, his flowering will be short-lived, and his momentary brush with beauty will give way to the unfortunate balding and beaking of his Norman-Saxon genes. At present, though, Lytton would have called him defilable.

Through Julian's introductions, Stephen (as they have been urged to call him) has become something of a friend and regular at the Woolfs', so when he sees Virginia, he leaps to his feet as if cured, and kisses her firmly and wetly on both cheeks.

"Good God," she cries, "but you are eager today, Stephen."

"Yes," he drawls, turning immediately to Yeats. "Forgive me. But this venerable gentleman here is the eager one. He has been waiting with misted eyes for your arrival ever since Ottoline importuned you to save him from me."

Yeats shakes his head as if to demur, but he has clearly been pained by the intimidated lad and is every bit as relieved to see her as Stephen is. Though Yeats would not say so, he does have the grateful look of someone saved — and this much he might say when they are alone, for he has said as much elsewhere, she knows — how sharper than a serpent's tooth they are, Spender and his lot, this thankless gaggle of lettered offspring. Dreamless, angry, dialectical materialists, he calls them, beating their poems into ploughshares. And she agrees. She has said the same herself. Yeats must be nearly seventy now, and Stephen is just about Julian's age, give or take, a mere toddler of twenty-six. They are indeed so young, so brash, so chipped against the shoulders they have stood on. Yeats, meanwhile, does resemble the woeful parent Lear. Today he is open-collared and windblown, yet rosy with the vigor of something suspect. Or supernatural, perhaps?

He is not shy in telling her his secret, though the moment he does, Stephen seems to petrify with shame or disgust and fall into his former vegetative state, for succor, if nothing else.

"I've had the Steinach operation, my dear," Yeats announces. "It's marvelous. I feel sixteen again."

She does not want to know what the Steinach operation is—something gonadal, she gathers—but she is grateful for the bloom it seems to have given him. Though she has not read it yet, she knows that he has just published another collection, *The Winding Stair*. He seems as prolific as ever. A prick of envy catches her, but it is soon dispelled by his enthusiasm, which is as brimming with her as it was dry when he was with Stephen. She feels for him, Stephen, being alone with an icon. How can one help but dry up and turn into a tuber? Unless one is an icon oneself? The puckish thought wanders through her brain, but she dismisses it in favor of a better formulation, mystic. She is a fellow mystic, and this time she is prepared.

But she needn't be. Yeats is doing all the spinning.

"Oh, Mrs. Woolf," he cries, "do you know I wrote a little poem after we met the last time? It is in this new collection. You are an inspiration to this withered vine. I grow the vaunted grape once more."

Again, this is not a metaphor she wishes to pursue, but she is cheered by his zeal.

"Ah, youth," she sighs, a little caustically, casting a slightly suspicious eye on Stephen, who is still catatonic and stiff in his chair, as if he has changed ages with Yeats or had all his natural verve siphoned from him by the old wizard. "It has so many secrets," she adds, glancing now at Yeats, who is—she must agree—sitting oddly pretty to the youngster's left and looking almost sinisterly sated by *some* juice.

Yeats smiles meekly at this, but does not reply, and so she goes on with her thought.

"I had a similar conversation with Tom Eliot several years ago about De Quincey's purported secret of youth, but as I remember, Tom was quite drunk at the time."

Yeats is roused. "Ah, yes. Tom Eliot. He, too, has heard the mermaids singing. What did he say De Quincey's secret was?"

"Drink," Virginia says. "Well, that and other substances, both ingested, I believe he said, and excreted. He came to De Quincey via Baudelaire, it sounded, and was very keen on *Les Paradis Artificiels.* Mysticism achieved through derangement of the senses and all that."

"And you disagree? Or is it disapprove?"

"No. No. Neither," she says. She is going to be surprisingly honest with the old man, she realizes. "I think that in his drink, Tom has an excuse for mysticism, not a method, and his newfound spirituality, such as it is, while it scans beautifully in print, is cover."

Yeats's eyes light up with what Virginia takes at first for a fellow gossiper's glee at the bitchiness of her remark, but he is no Lytton or Ottoline, and he will not contribute to slander.

"I think you do him a disservice. You know, of course, that in his poem 'Ash Wednesday,' Tom and I have shared the metaphor of the winding stair. We have done so unwittingly, I would say, except that there is nothing unwitting in the Spiritus Mundi. We are drinking from the same spring. As are you, dear lady, as are you."

She cocks her head, saying nothing, then looks down, both because she has been caught talking idly and because Yeats, as always, has seen through it.

"*We shine with brightness,*" Yeats pronounces, but she does not understand that he is quoting. Seeing this, he adds, "That is from 'Ash Wednesday.' Tom's conversion poem, I believe it is called?"

She nods meekly. "So it is."

"And then there is you," Yeats says. "*I feel myself shining in the dark.*"

He is quoting again, this time from the mouth of Jinny, her own half self in *The Waves*. But she cannot acknowledge it. How can she now, when this repository of a man has plucked seven words from the middle of her book, as if once again they are written on the palm of his hand, and matched them to five nearly identical words in Tom's latest poem?

"It is the same thought," Yeats continues. "Coming from the same vast permeating source. In *The Waves* you have captured this in fictional form. You have given linguistic expression to this oneness, this continuation of universal consciousness and the pulsations of energy that are coursing through it. You have shown that the individual and the collective mind are one and the same. These are indeed the very waves, as you have so aptly called them, for whose existence today's most innovative physicists are producing the scientific evidence, and which the newest developments in psychic research are beginning to corroborate."

Bless and damn him. She is on the verge of tears of sheer joy and relief that someone outside her immediate family has understood *The Waves,* and said so. The words, the labor, the pain have not been wasted. God, but he is astounding.

"And did you speak with Tom of Baudelaire's 'Correspondances'?" he asks.

"No. Not specifically."

"You know the poem, of course."

"Yes, but not by heart. My French is poor."

"By mind." He smiles, and she nods gamely.

He begins once more to recite: "*La nature est un temple où de vivants piliers / Laissent parfois sortir de confuses paroles.*" And then to translate: "Nature is a temple where living pillars / Sometimes let fall confused words."

She furrows her brow.

"Living pillars," he says. "The stones are alive! All around us, they are alive. And speaking, what's more. Speaking!"

She immediately recalls the time, so many years ago, when she and Leonard were courting. She had told him virtually the same thing. You are my rock, she'd said, meaning it in just this way, as a compliment, but he, of course, had taken it as a slight. Then, as she had proceeded to explain that no, no, rocks were as sentient as everything else, he'd looked at her for the first time with that mixture of awe and worry that would cross his face so often over the course of their marriage.

This, for some reason, makes her remember Stephen, and she looks across at him to see how his brain is taking this assault. He is now sitting forward in his chair with his head in his hands, but from between his splayed fingers she can see his goggle eyes swiveling frantically back and forth between Yeats and her, as though he is watching a game of tennis being played between the undead with a ball of fire.

Then, out of nowhere, as if she, too, is energetically in tune, Ottoline appears at Virginia's shoulder in a flash of trailing purple silks and floral headscarves. She leans in, levers rigid Stephen out of his chair without a word and shuffles him to a chaise across the room, where what appears to be a troop of truant brokers and their daytime tarts are gathered round, sipping champers and talking political rot. Just the thing.

Virginia turns laughing back to Yeats, who is chortling avuncularly at the sight of the overcorrupted ears of a tyro being scuttled on their wobbling pins to safety among the starched shirtfronts.

"I take it you hear voices, Mrs. Woolf?" he resumes, now that they are alone.

The question is as artless as she feels, yet rather lawyerly, too, she thinks, in the way it is phrased. He knows the answer, or he would not have asked. And for her part, she is as liberated as he has been by Ottoline's rare showing of good sense. Perhaps the two of them are emanating, after all, levitating there on their side of the room, speaking of things that are, like demonic charms, dangerous to say aloud.

"Sometimes," she says. "Yes."

"And do you know how?"

This is startling. How? The whats of her illnesses have been far too preoccupying for her to have ever considered the hows. And she gave up hope long ago that any of her doctors would ever know anything of cause, so why should she?

"No," she says at last, politely but a little disapprovingly, as if she is a teetotaler refusing a stiff drink.

But Yeats is determined.

"It is not mysterious," he asserts. "Have you listened to a wireless?"

She shrugs. "Of course."

"And do you know what makes a wireless work?"

Again she makes the flat response. "No."

And again he urges past it without pause.

"To keep it simple," he says, "the metals and the carbon in the vacuum tubes inside your wireless are receiving, converting and then amplifying waves that are running through the air. Radio waves, to be exact."

She shrugs again and says nothing.

"This is clairaudience at work. Do you see?" he insists. "The mechanism of it man-made, already in many houses in the land, as accepted and commonplace as pudding."

"Man-made?" she repeats, a bit dazed, and not quite caring to contest.

"Yes. The wireless is"—he puts up his hands to bracket the

words—"an 'invention.' But in fact it is only mimicry, a reinvention of what already exists all around us in the earth and in ourselves. All the elements and conductive metals in a radio are not only in the hills, the mines and mineral deposits in rocks, in air, in soil and in seawater, they are also in your body. Did you know that zinc, copper and iron are in your blood? And you yourself are made primarily of salt water and carbon? Water is a marvelous conductor, which, as the latest techniques in neurological research are showing, acts as a kind of bioelectrical charge on our skin when we sweat. They are calling it the galvanic skin response and have used it to measure states of psychoemotional arousal in the human brain. Notice the word 'galvanic.' In common usage, as you know, it means to cover something with a metal coating, specifically zinc, and also to electrify or spur something into a heightened state of activity. And that, my dear, is the metal in our sweat acting on us like a conductor, and turning a human being into a wireless."

Now she is nodding politely and thinking that he is as mad as she sometimes is. Yet he is talking of things she knows, or has sensed at least and felt. She cannot deny it. And he does talk so like an Irishman. The blarney is rolling over her like a cascade of hands. She cannot help but lose herself in the feel of his voice.

"We will not live to see it," he continues, "but one day people will be communicating across seas and continents, their messages traveling through nothing but air, and they will be doing so through yet another of these so-called marvelous inventions, which will in fact turn out to be nothing more than what we ourselves are—modifications of the same earth, air and water that are all around us and babbling all the time."

Now he can see that she is addled, and slightly afraid, somewhere back behind her glazing eyes.

"I did not mean to frighten you, Mrs. Woolf."

She surprises him and herself by coming suddenly and rather fiercely out of her daze to assert her side of this description. She does not wish to have the tortures of her mind swept so nonchalantly into the speculations of this wild-eyed Fenian shaman. In any case not without a fight.

"Why is it, then, Mr. Yeats," she says testily, "if all of this activity you speak of is so real, if it is going on always and everywhere, why do I, and, alas, some of the unfortunates who are caged and so cannot be among us, seem to be the only ones who hear or see or feel it? Tell me that."

"Wonderful," he says in a strange tone of voice. "And brava, my dear. You have hit the pith of it in one."

She frowns, regretting that she spoke at all.

"Think of Melville's whales," he says.

She looks at him quizzically, and still annoyed. But then, she thinks, at least they are back in the neighborhood. And besides, what can she do? He is off again like a crier before she can protest.

"Melville spends a great deal of time, you may remember, on his cetology, the science and classification of whales. He tells us of their singing. The humpback, one of the baleen whales, which is also called the Mysticeti whale, is perhaps the greatest composer among the whales, propagating his song through the waters in waves of sound. Many of these vocalizations are too low for us to hear, just as our very own Sir Francis Galton's dog whistle is too high for us to hear. But humpback whales can hear these sounds, and they have been making these sounds to each other for thousands of years, unheard by us, because they are specially equipped to function in a wider range of frequencies."

He fixes his eyes on her like pins.

"I ask you, then, if we are able to hear what is indubitably only a fraction of the whale's deep-throated symphony, and we cannot hear Galton's dog's whistle at all, does this mean that these sounds do not exist?"

She shakes her head.

"Of course not," he cries, his voice rising sharply. "That was what I meant to show you with the example of the wireless. There are many, many more things in heaven and earth than are dreamt of in our philosophies. That is given. But some of our wildest dreaming is coming true and being made real through discoveries in science. What's more, these *dis-coveries* are just that, uncoverings of what has always been there, in the songs of the whales of the seas, and the *babbling gossip of the air* that is being heard and answered by the mountains."

She does not like the manner of this much better than she did before, but she does love that they are back to poetry, and that he has quoted Viola, the androgyne, whose speech of love is among her favorites in all of Shakespeare. *If I did love you in my master's flame / With such a suffering, such a deadly life ... Halloo your name to the reverberate hills / And make the babbling gossip of the air / cry out ...*

She is smiling without knowing it.

"So, at last, Mrs. Woolf," he is saying, "I submit to you the notion that you and I, and Tom and others, who are able to hear and see and smell things that others cannot, are not perhaps mad, after all, but only distinctively equipped to receive the *complete* experience. And that, again, is Baudelaire: *Les parfums, les couleurs et les sons se répondent.* Perfumes, sounds and colors correspond."

He is finally done, yet he does not have the look of a man who has just delivered a psychotic's sermon, or, by chance, encapsulated the mysterious workings of the world within an hour. He does not seem enervated in the least. He is glowing, as he was when she came in, and now she is beginning to see just how he may have sucked the spleen out of Stephen. Yet in her chagrin, she is nearly his disciple, too. She is truly mesmerized, and now, it appears, unwisely encouraging him as well, for what she says next seems to come from someone other than herself and without her consent.

"You said the Mysticeti whales."

"Ah, yes," he gushes, "well, of course, the root of the word 'mystic' is the Latin *mysticus*. The root of the word 'Mysticeti' is unclear, though it appears to be *mysticetus*, meaning 'mouse,' a corruption of a translation from the Greek in Aristotle's *Historia Animalium*. But much more interesting is this: Melville named his ship the *Pequod* after the Pequot, one of the indigenous peoples of what would later become the Massachusetts Bay Colony. New Bedford is the primary seaport of whaling in North America from which Melville's ship departs in its search for Moby-Dick. As you may know, there is a river in that area called the Mystic, as well as a town of the same name. The name comes from the languages of those same indigenous peoples, either Muhs-Uhtug or Missi-Tuk, both of which mean 'big river,' though the latter term is more literally translated as 'great river whose waters are driven by *waves*.'"

"Like the Ouse," she says.

Yeats looks at her curiously.

"The Ouse River in Sussex, near where we live in the country. It is tidal."

She looks at him for help, as if she has said something terrible that cannot be taken back, but he is only hearing again what he has already heard.

"And so," he says, "here is yet another coincidence, as the skeptics would say. But you and I know from Baudelaire to call it a correspondence."

She nods, but she is utterly spent and, mesmerized or not, she can say nothing more. She does not quite know how she disengages herself from his clutches, or if he lets her go, but when she is aware of herself again, she is standing in Ottoline's foyer, going through the motions of departure with the grande dame herself. Yeats is there, too, but only to see her off. He is staying — to enthrall some other unsuspecting mark, no doubt, and invigorate himself still more.

As they are saying their goodbyes, Yeats leans in and whispers to her, "The poem that I wrote for you is called 'Spilt Milk.'"

She nods stiffly and a little guiltily, but he seems unperturbed by her failure to have read his latest work. As always, he simply knows.

The moment she reaches home, she bounds up the stairs to her room and rifles through her books. She has it here somewhere. She is pulling out all the newer ones that she has either shoved in sideways on the bookshelves atop the rest or crammed in nooks by the bed and elsewhere in the room, but it is not there. She stumbles, twirling anxiously around the room, more determined than ever to find it. She goes flat on her belly beside the bed, and retrieves it at last from the depths of a pile of toppled quartos, newspapers and journals that she has let accumulate there.

The Winding Stair, a pale turquoise and black-checkered volume on which is depicted the winding staircase of the title, a coiled serpent, confrontationally open-mouthed, and a woman riding a dolphin. She flips to the table of contents and runs her finger down the page until she sees it. "Spilt milk." She opens to the place and sees that the poem is only four lines long. She reads it over many times. She reads and reads, and her eyes begin to water and swell. She closes and reopens the book. She sits staring blearily at the text, the cover, the walls. Then, finally, she allows herself to cry.

There is no escaping these links. She will not use Baudelaire's word for it yet, but the sense is clear. These are the words of Mr. Wolstenholme coming back to her out of the past in another form, steeped, exactly as before, in her unutterable sadness. They are a prophecy. They are a recollection. They are an epitaph. They belong on a stone.

NOVEMBER 1936

LEONARD IS SITTING by the fire, listening to the wet, green logs hiss and crackle, not caring that he has been soaking in their smoke, almost to the point of asphyxiation, for hours. His smarting eyes are doggedly fixed on the page in front of him, which he is holding up vertically and very close to his face, trying to obscure his expression from Virginia. She has been sitting across from him all this time pretending to read, but she has been watching him like prey.

The rest of the proofs for this, her latest novel, *The Years,* are balancing on his lap. He is almost through. She has not let him see the work before now because she has been in such an almighty swivet over it. True to its new title — it had formerly been called *The Pargiters* — she has been wrangling with this tome (it is six hundred pages long) for years, and in the past six months she has been as unwell as she has been since those last worst days of 1913.

He is staring at this page, has been for some time, not reading it, because it is the second to last and he does not want to finish. She is waiting for this, as she always does, for his verdict, but this time, because of her state, there is far more at stake, and they both know it. His judgment carries all the fatal thrust — sadly, this is not an exaggeration — of a Roman emperor's up- or downturned thumb in the gladiatorial ring, which is why he cannot give it truly, and why her hunkered waiting has become so immense and terrible.

It is the worst feeling he has ever known with her, even after all they have been through together in the almost quarter century of their marriage. This feeling, this brainwave of hers, call it, has a menacing life of its own. It brings to mind recent broadcasts from the Continent made by that foaming maniac Herr Hitler, who had positively desecrated that summer's Olympic Games in Berlin, and by technological extension the rest of the world, with his plosive spattered outbursts into the Reichrophone, which had come lashing over the wireless into every home and mind like a fist full of rusty knives.

The comparison is unfair, of course, and yet, he thinks, how her thought pattern beams so acutely between them as if it would indeed cut. It hangs, it hovers, it protracts and somehow seems to ping overhead, ever so softly and metallically — he cannot escape this association with sharps — like a guillotine in the wind in those last interminable moments before it falls on the unfortunate's neck. She has not meant to put him in this position, nor would she were it up to her, but it is not up to her, and so she has.

No wonder, then. He is in a mighty paroxysm of angst, desperate to summon his powers again. Quietly, wretchedly, his senile tremor making the page before him shake violently in his hand, as if it is indeed in the throes of some supernal force, he has spent the last however many minutes — seconds, quarter of an hour, he does not know — petitioning a God in whom he does not believe to descend in his rickety machine and relieve this denouement. Solve this, he begs. Give me strength. Give me conviction. Give me the mendacity to deceive, to assume again this unwieldy burden of her doubt and embellish what I do not feel. Let me not say what I think — though what I really think is not at all bad — but rather what she is waiting, what she is so wanting and needing, to hear. Somehow, he wagers recklessly at last, at the cost of my own perdition if it must be so, please, this once, this once more, let me save her life.

At this, as mechanically as his convenient God, with his free hand, he takes up the last page, and, holding both it and the other before him at chest level — he no longer has the wherewithal to hide his face — he runs his eyes across the final words. He pauses this way, held fast for a moment by whatever potency he has managed to conjure in himself, and then, quite suddenly and utterly, in a way that he has never, ever allowed himself to do in her presence before, he breaks.

He breaks the way he had once broken as a child of five or six, when, upon returning from a blissful summer holiday in the country, he had rushed out to the family plot behind the house in Lexham Gardens to inspect the garden. Much to his dismay, though not entirely to his surprise, for they had been left untended all season, the beds lay sprawled there pitiably in all the decrepitude of their neglect, far uglier and more upsetting to behold than he had anticipated. The few remaining plants, drooping and bereft, had been overlaid with a thick and dreadful coating of soot, the remnants of the famous clinging smog — not fog — of the coal-fired London of those days.

Standing there looking at this scene, such a young boy in his

Eton collar and worsted suit, in the year 1885 or '86 it would have been, he had shivered top to bottom for the very first time with what he would one day come to understand had been the great abiding sorrows of the world. *Weltschmerz,* as the Apostles would invoke it.

But at the time, it had only seemed as bizarre and separating as all the rest of his experience. That time — which had been the zenith of Victoria's reign, of industry and of the Empire, yet also the nadir of social inequality, poverty and filth — had always been to him so thoroughly other, so inherently unreal, even then, as he was living it, that looking at the people and things materializing before him had been like looking through a rent in time itself, or through a stereoscope, into a picture that he did not believe he could touch. It had never quite seemed to exist.

And the sight of it, many such sights, in fact, and their accompanying sadnesses, had broken him, just as they were breaking him now, way down inside, and without his consent, in all the hidden nodes and ducts and apertures where his reason has no say, and where the somatic betrayals of grief come furiously, and of their own accord.

As the first convulsive sob seizes him, he snaps forward from the waist and then immediately back, caroming against the wooden upright of the chair with a resounding thwack. The proofs whoosh and flurry to the floor around his feet, as if he has thrown them down in disgust. His mouth cracks open obscenely, red and mute, as in a Goya still life, with its lurid centerpiece of rotten fruit. And finally, spasmodically, with the same intemperance, the tears come all at once, drenching his cheeks in sheets and darkening the collar of his shirt as if he has plunged his head into the washbasin.

Good God, Virginia thinks, the sought relief of all these

stranded months flooding her parched and isolated brain. I had not hoped for such a reception; he is moved to tears.

She had spent much of the summer in bed with Adeline, reading aloud—when she had been able to read—passages from the manuscript of Vita's new biography of Joan of Arc. Adeline had become convinced, though of course Vita knew nothing of Adeline, that this was Vita's long-awaited answer to *Orlando,* a book written specifically for, about and in honor of not Virginia, but her.

Yet the truth was that Vita had mostly waned from view. At some point in the previous year it had crossed Virginia's mind that their demoted friendship, which had slid a long way from its erotic heights over the years, had reached its end.

But that had not happened. Though diminished, it had gone on, and at a considerable remove, for Vita could not—she had never been able to—handle Virginia's spells. She had always been afraid of the turmoil that lay behind Virginia's brilliance, and she had never doubted that something truly alien and frightening *was* there, and waiting to pounce. However intimate they had become, Vita had always maintained a safe distance from Virginia's "other side," and she had, as she had done in all of her affairs since the disastrous tryst she'd had so young with Violet Trefusis, kept her hand safely on the door handle at all times. In her own way, Virginia had done the same, knowing that the donkey could not fathom the asp.

Yet Adeline would have no truck with this view. She had seen herself in the Maid of Orleans, as well as a tribute in Vita's love, and that had been that.

The visions, she had cried, as if the concordance were unmistakable. *The headaches had come upon her at thirteen.*

And, of course, as she had gone on to point out, the Maid had also shorn her hair and donned the clothing of a boy. Was this not proof enough?

Orlando! She had wailed decisively.

There had been no dissuading her or curbing the effect that this perceived flattery had had on her. This, as well as Virginia's seriously deteriorated condition, had given Adeline a degree of confidence and strength that she had not enjoyed for many years.

In their exchanges, Adeline had often had the upper hand, and she had, at times, been remarkably strident, as inversely hale as Virginia was ill, and full of the pride she had always drawn from Virginia's falls.

The martyr dies, she had insisted one morning while yanking Virginia's breakfast tray away from her. *She always dies.*

Then, quite without precedent — presumably it had been the boldest thing she could think of, and an attempt to show who she'd thought was now thoroughly in command of their partnership — she'd taken up the boiled egg and, with a disturbing and ghoulish relish, popped it into her mouth, shell and all, and summarily crunched and swallowed it as if it were a soul and she one of Satan's subalterns reclining on the burning lakebed of hell. She had, alas, been introduced to Milton.

How awful, Virginia had thought with a shiver, watching the long, flexing muscles of Adeline's throat pass the object like a snake. Still, she had thought staunchly, I will not show her my fear.

"That may be," she had heard herself saying, "but we are simply not going to self-immolate." After an angry pause, she'd added, "Nohow," a strangely slangish turn of phrase that she had not even known she'd known, and one that she certainly never would have used with anyone else. "Never mind," she'd said finally, pulling the breakfast tray back and replacing it on her lap. "That is not how we are going to die."

But is it not a purification of the soul? Adeline had said, as if she had not heard the reprimand.

"Don't be a fool. They burned that poor peasant girl at the stake. It was a barbaric method of execution imposed by religious fanatics on a pawn."

But what of holokaustos?

"Don't be clever. That was an inane and useless pagan ritual which—"

And so, to wit, Adeline had cut in—something else she'd never done before—*we have the ceremonial cigar instead.* It was, word for word, what Virginia had said to Lytton in the garden years before when they had been talking of the pagan ritual of sex. Hearing it again, Virginia had marveled at how precise, yet how blank, Adeline could be. Her recall in some things was like a child's, perfect yet ignorant. She could say the words in order by rote, as if they were a line in a play, but she did not know what they meant.

Still, in those long, hot, cloistered summer days that Virginia had spent alone with Adeline in the bedroom, there had been something else fueling the girl's insolence—something more than the usual smell of the sickroom and the near persuasion of death, or even Vita's perceived *hommage.* She had been overjoyed, quite literally. She had spent a great deal of time dancing about the room with her skirt raised above her knees, singing nonsensical ditties and bouncing on the bed.

The occasion? This had been the year of Virginia's menopause, or still was. She did not know how long it could be expected to last. She did not know if this latest trouble was the aftermath or if it was still the phenomenon itself, her hormones having their last gush and making it damn well count. *Exit, pursued by a bear.*

In any case, Adeline had been elated by the demise of her old nemesis. In fact, if Virginia hadn't stopped her — she'd actually gotten as far as assembling the necessary items — she'd have fashioned one of the hated menstrual rags into a doll, tied it to a stick, set it alight and marched about the room hoisting it aloft, belting out the "Marseillaise" like a Communard, burning her bloodied bandage in effigy.

Virginia had, of course, been as pleased as Adeline to see the hated womb-leakage go, but if its going presaged, as it was threatening to do, some ineluctable drive to do herself in, and in some hideously torturous and symbolic way devised by Adeline, the piping part of her was not for it. And there was still a piping part, the part of her that was still propagating ideas and intent on breeding art, the same part of her that had been of late both gravely provoked and disgusted by the creeping lamia Adeline had become. How dare she feast on my weakness? she had thought. How dare she amble and jig, and yet smile and be a villain? I am the progenitor, not she.

Well, they had had their wars together, she and Adeline, and for nigh on a hundred days, stamping and flailing, sweating and groveling, fretting as they fell, indeed like the petty demons in Milton, grappling well out past the stratosphere of sense and down again into chaos. But now, sitting by the fire watching Leonard weep into her book, that is all quite over. A bad dream.

For Leonard has made the miracle happen again. He had done so months before, actually, though only now does it truly resonate.

Was it not wonderful to see Godrevy again, and Talland House? Adeline had said excitedly at one point during their trial, the innocent girl emerging for a moment once more from behind the provocateur.

In May, when Virginia had begun her decline, and everyone,

including the servants as well as anyone connected with Hogarth, had become sufficiently alarmed to stop the presses, Leonard had insisted on a complete break, a two-week holiday from all work.

He had driven them to Cornwall, thinking that a visit to this idyll of childhood memory would heal her. And so it had, briefly. How could it not? She had walked in the garden at Talland House and peered through the high, thickly moted windows into the molting yellowed rooms, just as she had done in her mind's eye when writing *Lighthouse,* with the caressing, slow and heavy-lidded gaze of passing time. Yes, it had been a return to that time, both to the time of Mr. Wolstenholme and of Adeline sitting on the grass having her vision (he being a shattered witness to it), and to the time, many years later, of her fullest creative outpouring in *Lighthouse.*

What a monumental kindness Leonard had done by taking her there, to that place, to that very day and to its elaborated twin, that other day in the garden at Monk's House in 1925 when it had all come rolling out into art. It had been the perfect reminder. She could heal herself once more, as she had always done, by looking into the past, planting her feet again where she had once been whole, when she and Adeline had not yet diverged, and where they had been so very, very happy as one.

Leonard had known all of this without knowing explicitly of Adeline, and he had also known that by recalling what she had achieved both symbolically and actually in her work in the recollection of this place, she could find again the encouragement to live a little longer. All at once, and while himself saying nothing at all, this simple act had communicated the profoundest, most rectifying message that anyone could: Here you have been happy, and so you will be again; about this you have written beautifully, and so you will again; here is life; these are the things that belong to you, and they cannot be taken away.

Afterward, she and Leonard had stood together for a long while, hand in hand, on the gouged and pitted limestone promontory of Godrevy Point. With the waves pounding beneath them, the spindrift dashing up into their faces, they had looked out across the raucous waters of the bay at the proud gleaming tusk of the lighthouse, with its moody cumulus above and its walled lawn below. There it had stood, even still — and also still, it stood so remarkably still — the defiant finger and the stamping foot, so white, so green, lofty and grounded both, always flying, always holding fast amid the graft and torment of the sea.

"Shall we?" Leonard had said at last, loosing her hand and turning to go.

She had looked at him then with all the gratitude of a lifetime, which had owed its extension, each bleak and obstreperous time, to moments, to gestures such as these. But with his usual grace and exquisite kindness, he had merely narrowed his eyes at her and blinked: There is no need, my love, no need.

And so they had come home, and she had spent her summer *in camera* with Adeline, waiting for the medicine to work. But, of course, the real medicine had been there all along. She thinks she sees it now in Leonard's suffering, though, like Adeline, she has not understood it.

But no matter. He has succeeded in this ruse without using one. His anguish has been interpreted as love, which, in fact, it mostly is, the intolerable awareness of his growing weakness against the recurrence of her disease. He is crying because this grief, happily misleading though it may be, is only one more temporary hold against the enemy, a mere postponement of defeat. He cannot foresee how or when, but he knows that failure is assured. Someday, it *will* come.

Yet, sitting across from him, now beaming, Virginia — and this is really so unlike her — is seeing nothing but praise. Can she not see the pain? Well, he is thankful, then, if she cannot.

But this is not the whole reason she is beaming. He, too, is off in what he sees in her, for over the past few hours she has at times actually been reading, or, to be more accurate, thinking quite hard about something she has read. She has had Tom Eliot's latest collection of poems open in her lap, and there is a piece — "Burnt Norton" — a single line from it, that has held her in its grip for some time in the profoundest state of awe and disbelief.

The trilling wire in the blood.

It is breathtakingly beautiful, as so much of what Tom writes is. In whatever time or place she might have read it, the line, the words themselves put together in this way, would have made her stop. But, again like so much of what Tom writes, if she had read it only two years ago, it would have made no sense. She would have admired it the way a savage might a foreign god, for the phenomenological fact of its beauty and power, but she would have knelt apart in ignorance and never dared approach. In the end, she would have done what she had so often done before with Tom's work. She would have shut the book and, with the sourness of envy in her heart, dismissed as fancy whatever she had felt.

But now. Now it is too clear. Hauntingly, thrillingly clear. It is Yeats's prophecy come true, the very thing he had said to her two years before at Ottoline's. "Tom — he too has heard the mermaids singing." And again, "All the metals are in your blood . . . and so a human being becomes a wireless."

So, now there it is, at last writ down as the old man had said.

The trilling wire in the blood.

But that is not all, for, as she had asked herself just moments ago, moving her finger along the page, What is the very next word? What is the noble function of this blooded wire? *It sings.* It bloody well sings, just as Yeats's whales and seas and mountains are singing, and thereby it resonates the world.

At this she had gasped rather loudly, just as Leonard had been gasping out the first of his tears, and she had looked across at him with such surprised relief, yet also with the trill of Tom's blood and the wail of Yeats's Mysticeti in her ears. But of course Leonard, dear man, had not known this cause. And now he, too, is looking at her — a little oddly, she must allow — with his own — is it relief? — because he thinks she is gasping only at him.

"It is as good as anything you've ever written," he says at last. "Extraordinary."

"Oh," she sighs, leaping up and crossing to kiss him on the forehead. "I am so, so, so, so very pleased you think so."

He takes gentle hold of her wrist, looks up at her and smiles weakly. "You see," he says, "it is all all right."

"Yes, so it is. After all this blasted suffering, it is."

"I told you it would be," he murmurs, but he cannot quite look her in the eye as he says so. His gaze slides a little sideways from her face, seeming, he hopes, to muse in the middle distance. But he needn't worry. She is no longer looking at him either. Or, not at his face.

She is looking down at his hand, which is still holding her wrist loosely and distractedly, tossing it gently between his thumb and forefinger, as if it were the worn willow handle of a cricket bat idling between his knees.

She remembers that she had seen him do this once over tea that day so very long ago when they had first met, when she and Nessa had come up to see Thoby at Cambridge. All through the visit,

Leonard had been fidgeting with a cricket bat between his knees, and because of this — he had done it expressly to disguise his defect — she had not noticed his tremor. But she would not have been likely to notice it in any case, for she had been trembling herself that day.

She had been as nervous as he. And so, there they had sat, awkward among the others, two fiddlers, he with his bat, she with her parasol, ticking at their props for comfort. And once — she remembers this bit only now for the very first time — just for a moment, their eyes had met. Immediately and synchronically, like the pendula on a pair of magnetized clocks, their fussing hands had stopped, and shyly, tenderly, they had smiled together at being caught.

JULY 1938

TOM HAD RUNG up this morning to tell her the news himself. Vivien had been committed to the Northumberland House
asylum.

"I didn't want you to hear it from someone else," he'd said, with
what, even for him, had seemed a new and chillingly clinical re-
serve, as if he were not still the husband — astoundingly, they were
not yet divorced — but some bureaucratic adjunct assigned to the
case, making the obligatory calls to forestall any fuss.

By way of justification, she supposed, or to gild his little household catastrophe with the precedent of genius, he'd told her that
Joyce had been forced to do the same with his own daughter Lucia, not three years before.

Ah, well, in that case . . .

She had said all the right things and given nothing away — so sorry, how awful, perhaps it's for the best—but all the while she'd felt a fearful nausea creeping through her. Before long, as she'd sat listening to Tom drone, all at once she had been horrified to find herself clammy and shuddering and foul-smelling beneath her arms. In the end, she had had to ring off quickly and rush to the lavatory to be sick.

So Tom, she thinks, her arm still slung around the toilet bowl, there you are. The reptile is out of his hole, having shed his un-sightly skin. Now, all slick and freshly shining with treachery, he suns himself in the full light of day.

Her hatred for Vivien, she realizes, has mostly slipped away with the years, lost its hold on her, in spite of the horror show of their last day together. Perhaps that had been the actual breaking point for Tom and Vivien. She had wondered ever since if it might have been. Certainly it was one of their last outings together. Tom had left for Harvard later that month, as planned, and that had been the end of the marriage. He'd simply left, and a year later, in absentia (as she'd predicted), he had had the separation papers drawn up and delivered to a bewildered and bereft Vivien, who had been, by all accounts, still reeling from the abandonment, as well as the thorough shunning that Bloomsbury had given her on Tom's behalf. Virginia shudders now to think of her own part in this. The cruelty, the hypocrisy, the pettiness.

As she had watched Vivien from afar, growing more and more frantic in the shadow of Tom's rejection, and finally seeming to self-destruct in embarrassing public displays of recrimination, Virginia had sensed her distaste for the woman obscurely giving way to the feeling of kinship that had always underlain it.

Perhaps, she thinks now, it was finishing *Three Guineas* that had finally done it. Its shrill denunciation of patriarchy, or so the harshest critics have opined, had had a jarring effect, even on her. The first reactions have been absolutely scorching on this point: This is a screed, not an argument, and one that has only served to reinforce the very stereotypes about women's minds that the author intended to refute, etc., etc.

She had been painfully aware of this stylistic vehemence all along—for it was indisputably there, that much was true—yet she had found herself unable to dampen it in later drafts, despite repeated advice from Leonard and others that she do so. On the contrary, she had grown angrier and angrier on behalf of her fellow women as the writing had progressed. Now, in its first month of publication, this tirade, as the book has been tarred, has drawn more fire than anything she has written, and she has grown angrier still.

Tom's news could not have been timelier or, indeed, more predictable, yet it has hit her like a train. There had been signs, and she had noted them, albeit with a subdued alarm. Yet she had behaved terribly nonetheless.

In perfect inversion to Vivien's decline, Tom had flourished in recent years, at times it seemed almost malignantly drawing vigor from his wife's demise. It had been horrid to observe, all the more so because Virginia had felt complicit—no, she had been complicit—yet she had been unable to stop herself from licking her lips and presiding, every bit as shrewishly as Ottoline, over Vivien's exile from their club. In her usual convoluted way—all cryptically subconscious, of course—just as Virginia had begun softening toward Vivien, and even vaguely descrying in this mistreated woman the fragile likeness of her own mad self, she had also begun to experience an equal and opposite surge in her affection for Tom.

It was indefensible, and she sees how expertly she had hidden it from herself, all of it, buried and denied, very deeply and heatedly, in the sharp, expository prose of this new polemic. There in plain view, in the pages on her desk, she had held the whole disgraceful mess of her personal feelings conveniently at arm's length.

Until the call. This awful call from Tom. Now, swilling up in her all at once, the broth is too shameful to stomach, hence the sickness, coming on so hard and suddenly. Listening to Tom had been like having some poisonous serum of truth poured into her ear, and it had done its worst, making its nauseous way through her guts. All the rot had come up.

She looks at it now, the viscous brown stripe of bile lying along the curve of the toilet pipe, having slithered down from the bowl. Bile is thicker than water, she thinks, but there is no cleverness in the thought, only rue, and the vile reflection of this unflattering Narcissus staring back at her, having morphed into an eel.

Ugly is as ugly does, warbles Adeline. She is sitting on the edge of the tub, her hands hanging limply between her legs in the folds of her skirt. She looks both removed and pitying, like someone who has come upon an accident in the road and can do nothing but stand and pray. Except that Adeline will not be praying. She has declared herself a rationalist, because Thoby had once done the same. She worships her older brother still, and in the usual way, as a god.

She is full of his memory. They had traipsed up and down the stairs together, playing games and talking about Greek and Roman literature, which he had been studying at school. Once, while arched heroically on the stair head, preparing to vault the rail and drop like proud Achilles into the foyer, he'd proclaimed himself an atheist. "God is a myth like any other," he'd announced. "The Bible is simply our Homer, Hesiod, Virgil, Ovid and so on, all folded into one."

But Adeline's taunting now is nothing like Thoby's then. Virginia presumes this is deliberate. She is being as irrational as it is possible to be. But Adeline is not one for making a point. She is the point, the reminder, which is why Virginia's first answer is contrite.

"Yes," she whispers, still hanging over the bowl to be sure that the spasms have ceased. "I have done wrong."

She detests this idiotic adage about ugliness, but it has emerged of its own accord, like the lyric of a popular tune that has lodged itself in her mind.

She remembers the barbershop standard that Tom had once sung to her, to tease her about her discarded first name. Sarcastically, she begins to sing, putting her head right down into the bowl, so that she can add an extra touch of scornful twang to the insult.

> Sweet Adeline,
> My Adeline,
> At night, dear heart,
> For you I pine.

But the tone is lost on Adeline, and cheerily she joins in.

> In all my dreams,
> Your fair face beams.
> You're the flower of my heart,
> Sweet Adeline.

As Adeline leaps clumsily from the chorus to the verse, her voice careering from its first breeziness to a sudden heartsick vibrato, the song begins to swirl cacophonously in Virginia's head.

There's a picture that in fancy oft' appearing,
Brings back the time, love, when you were near.

Adeline is holding her arms out stiffly in front of her, bent in the position for a waltz, but by the way she is squeezing them slightly inward toward her, she appears to be pantomiming an embrace.

It is then I wonder where you are, my darling,
And if your heart to me is still the same.

There is nothing remotely festive about this anymore. There is a tear rolling down Adeline's face, and her tempo has slowed so painfully that she is virtually sobbing out the last lines.

For the sighing wind and nightingale a-singing
Are breathing only your own sweet name.

"Stop," Virginia cries, and obediently Adeline does. For a long moment, the harsh ring of Virginia's command hangs over them.

It's my song, Adeline bawls at last. *You taught it to me.*

But Virginia is ruthless. "Well, you should unlearn it," she rages, "along with all those other pious little aphorisms of nannies that you have been inane enough to repeat. *Ugly is as ugly does.* What *is* that? Thoby would have thrashed you for saying it."

At this, Adeline dissolves into tears and fades.

Thoby, Virginia thinks, would have had hard words for me, too, over this. *Bullying a child. Honestly.* No, he would have been more strident than that. *Raving at yourself in the lavatory like some demented guttersnipe. Do you imagine such a thing can be overlooked? Tell me, how, precisely, are you different from this Vivien? Or from our very own Laura, I should like to know. You do remember our sister Laura, yes? In what way are you not her copy? And furthermore — ah, yes, we are at the crux of it now, I believe — why have you not suffered the same fate?* He cocks a hand to his ear. *What's that? No shouting now? No slapping down? Right, then. I will tell you. The only thing that stands — the only thing that has ever stood — between you and the madhouse, beloved sister of mine, is not your talent, and certainly not your fabled divergence from the common follies of your sex, but us, my dear girl, us. The swains, the grooms, the* pères, *the* fils *and all the other common brutes presiding in your life. In short — dare we say it outright to the fearsome Mrs. Woolf? — the men.*

This is the tone of her worst reviews, as if all the deceased men that she had so admired and fought with in life — Thoby, Father and now Julian (he is most painfully apt) — were towering over her, brandishing a copy of *Three Guineas* and bringing it down on her head.

Yes, though doing so feels somehow obscene, she must include her nephew in this company, for now Julian, too, is among the dead. She repeats this to herself many times these days, because it will not hold. It is an empty phrase. Julian is dead. What can it possibly mean? How can it possibly be? Sweet, cherubic Julian with his *Gioconda* smile, her very own borrowed child, perished in the corner of some hellish foreign field, and in Spain, for heaven's sake, of all the baked and tattered hells to die in for a cause.

But what cause exactly? War? It simply does not signify. The waste. The contradiction. He had been raised in Nessa's embrace, in their bohemia, suckling the daffodils and making love. So what the devil had happened to him? Why had he insisted on enlisting himself in someone else's civil war, when doing so had only broken his mother's heart? His great (and only) concession to Mama Nessa had been to drive an ambulance rather than fight, but driving through the battlefield foraging for wounded had proven to be every bit as dangerous as the battle itself. He'd lasted little more than a month.

She still cannot accept it, though it had happened a year ago nearly to the day — all these morbid anniversaries — but she knows well enough what it had been for. The necessity of using force against fascism. That had been Julian's line, and the thing that had brought him into conflict with Virginia and others, in person, over many a vituperative dinner, lunch and tea, as well as in writing, the letters, the essays, the articles.

"Violence must be met with violence," he'd railed, "when the perpetrators are beyond human decency." He'd detested what he called the insular humanism and conciliatory nonpolicies of the residual Left, who he'd said still blindly clung to the threadbare pacifism of their youth, as a child does to his blanket when the monster is beneath the bed. "Well," he'd scolded, "this monster is no longer bound by the conventions of fairy tales. He is not beneath the bed. He is tearing apart the room all around you, yet you remain holed up in your cribs, squeezing your eyes as tight as they will shut, and clutching the covers over your heads, in the infantile hope that the scary thing will simply be a good chap and go away."

It was, of course, his generation's view of theirs (i.e., Bloomsbury), though Julian had mostly excepted Leonard from this attack on account of what he'd called (and rightly so) Leonard's longstanding penchant for seeing sense and for taking a well-informed and consequently more nuanced view of the lessons of history. Still, they had all been squabbling like relatives — cleaving the age-old rift between parent and child — for the better part of the decade. But now there was no more talk. Action had taken its place, and duly exacted its consequence.

The death of one's child. There is no name for it. Children without parents are orphans. Spouses are widows and widowers. But a

208

mother who loses her firstborn child, what is she? Her condition is unspeakable, yet she is the very essence of tragedy, and therein she is given many proper names: Medea, Clytemnestra, Niobe.

But Nessa is none of these. Hecuba bears the closest resemblance. Her Hector also died in war. But Julian was no Hector, even if he fancied himself as such. He did not die hot and quick on the sword of a demigod. He went slowly cold on a slab, riddled with anonymous shrapnel — it had been too far-flung to know whose, as if that would have somehow made a difference. Though maybe it would have. It might have seemed less futile if they'd at least known who the bastard was — the Hans or the Hermann or the Heinrich, for it had been a German plane, they knew that much — who'd dropped the bomb that had landed in Julian's plot and thrown its scraps into his lungs.

Damn it all, it will not go away. War and peace. She can keep having this same argument, heedlessly, endlessly — she does, in fact, almost daily, traipsing over the downs, rowing openly with Julian's ghost. And who cares who sees her. Who cares that she had bled it all out again publicly in *Three Guineas* — for Julian, to Julian — or that most of the cognoscenti, and even many of her friends, had deemed it a load of tripe. The book is her child, and for the child, and the child is her property. For her, there is no argument about that.

It is like Thoby dying all over again, and at nearly the same age — Julian was so like him — except that now she is nothing like the young Virginia who mourned her brother's death as a contemporary. Now she is a fifty-six-year-old woman, a veteran mentor, disputant and aunt, who never felt right in any of those roles. Whereas Julian had been the young poet, threshing his own course, as young men must, defining himself against everything his elders stood for, yet also asking for their response, their advice, their — no, not their, her — her criticism, her match for his intellect, his ambitions and his art. He was the phantom limb that ached, and right in that telltale part of her where no limbs had ever grown.

Now she must go on comforting Nessa. She has been doing so all year, and in that time she has been tortured by the duty, which by rights should have been the most natural, most reciprocal of acts. Yet it has often felt like something out of Dante, a diabolical ordeal devised for the punishment of special sins.

To Virginia, as much as nursing Nessa has been tender, at times wrenchingly so, it has also been nothing short of perverse. Now, as never before, their bond has developed a caterwauling life of its own, and seems always to be flipping capriciously between extremes, so that one moment she feels almost subversive, like the mistress ministering to the wife, and the next she is just the sister again, shoring up the sibling who had done the same for her.

Julian had always been the focal point of all their love and conflict, the nexus of everything sweet and ugly that had ever been between them, the support, the competition, the camaraderie, the jealousy, the passion, the hurt. But now that he was dead, all of this had been magnified tenfold, had become more convoluted and — this was the most difficult part — instantaneous than she had ever thought possible. It is as if everything from the past, the present and even the future is capable of happening all at once, at any time, and exploding between them without warning. This newly old relationship with Nessa is more difficult, and more charged than any she has experienced, Vita included. Perhaps it always had been, but it has taken this atrocity to synergize the whole.

"Mrs. Woolf?"

The voice is startlingly close, and Virginia jumps at the sound of it. She might have thought it was one of her own, were it not for the formal address, but it is only Louie calling from somewhere on the stairs. "Mrs. Bell has arrived."

In fact, Nessa had arrived a quarter of an hour before, but Virginia has been in the lavatory all that time, and Louie knows from experience not to disturb her there unless it is a matter of life and death. But Nessa's presence in the house has made Louie anxious, partly because she does not wish to be perceived as a servant who, at this late date in her tenure, is incapable of performing the simplest of tasks, such as announcing a guest, especially this guest, whom she knows so well, and knows to be in no fit state to endure much of anything. But she is also nervous because she knows that Virginia has been in the lavatory for much longer than a quarter of an hour.

She knows, too, that Virginia has not been bathing in there or answering nature's call. It had been she, Louie, after all, who had first answered the telephone this morning, and given the familiar caller's famous name. It had also been she who, while upstairs making the gentleman's bed, had heard Virginia stomp across the hall, slam the lavatory door and begin retching like a dog. The retching had gone on fitfully for some time. And yes, she had heard the lady talking to herself as well. She has heard her do so many times before, and not—begging your pardon—because she has been listening, but because it can sound as loud as the pub at last orders in there when ma'am is going strong.

"All right," Virginia calls, trying to sound gathered, but she sounds throttled instead.

By now Nessa, too, knows that all is not well, and she does not expect Louie to intervene. She can deal with this herself. She has followed Louie onto the stairs, and hearing Virginia's gurgled reply, she pushes past the servant and takes the rest of the stairs by twos. When she reaches the top, she flings open the lavatory door and glares across the threshold.

Again Virginia jumps at the sound of the door as it bangs against the far wall. Terrified, and still clinging to the toilet, she turns to see her sister standing with her legs sturdily apart and her arms stiffly crossed, looking like a murderous landlady.

"Nessa!" she gasps. "You frightened me."

At nearly sixty, Nessa is still a very attractive woman. Her greying hair is gathered at the base of her neck in an elegant chignon. She is wearing little or no makeup, yet her pale skin and hair are so clear, and they complement each other so becomingly, that she glows with the lustrous monochrome of a photograph. Age has merely softened her beauty into the comeliness of a life well lived.

"Yes, well," she says hotly, "I wasn't going to wait down there any longer. Not with you up here doing your usual God knows what."

Taking in the view of Virginia on the floor, hovering over the dregs of her vomit and gazing into the bowl as if she thinks she can read her fortune there, she adds, "Honestly, Virginia, must you always be so eccentric?"

This breaks the tension and makes them both erupt with laughter. Nessa rushes to her sister's side to lay a nurturing hand on her shoulder. "Dearest, come away," she says. "Shall we sit in your room?"

Virginia nods and allows Nessa to help her to her feet. As Nessa turns Virginia around and begins guiding her toward the door, she reaches behind and pulls the toilet chain.

When they are comfortably installed across the hall in Virginia's room, Nessa in the writing chair, Virginia on the edge of the bed, Nessa says, "This isn't over something to do with Ottoline, is it?"

"Ottoline!" Virginia scoffs. "God. She died in February and, would you believe it, I'm still quite over it."

Nessa frowns.

"Oh, I know, I know. I'm wretched, and you know I don't really mean it. But how could you think that I would be sick over Ottoline? Unless, of course, her journals have been unsealed." She makes a scandalized face and covers her mouth coyly with her hand. "What then?"

Nessa smiles weakly, knowing, as everyone does, that Ottoline's infamous journals are rumored to contain more incriminating information about the whole tangled web of Bloomsbury—at whose center Ottoline lurked like a black widow for more than thirty years—than the files of British Intelligence contained about the Nazis. And they had been sealed every bit as tightly, too, at her behest, by her husband Philip, who, without exception, did absolutely everything he was told.

But Nessa has never been attracted or susceptible to the martial art of gossip the way her sister has. Virginia might pretend otherwise when it suited her, but Nessa knows that a good chin-wag has always been a favorite pastime of hers. It was the virtual linchpin of her friendship with Lytton—perhaps "friendship" is the wrong word—and the coven she assembled with Ottoline. Virginia had wasted a great deal of time and idle talk with Her Ladyship over the years, and in the blood sport of society she had given every bit as good as she'd got. She did not like to be reminded of this fact.

Nessa, meanwhile, had always thought of herself as actually living the life—and happily—that so many others had lived only vicariously—or in Ottoline's case, relived convalescently—by yapping about it. The postmortems of love affairs have never in-terested Nessa much, but when it comes to Virginia (*vide* Vita), she knows that there is often a great deal more than hurt feelings at stake, even just in what she overhears.

"So, what's happened?" Nessa asks.

Fiddling with the lamp cord on the night table, Virginia says nonchalantly, "Well, I suppose it does have to do in some manner with Ottoline. But then"—she laughs—"what doesn't?"

They both smirk at this, Nessa less so than Virginia, and Virginia goes on, trying to distract herself from the mild constriction that is still there in her throat.

"You know she filled Vivien Eliot's head full of nonsense about Carrington after she and Lytton died."

"Well, she would, wouldn't she?" Nessa says. "You said they'd been lovers once."

"Who?" Virginia cries. "Vivien and Ottoline?"

"No. Of course not. Don't be a fool. Ottoline and Carrington."

"Oh, yes. That. Well, as I said, Ottoline had her hand, so to speak, in every pie. But I mean something else."

She pauses here, still fiddling with the cord. After a moment, she adds sheepishly, "I mean how badly Ottoline and I treated Vivien after all that. After Tom left her."

"But that's ancient history," Nessa says, not wanting to discuss Ottoline any more than necessary. She is pressing for the real cause of this morning's events. "Why are you thinking of that now?"

"Not that ancient," Virginia balks. "Anyway, I feel awful. It's all a muddle. Everything is bound up with everything else, and I'm thrown over. I just—"

"Virginia," Nessa interrupts sternly, "what have you heard?"

Throwing up her hands, Virginia says, "I received a phone call this morning from Tom." She looks candidly at Nessa, as if this should say everything, but it is obvious that she has stopped short of the main thing.

"And?" Nessa prompts. "What did he say?"

This is more difficult than she thought it would be to repeat. She is beginning to feel sick again at the thought of it. She swallows hard several times to clear the saliva that is filling her mouth, and takes several deep breaths.

"Virginia?"

"Yes, all right," Virginia snaps, cracking the cord against the nightstand and nearly toppling the lamp. Nessa leaps up to steady it. Virginia takes full advantage of the delay, and the fact that Nessa's attention is, for the moment, focused elsewhere. She breathes deeply several more times, and clutches at her throat and belly in a way that she is relieved Nessa doesn't see.

When Nessa has retaken her seat, Virginia swallows again and says, "Tom said that Vivien has been committed to an asylum."

The words "Oh, dear" slip out before Nessa can stop them, and Virginia's eyes pop up at her. "You see?" she says accusingly.

But Nessa immediately recovers. "I see that it is a very sad thing for Vivien and for Tom," she says, pausing to emphasize her verdict. "And that is all."

"That is not all," Virginia cries.

Nessa starts slightly at this and tries to soften her tone. "I know it isn't. I'm sorry. It's just that I don't want you spinning this out, making more of it than there need be. You know that at times like this you blame yourself for everything. You must stop this now."

She had meant to express her sympathy and the profound understanding that she has gained by helping Virginia through these bouts since they were adolescents, but by the time she finishes, she is surprised to find herself nearly shouting.

Julian's death has both sharpened and dulled her. She feels less, she rages more. She can seldom suppress the tantrums that seem to lurk most threateningly when she is with Virginia. The persuasion of her grief is too strong: This is not your burden anymore, it tells her, this constant shoring up of your sister. *You* are the one who is destroyed. *You* have known the blankness of actual pain.

In this mindset she has very little of her famous patience left. She can no longer tolerate these petty exacerbations.

"Oh, Nessa," Virginia moans, fearing Nessa's thoughts. "It is I who am sorry. I didn't intend to tell you. Not like this. I didn't mean for you to find me as you did. I know that all of this is nothing beside Julian."

Nessa feels the momentary urge to contradict, but there is no real feeling behind the impulse, and so she merely stares at the floor beneath Virginia's feet.

"It was you, you know," Virginia says softly.

"Me what?" Nessa says without raising her eyes.

"Who saved me from ending like Vivien."

At this, Nessa looks up with a puzzled expression. "Saved you?"

But Virginia only returns Nessa's gaze, her own eyes filling with the sudden tears of gratitude that have overcome her.

Nessa can feel a shudder of discomfort go through her, and then a hot surge of resentment overtaking it, thickening in her throat and filling her ears with blood. It is too typical. She is being ambushed yet again by a show of unaccountable emotion whose true cause Virginia refuses to expose. But she will not let herself be thrown. With a stilted matter-of-factness that for the moment conceals her displeasure, Nessa says, "But of course it was Leonard who saved you."

Virginia smiles. "Yes," she says. "But it is more complicated than that. Our family. Oh, Nessa, it frightens me so even now just to think of it."

This sends another rush, this time of near fury, up Nessa's spine. Her brain is beginning to simmer. There will be no avoiding this scene, but she will not be the one to provoke it.

Looking at Virginia now, Nessa sees her sister's strangely pained expression, as though she is trying to sweep aside her first feelings as quickly and ruthlessly as possible to make way for a more dispassionate pronouncement. This has a slightly cooling effect. Nessa settles in the chair and lets the cushions plump soothingly against her stiffened back.

"It is always the men who appear to be in control of these decisions," Virginia resumes at last. Her tone is now pedantic, but forced. "And, ultimately, they *are* in control, of course. The doctors, the fathers, the husbands, the brothers are all holding the keys, but—and this is part of what I have been sick about this morning—perhaps it is in fact the women, the mothers and sisters"—she pauses briefly to say the next words with special emphasis—"or the *step*mothers and *half* sisters, who are turning those keys in the locks. Might it not, in the last analysis, be the acquiescence of one or more female relatives that permits, or overlooks, or obscures, another female relative's confinement? Vivien's mother, Lucia's mother and, not least, let us say it aloud for once, our own mother, poor Laura's stepmother—where were they?"

"Lucia?" Nessa says, because she does not want even to begin to entertain what Virginia has just suggested about their half sister Laura and their mother. They have not spoken of Laura in many, many years. The mere mention of the name is evidence enough to Nessa that Virginia is much farther afield this morning than she realized.

"Lucia Joyce," Virginia says perfunctorily. "Never mind her. It's just . . . I wanted you to know that I know that it was you."

Still Nessa says nothing, though she is looking searchingly and skeptically into Virginia's eyes. Why is she on about Laura?

"Don't you see?" Virginia says. "Laura lived with us. She was there with us in St. Ives. And then, magically, she was not there. She was put away, and long before Mother died, when we were too young to know what it meant. Then Mother died, and sister Stella died not long after, and it was only us, you and me, with the boys and Father. Then Father died and Thoby died, too, and we were left at last only with Adrian, who, you'll agree, was always a nonentity, and with George and Gerald Duckworth, who, well, we know what they were."

Nessa looks down again at the mention of their half brothers' names, for she, too, has very sore and shaded memories of both of them. This is something else of which they have not spoken for many years.

"I'm sorry," Virginia says, seeing Nessa's eyes fall. "I know what it means to say these names. All of them. But I must tell you what I mean. It was then, after everyone had died, that I began to decompensate. It was when they alone were our proprietors, our three so-called brothers, two pigs and a midge, that I was most lost."

"And Leonard!" Nessa angrily interjects.

"Yes," Virginia concedes, "and then Leonard came along to civilize everything, the only noble male in our vicinity."

"Yes, and the one who kept you from ending like poor, maligned, forgotten Laura. Isn't that your point?"

"Has she ended?" Virginia says remorsefully. "Has Laura ended? I do not even know."

This snaps the fragile equanimity that Nessa has held so carefully intact. She puts her head into her hands with a cry of utter frustration and begins to weep.

"That is my point," Virginia says quietly, watching Nessa react. "People might have said the same of me, in passing perhaps, or because something reminded them of that strange, mad girl they once knew: Whatever happened to Virginia?"

She pauses here to raise herself from the edge of the bed, cross to Nessa's chair and kneel at her feet. Taking Nessa's wet hands away from her face and holding them in her own, she says, "They would have said so were it not . . . yes, for Leonard, his credit is assured, but"—she beats the air assertively with their held hands—"but for you, dearest. Were it not for you."

Nessa drops her head against the rear of the chair, exhausted, and sighs heavily, the sobs still hiccupping her breath.

"And this is how I repay you," Virginia says bitterly, as she drops Nessa's hands and lets herself fall backward onto the floor. She lands with a whimper of dismay and looks away.

"No, Virginia," Nessa says, raising her head from the chair to glare down at her sister, "this is how you *are.*"

Nessa's voice is still thick with tears, but the sudden fierceness of the words has jerked Virginia back, and she is staring into Nessa's angry eyes.

"You do this whenever you are distressed," Nessa says. "You mix and equate things that are not the same. You confuse and you contradict, just as you have always done, because it is your most effective means of condemning yourself . . . Well, I'm sorry, but this time I will not let you do it. I will not let you have it both ways. Not about this. Not in the state I'm in. I will not sit by and listen to you revise and indict our entire family because on this particular day it happens to suit your spiteful habit of mind."

Nessa is now sitting on the edge of the chair, her hands flying.

"You pretend to credit me with saving you, yet in the same

breath you condemn me for not saving Laura. Don't you see that? Oh, of course you do. It's all just another part of this sick dance we've been doing since—" She stubbornly shakes this away. She will not to be put off by the mention of Julian's name. "What you are really saying is that because I saved you, why did I not save Laura? Why in all these years have I, like you, never sought my half sister out? How is it that I do not even know if she is dead or alive? Perhaps I—we—could save her still."

Virginia cannot contradict this, because she knows it is all perfectly and miserably correct and, as Nessa said, just more of the same perversion that has been pulling them together and apart since Julian's death. She does not really want to think about the fate of Laura any more than Nessa does, or about Vivien for that matter, or, God's sake, Lucia Joyce. She wants her Nessa. She wants her Nessa to tell her that it has all been, and that it will all be, all right.

"Do I always?" she asks plaintively.

"Yeeeeessss!" Nessa wails. "Yes. Always. There isn't a single consistent thought in your head or feeling in your heart except, occasionally, the ones you manage to put down in your books. You've just published the most scathing attack on men, accusing them of disempowering women for centuries, but now you want to tell me that it's the women, after all, who have been putting women into the madhouse, or, occasionally, when they are the mildly good ones like me, saving them from it."

"One is entitled to adjust one's opinions after the fact," Virginia says weakly.

"And then there's Tom," Nessa says, ignoring this remark. "The source of today's avalanche, apparently. It's truly incredible. You told me once that you thought you might have loved him. I have the proof. You put it in a letter to me not two years ago. As for Vivien, well, you virtually threw her down the well after Tom left her. But now that she's been put away — though again, apparently not by Tom alone, but somehow by the machinations of her mother as well — Tom is the devil, Vivien is a saint, and you're a wreck who only narrowly escaped being carted off like Vivien, like Laura, and like this Lucia, whoever she is, to the darkest hole in all of Britain, had it not been, heaven be praised, *for me!*"

Nessa is purple with rage. She has been screaming all of this, hardly pausing to breathe, and subsiding only when she has run out of air, as she has done now. But she is not finished. She gasps as if she has just fought her way to the surface from fathoms deep. Her voice has roughened with the strain of the attack, and what she says now growls out of her so harshly that Virginia is truly frightened by the sound.

"All the extremes," she snarls contemptuously. "Love — ha, now there's a specimen — you thought you loved Lytton once, too, remember? And, dear God, let us not even tread on Vita. But then there are all the other emotions as well — hatred, fear, like, dislike, envy, faith, pride, jealousy, lust, adoration, accusation, and on and on and on. They're all one and the same to you. They make no sense, and they mean nothing. You apply them all. Julian is, of course, their nearest target — the great love, the great enemy, the measure of all things that you haven't *conceived* — but who, really, has escaped your onslaught? Who haven't you tried to possess, and then just as quickly discard with all your downpouring of nonsense? . . . But in the end there is only you. You, who put it all into your one and only true obsession — yourself — and spin it round and round in that hopeless roulette you call a brain, and then, when you're finally through with it, when it serves no further purpose in that lethal little game you love to play with your-self, well then, you simply spit it out. You spew it as far and wide as it will go. And they call it your wit, your charm, your brilliance, but all it really is, or ever was, is waste."

Now Nessa is panting to regain her lost breath, and she has fallen once more against the chair, weak-eyed and faintly blotched, like a person who has been released at long last from a sickness that has convulsed her for days.

But Virginia has not turned away or broken down under this abuse. She has heard everything. But she is not incensed. This time — which in most ways has been so much like all the other times that she and Nessa have fought this fight in the past year — this time it is different. She is amazed. She has been looking on and listening in awe as this same, familiar lifetime's worth of sib-ling rivalry and grievance, pressurized by time into a gorgeous, clear, diamond-hard expression of hate, has come roaring out of Nessa word-perfect. And the most perfect word of all is right there where it should be, in the center.

"You have said it in a single word," she says, with what is pos-sibly more love and admiration than she has ever said anything to anyone, and Nessa cannot believe it. She is dumbfounded.

"What?" she croaks, turning limply once more to look down at her sister, as if she has just materialized from within the lamp on the night table.

"Conceived," Virginia says.

"What?" Nessa says again, this time truly vexed that her sis-ter cannot respond like a normal human being and simply take a tongue-lashing for what it is. I beat her, Nessa marvels, and she will not go down. She will not cry or just bloody well go to the devil under the punishment. No, not Virginia. She's in heaven.

Harm is manna to her. She doesn't know up from down, and now, of all these damned, demented manias of hers, she is cuckoo over a common word.

"I have not *conceived,*" Virginia continues deliberately, undaunted by Nessa's caustic stare. "I did not have a child . . . and in that . . . is everything. Everything of me, and everything that is between you and me. Everything that you have said, and everything that has happened here this morning.

"It has been one long, relentless progression. Cause and effect." She pauses. "Shall I enumerate?" She raises her fingers to tick off the links in the chain. "Because I was mad, I could not have a child. Because I could not have a child, I could not be a mother. Because I could not be a mother, I could not be a woman, or a wife, or a sister, or a self. I could not be sexually free. I could not give my husband what he wanted. I could not nurture and take care. I could not learn how to love. I could not feel anything properly, and so I could not be whole. And in all these ways, dear sister, I have hated you, because you have been whole, and you have done all of those things. Always. And in that hatred of mine for you, it is all contained—the closest thing that I have ever felt to what you know as love."

She scrambles to her feet. "So yes, Nessa," she says finally, commandingly, looking down on her sister from her full height. "That is my response. Your one word has said what I could not. Not in all the circuitous obsessing that I have done this very morning. Not in all my life, in all the reams and reams of paper I have covered with ink. And so, as ever, as always—my precious, my astonishing sister—I am here, standing aside, admiring you."

Virginia falls back onto the bed, exhausted. They are both spent. Nessa cannot bring herself to say a word. There is no point.

The venom is out, the festering wound lanced and drained. The treatment will do for now, until the blister fills once more, and they must go through all of this again. It is what they do.

There is a tap on the door, which they have left wide open, and Leonard has appeared in the doorway, knowing all. Not that overhearing is the reason he knows. He is well acquainted with this match. He is often its umpire after the fact.

"Shall we go downstairs and have our tea?" he says quietly, but they are all quite aware that this is not a request.

Virginia rises mechanically from the bed, and Nessa from the chair, and they file past Leonard into the hallway and down the stairs to the sitting room, where Louie has set out cups and a warming pot and a plate of forlorn-looking lemon curd scones.

Act V

THE VOYAGE OUT

～

Saturday, 22 March –
Friday, 28 March 1941

SATURDAY

LEONARD IS SITTING smoking his pipe in one of the armchairs in the sitting room. Looking around him as he puffs, he thinks of how, years ago, he and Virginia had painted these walls themselves. They'd chosen what they considered a suitably unconventional and vibrant mint green to bring a touch of much-needed whimsy, as well as an illusion of spaciousness to the low ceilings and thick, dark exposed beams of this seventeenth-century cottage. They had done well, he thinks. He has always been happy in this room.

Today, however, is an exception. Today he is thinking through the strategy he has devised for how best to deal with Virginia in the coming days. For some weeks now she has been showing all the recognizable signs of becoming unwell again, but he has been more uncertain than usual how to proceed. In desperation — he has admitted this only in the past twenty-four hours, and then, only reluctantly — he has turned to their friend Dr. Wilberforce for help.

Leonard and Virginia have known Octavia Wilberforce since 1928. She is a wonderful woman, solid, dependable, and though she is only six years younger than Virginia, and eight years younger than he, she is not a woman of their time. She has lived her life with great fortitude and dignity, Leonard has always thought, and delightfully against the grain.

She was born and raised in a large upper-middle-class family in Sussex, the daughter of a typical English country gentleman. But early in life she set her mind on studying medicine, and despite the many obstacles that stood in the way of any woman pursuing such a career at that time, she succeeded in qualifying as a physician in 1920.

She established her practice in Brighton in 1923, not far from Rodmell, and Virginia and Leonard have had her and her longtime companion, the American actress Elizabeth Robins, to tea frequently at Monk's House over the years, more so since the war began. Octavia brings them fresh milk and cream from her own Jersey cows, and they give her figs and apples and anything else she wants from the garden.

Leonard has grown quite fond of her, and for one reason above all: because he trusts her. She has been Virginia's unofficial internist for some time, and, as far as he is concerned, the only consistent antidote that has ever presented itself to those quacks and crackpots of Harley Street.

There have been no bona fide psychiatrists. With due respect to their friend Freud, Leonard does not believe that such an entity exists. Not for Virginia certainly, and never, as now, in extremis, when she both needs and refuses help most.

In her case, surely, but in all such cases, he thinks, when one is dealing with the most complex and intimate terrain of an individual, the term "professional help" is an oxymoron. None of these so-called specialists has ever understood Virginia well enough to navigate her mind. No one knows the topography as he does. No one knows the risks.

When Virginia is like this, at the crisis point, she is like a wild animal being hunted for sport in her own back garden, and he is like some softhearted gamekeeper creeping up on her, trying to keep her out of harm's way as a pet. There are only two choices: death or captivity.

If he moves to cage her she may run, back into the hostile territory of her own mind. Eventually the hounds will run her down. If, on the other hand, he leaves her to her will, the end result will be the same. The right course is not obvious. It never has been, but this time it must be carried out against the backdrop of another world war, which is buzzing and booming all around them at very close range like some cruel manifestation of her madness. He does not think that he can handle her alone, and no one else will do. Octavia is their only hope.

Yesterday, when she'd come to tea, he'd asked her, and she'd agreed, to give Virginia a full physical examination at her surgery in Brighton on Thursday, as well as a mental evaluation to follow, though this, they both emphasized, must happen in the strictest confidence and under the guise of a friendly visit. It is the only way that he will be able to persuade Virginia to go at all, much less to engage in anything resembling a discussion of her state of mind.

He'd finally been able to tell Octavia the full extent of his concerns, and to ask her to help him coax Virginia into a rest cure, but only after having spent three days agonizing over the decision. He'd gone back and forth with himself about how much deceit might be allowable if it was in Virginia's interest, or how much it was even possible to deceive Virginia when she was in such an anxious and watchful state. Yet a decision had to be made; that much he'd settled on. The breaking point had been reached.

It had happened last Tuesday afternoon. He'd been working in the garden when Virginia had wobbled in from one of her walks on the downs, wet to the skin and shivering, looking very rattled and tossed about, as if she'd been in a fight. He'd asked her what had happened, and she'd said she'd slipped and fallen into one of the drainage dykes along the Ouse. Outwardly he'd accepted her explanation, but inwardly the high wire of indecision he'd been walking for the previous five or six weeks finally snapped. Then and there, he'd resolved to act.

Nothing about the war — not the air raids, not the destruction of their old London house at 52 Tavistock Square (which, thankfully, they had already vacated) or the damage inflicted on the new one in Mecklenburgh Square, not the threat of invasion, not even the plan he and Virginia had made to asphyxiate themselves in the garage rather than be taken alive by the Nazis — none of it had made him feel anything remotely this intense.

In fact, in comparison the loud, acrid reality of the Blitz had left him cold, bored even, by the waiting, the constant waiting in shelters, in queues, on trains and in stations, sitting out the interminable delays and tortuous detours on his trips to and from London. Even Dunkirk had seemed unreal, and that had been a village event. He had seen the boys from Rodmell and Lewes scarpering home in tatters, each to his sobbing mother's embrace. Yet he had felt only the thin, obligatory disgust and indignation that he'd felt in one form or another since Hitler had come to power in 1933, but which had atrophied since with overuse. The war had resigned him to the slow, steady onset of barbarism and his fate.

It was nothing like this.

He is a man at odds with himself. He has always been so, a misanthrope at home who has been nonetheless compelled to do right by his fellow man in the public sphere. In his heart he condemns most men as idiots and churls, yet out in the world, by the rule of international law, he is bent on saving mankind from himself. In this way, the war is like the manifestation of his madness, too. It is his deepest mental conflict writ large, blazing across the sky in burning fuselage and gunfire, exploding the foundations, the very bricks and mortar of civilization as he sees it, in the city that he loves, and, worst of all, staring blankly out of all the loathed and filthy faces of the brutes who are fighting on behalf of his cherished cause.

And where is Virginia in this? She is one of the exceptions, one of the few bright lights of his existence and of the species, that make the rest of this Pandæmonium endurable. She and the others like her, the artists, the philosophers, the best in mind and spirit, are all that can be salvaged from the catastrophe we call Earth, and all that keeps whatever godlike power may exist from tearing it all down in disgrace.

The threat to her is a threat to the idea of everything he stands for and to the only thing he believes in. It reawakens him to the terror of meaninglessness. It shakes him all through, like a dull iron bell tolling a reminder of the defining contradiction of his life: He has indulged himself in the delusion of progress, to inching ever upward on a journey that he has always known was going downhill. It has never changed. He has never changed. It is like a puzzle turned upside down and backward, wrapped inside a lie. He has never been able to stop caring about something that he knows will come to nothing, and he has never been able to stop trying to forget what he knows.

That is Virginia. That is love, a justification, a corrective walking around in the flesh, which is simply, always there, and for no good reason, but is beautiful enough, redeeming enough, purely in its essence, and just because it happens to exist, to ameliorate the futility and the savagery of being alive.

But she is not the only source. He has made sure of that. She is an example, one incarnation picked out of chaos that he has chosen to live with every day so that he might point to her and tell himself: This is why I do it. This is how.

But there are other people, other creatures, other ways. There are the Apostles (who survive), his animal companions, his garden, music, art, books. They serve the same purpose, and he has placed them carefully around himself as touchstones. They are always within reach, and that is why the thought of Virginia's death shakes him as profoundly as it does, but it does not shatter him. He has never, he would never, give so much power to one hope.

And yet Virginia is singular. She is in fact not of a kind, but her own kind, and there will never be another. He does not want to see her go so soon. And she needn't.

Not long ago she was happy, perfectly happy. She had said so. So had he. They had been walking together on the downs one afternoon, talking about her work, and the work of all writers, speculating about what a writer is and what he might be for, and there had been — they had both noted it — that low pleasant hum of contentment between them, the deep sense of satisfaction that always swelled in both of them when they were flying together in thought. It was another of their jokes. They called it being in a state of classical grace. When they were walking out there across the fields, side by side, heads turned in the same direction, eyes and minds on the horizon, they said they were like the Greek ideal of friendship carved in an Athenian frieze, or painted on an ancient urn such as the one Keats immortalized.

He had been free enough that day finally to tell her the truth about *The Years,* that he had not thought it her best work. She had even agreed, and allowed him to elaborate. It was, he'd said, the very thing that it had been to her in the making: too labored. It was too fussy on structure and fact—which in fiction had never been her strength or her mission—and too short on atmosphere—which *was* both her mission and her strength. Again she had agreed, and this had led to their discussion of writing and writers more generally.

He remembers clearly what she'd said next, and he knows that he will always remember it, because he'd found it so unexpectedly piercing and beautiful, and because it had reminded him of a similar discussion they had once had about her work many years before, when she was riding the crest of her genius into her prime in *To the Lighthouse* and *The Waves.*

She'd said that perhaps every writer is meant to express only one idea, one mood, one version of what this strange human experience is about, and that he spends his life and work repeating it over and over. If he is fortunate, once or twice he gets it absolutely right. He delivers his single given message more purely, more uniquely than any other writer has or will. But the once or twice is usually all he gets. Either he builds to it slowly, gathering strength and particularity as he goes, and it happens toward the end of his career, as it did to Joyce, the last expressions being the best—this is the most blessed outcome, she'd said—or it comes all at once in a bolt and then never again, as it did to Conrad, or it comes, a hump somewhere in the middle, as it had—she'd paused only briefly here—to her, and the rest is just an echo, the congenital compulsion wearing itself out.

He wonders if he should have heard the warning then. Yet he had been so taken, as he is now, by the truth of what she had said, and the impressive presence of mind that she had shown in being able to say it. He had never heard her speak this way of Joyce, but he had also never heard her speak this way of herself. She had spoken of her own work dispassionately, yet at the same time with an undertone of resigned wistfulness, as one might remark on the ouster of a sick fledgling from the nest, or some other calamity of nature which was indubitably sad but couldn't be helped.

But then her tone had abruptly changed, and she had begun to talk of her most recent novel, *Between the Acts,* which she had just finished. The interregna between books had always been emotionally treacherous for her, he knew only too well, but this transition had been worse than the others, worse even than the terrifying time around *The Years.* In this case, her customary downward slide from the creative highs of composition to the postpartum lows of final edits had been more precipitous than usual. The contrast of moods, before and after, had been especially stark. She had enjoyed writing this novel more than most; every page, she'd said. But now that it was done, she'd set herself stridently against it, calling it trivial and unworthy. She'd gone so far as to say she wanted to withdraw it from the press.

Julian's old Cambridge friend, and their onetime employee, John Lehmann had come back to them after six years and was now part owner and managing editor at Hogarth. In '38 Virginia and Leonard had reconfigured the press in order to relieve themselves of some of the day-to-day burdens of running it. To that end, they had sold half of the concern to Lehmann and taken him on full-time to co-manage it with Leonard. They had established an advisory board over which Virginia, as well as the old hot Oxbridge set from '32 — Stephen Spender (who had become a friend), Christopher Isherwood (whose second novel, *The Memorial,* Hogarth had published in '32) and Auden (who was not a friend) — ostensibly presided. But the board never met. Still, the changes had brought the press more fully into the hands of the younger generation, a move Leonard and Virginia had hoped would ensure both its continued relevance and its longevity.

Leonard and Virginia had gone to London a week or so before to have lunch with Lehmann, and it was then that Leonard had given Lehmann the good news that Virginia had finished *Between the Acts.* Lehmann had been enthusiastic, asking to see the manuscript, and he had congratulated Virginia on her accomplishment, or he had attempted to do so, but she had cut him short in a flurry of the same disparaging remarks that she had made to Leonard on the downs.

Leonard had listened to all of it again, but he had offered no critical view. True, he had not considered this latest novel to be her best work, but he by no means shared her distaste for it. He'd fought her off on this point as tactfully as he'd been able, assuring her, quite honestly, that this was, in fact, a worthy book, and not trivial in the least. But he had done little if any good, and he had been relieved when she'd let the subject drop.

After this, they had walked in silence for some time, taking in the lovely roll and sweep of the downs and the dramatic span of what she liked to call a Constable sky, its bright blue back gleaming through great swaths of changeable cloud. They listened to the river chattering nearby, and spotted a grey heron in flight, its long, balletic legs stretching languorously behind.

Then they had begun to speak about death. This in itself was not strange. They had done so often since the fall of France the previous June, a debacle that had made Nazi occupation of the British Isles seem inescapable and imminent. They, as well as many of the couples they knew, including Vita and Harold, had spent the intervening months renewing their pledges to die together on their own terms rather than allow themselves to be interned in a concentration camp. As a Jew, he could expect no alternative, and as the nonconformist wife of one, she'd said she would not accept one.

This was all routine. War talk. But then — and this, he realizes now, had not been the strange thing, but the *strangest* thing — Virginia veered again.

"When a fetus comes alive in the womb," she'd asked, "what tells its heart to start beating?" As she'd said it, she'd stopped walking and turned to look at him quizzically, as if she were a girl pondering the mysteries of life and he was her father, the man of sensible remove, with all the answers. But she hadn't waited for him to speak. Instead, she'd begun walking again, leaving him standing there at a loss.

"And when it does begin," she'd added airily over her shoulder from a few paces on, "why then? Why exactly then and not a moment before or after?"

He'd begun to follow her, still a pace or so behind, still trying to work out what she was about, when she'd stopped once more, turned and said, "And why cannot death be as painless as that? Or as timely? The music simply ending, as it began, without struggle, without knowledge, without thought. Why must the life be shaken out of us when it has been so softly, so smoothly put in?"

He had had no answer for this, of course, and they had merely stood on the hillside facing each other with the wind gusting over the long grasses, whipping their hair and clothing and spooling the temperamental white-grey skeins of cloud across the valley.

They could see the river clearly from there, weaving through the sodden water meadows, the chalk escarpments and the whole of the wide majestic weald, mottled with grazing sheep.

At last he had moved to go, taking up her hand, which she had not offered him, but which she had merely let fall into his grasp and lie there, impassive and cold. He'd led her more than accompanied her home, and they had spoken only intermittently, of incidental things: the way, the smattering of rain they'd encountered a mile or so from the house, dinner.

He could remember nothing else important. Had he overlooked it? Possibly. What had brought about the change? They had been talking as they often did, more breezily even, more objectively, than usual. Then one of her anomalies had descended, a sudden barometric plunge, and that had been that. These are patterns he knows well—the only pattern, of course, being the lack of pattern. He does not really expect to find the tipping point, nor does it really matter if he does. The tip is the thing, the fact of it, the turbulence coming on and his response to it. "Right the ship! Right the ship!" blares the klaxon. "All hands on deck." But his hands are like her hands in this, undone.

The proximate cause had been the book, of course. It always was. And its connection to, its standing in for, bearing a child—that, too, was well worn. But it had been the leap from the likening of life's beginning to its end that had chilled as much as it had moved him, and as he thinks about it now, he is beginning for the first time to see why. It had not been the talk of death. That was usual. It had not been the transitive link she'd made between her creative output, the lack of children in their lives, and death. Given the atmosphere, her patterns of thought, it had made a Virginian kind of sense.

But something about this last thought throws him over, and the realization that he's been looking for overtakes him with painful conviction. No, of course, he scolds, those were simply the words, the ideas floating on the surface of her conversation. How could he have been so easily fooled when it was almost an adage with her? It was how she separated men from boys, how her method was achieved: Shiny pretty things conceal meaning. The dolt falls for them every time.

The obviousness of this strikes him with such a convulsion of conscience and shame that he wants to break something or rush out into the garden and tear apart all his handiwork. How can he have been so stupid? Now, when discernment is what is most required. Now, after all these years, and when he has just proclaimed himself *the* expert.

His brain is screaming. She was not saying anything philosophical or poetic in the least, you idiot. It was calculatingly practical. She was trying to work out how to kill herself, as quickly, as smoothly (that had been her word) and as painlessly as possible.

At this, he leaps up from the chair. He must find her. Where the devil is she? He calls to Louie and she comes, but she can tell him only that she thinks — she cannot be sure — that Mrs. Woolf has gone out for a walk.

THURSDAY

LEONARD AND VIRGINIA had arrived on time at Dr. Wilberforce's surgery, 24 Montpelier Crescent, Brighton, shortly after three. Leonard had agreed to wait for Virginia in another part of the house. He knows it well, for this is also where Octavia has made her home with Elizabeth. Since the start of the war, Elizabeth has been in the United States, but prior to this, Leonard and Virginia had called on the couple socially many times. Today Octavia will give them another ration of her milk and cream. It is too soon for fruit, so they have brought her a bouquet of the season's first crocuses and jonquils.

Though Virginia had insisted to both Octavia and Leonard that an examination of whatever kind was entirely unnecessary, to soothe Leonard's agitation she had complied with the arrangement. Immediately upon arriving, she had followed Octavia into the surgery, undressed, had her temperature taken — it was low — and allowed herself to be duly palpated and auscultated by the madam physician, none of which had resulted in anything more than a statement of the obvious. Virginia is not measurably ill, but clearly she is not well. One look at her will tell even a stranger on the street that something is very wrong. Everyone who has seen her recently has noticed. She is emaciated. Her eyes and cheeks are so sunken, her bones so prominent and the skin stretched so tightly across them at her clavicles and wrists that she looks like a marionette.

They have come directly from the surgery into the sitting room adjacent to have what they are calling their visit, but which Virginia knows to be some foolhardy attempt at psychotherapy. Let her try, then, she thinks coldly. See how far she gets.

Octavia Wilberforce is a stout, mannish woman of that particularly hearty old English country stock that was built to breed and to endure. Had she been born a man, she might have ridden the fields imposingly on horseback, overseeing the season's crop, or perhaps governed a far-flung colony, had her portrait painted and then hung it in the hall beside all the other somber, long-nosed forebears of her clan. Her forehead is very high and prominent and ends in a receding hairline from which her unremarkable but unruly brown hair sweeps back and outward in a crowning coif. She has a slight double chin and no lips to speak of. Her eyes are stretched lengthwise and rather far apart, which gives her the vaguely disapproving look of someone who is not easily played for a fool.

This is not the blessed face you would choose to behold on your deathbed, but it can be confessed to nonetheless. It has about it just the right bovine imperturbability, but with none of the stupidity attached. This might work in some measure after all, Virginia concedes, almost hopefully.

"Do you know why I called him Septimus?" she says abruptly.

Octavia is thrown. "Septimus?"

"Yes. Septimus Warren Smith. You remember, the mad young man in *Dalloway* who throws himself from the window to his death."

"Oh, yes, yes, of course," Octavia replies. "I'm sorry. Why did you call him Septimus?"

"Because I was the seventh child. There were eight of us in all, by both of my parents' two marriages."

"Yes, so there were," Octavia says. "So there were. I had not realized that you were the seventh. And, of course, Septimus is you."

"Well, in part, yes," Virginia says. "As are many of the other characters—Clarissa, Sally, even Peter. All pieces of me. You and I did not know each other then—it was almost twenty years ago now when I was composing it—but you have been kind enough in recent months to let me probe you about your own history, and I have only just put this naming bit together. You also came from a brood of eight, did you not?"

"Yes. I was the eighth of eight, and so named."

"Ah, then. So, you see, here we are, Septimus and Octavia, seventh and eighth. Siblings, almost. How strange these correspondences are. They seem to be multiplying just now. I am seeing them more and more."

Octavia does not like the sound of this. "Because you are looking," she says.

"And"—Virginia smiles to soften the correction—"because they are *there*."

They have always disagreed about such things. Octavia is, by nature and training, firmly on Leonard's side of the divide, brashly sensible and dismissive of any mystic tendency or shade of the oc-cult. Those are not really the right terms for what Virginia is get-ting at, but even "metaphysics" is a word Octavia would utter only with extreme prejudice, or as a rebuttal, exclaiming it above the fray, in the style of the logical positivists. She'd have done well at Cambridge.

True to form, Octavia pauses, unwilling to press the point of what may or may not be, so to speak, there. Instead, she goes back to the name, and asks, a touch reproachfully, "About Septimus, you were thinking of the past, were you not? The time when you, too, threw yourself from a window, and to the same purpose?"

"Not successfully, alas."

Octavia chooses to ignore this. She does not indulge self-pity in illness. And when it is mixed, as it is so potently in Virginia, with the grandiosity of social class — or perhaps it is simply bohemian pretense, she does not care to differentiate — it is a luxury she will not countenance.

"It was during the breakdown that followed your father's death, was it not?" she says, with an unavoidable clutch of the school-marm in her voice.

For a long moment Virginia does not answer. She is staring at the floor. Her hands are cold and shaking in her lap.

"I am not referring to my father," she says at last.

"All right. Then what?"

"I was thinking of Septimus's condition and particularly of the last war. The treatment and," she hesitates on the damning word, "the harm."

She pauses on the implication in this, to make Octavia hear it. She brings her hands to her lips, to warm and settle them and to prolong the effect of what she has just said, then drops the hands back into her lap with a dull thud, as if they are broken things with which she can do nothing. Shifting once more to her purpose, she continues. "As a doctor, did you never have occasion, at that time when you were at the war hospital, surely to . . ."

Virginia is troubled by how to say this well. Her eyes stray anxiously about the room. Her hands have come alive again without her realizing. They are fidgeting in front of her, seemingly of their own accord, as if they are trying to knit but do not know how. These are dangerous signs. Octavia leans forward in her chair and takes hold of the bucking hands. Their iciness is shocking, but she betrays nothing as she lowers her face very close to Virginia's and gazes firmly at her.

"To do what?" she says softly.

Virginia's eyes suddenly stop pinging, and lock with startling ferocity on Octavia's.

"To do nothing," she says emphatically. There is a pulse of anxiety in her throat that half strangles the words.

Octavia is not keen on this line of inquiry, nor on the obvious effect it is having on her patient. She has the familiar sense, as she so often has with her old friend, of being led, but she will follow only so far.

"What do you mean, nothing?" she declares more than asks.

The word "nothing" has a jab in it that warns, but Virginia evades it, taking a warier tone.

"Those soldiers, like Septimus, psychologically destroyed yet being forced to resume 'normally.'" She pauses, considering this, then changes her mind. "Actually, no, perhaps that's wrong. This will be more immediate for you—not those like Septimus, but the ones whom no one could mistake, those who had been defaced and mangled beyond resemblance."

Octavia pulls away.

"You know nothing of that reality," she says testily. "You know only abstractions."

"I was not there on the field or in triage, if that's what you mean," Virginia says, recoiling, too. "Though that is hardly a fault. Still, I believe I knew enough. I am thinking in particular of the drawings that were done in the surgeries, the places you were. At the time, my sister had access to some of Henry Tonks's pastels through the Slade, and she showed them to me. The faces of those men — it was a parade of horrors."

Octavia explodes.

"A parade? I have no need of your descriptions of the *pastels* you saw in a parade, or of the sanitized infirm you spied hunkering in Bloomsbury. I saw the beastliness raw, firsthand, unfiltered. And as for the renderings of artists on the subject, well, that was pure voyeurism and conceit. These were not subjects. These were not props for an argument against war. These were men. Maimed, denatured, sacrificed men."

"You sound just like my nephew Julian," Virginia says.

"Then I should think him a very sensible young man."

"He's dead. And he wasn't sensible at all about war. He died nearly four years ago in Spain."

That'll take the spunk out of her, Virginia thinks. And it does, momentarily.

"He joined the Republicans?" Octavia asks.

"He drove an ambulance," Virginia replies, making it clear that she will entertain no further questions about Julian or his views on war.

"Virginia," Octavia says, after a mystified pause, "why, of all things, are you speaking of this now, when we are in the midst of another war, the threat of destruction literally hanging over us so low that we can see the swastikas on their tail fins?"

"Now it is you who do not need to tell me," Virginia cries, her hands beginning to jump again. "Those planes have flown over our garden in broad daylight. They fly back and forth above us every night on their bombing runs to London. I am well acquainted, thank you, with the threat of these days. I am not linking wars frivolously, or their victims. I am not putting my abstractions in place of your carnage. You are missing—oh, you will make me too angry now."

She waves a dismissive hand and turns half away. Now they are both sitting very stiffly at attention. The ticking of the brass-faced mahogany clock on the wall and the tightness of their breathing are the only sounds.

Octavia will wait. She knows that she has lost her temper, which is a sorer point in her practice than it would be if she had not had to fight so hard for it. She has emotional control, but in this unaccustomed role as adjunct psychiatrist to a friend, not enough. Not nearly enough. She knows that she must listen less reactively, and Virginia must go on of her own accord.

There is a softening now between them that comes of knowing what is at stake. It happens quickly when they are sharp with each other like this, because of the strain. It is ever-present, the friendship, the struggle, women, the profession, the finer balance required, yet so often lost. They forgive each other instantly for all the harshest things, even as the disagreements persist.

"Fine, then," Virginia says. "We will speak in the present tense." She is in full possession of her forces now. "These horrors you point to, they are not fresh to me. But I assure you, they are quite familiar. I knew them first as a young girl, and they have been with me all my life. I have lived in their shadow always, even as I have gone on with what was expected. All these years, as the ghost of me proceeded, or seemed to, at meals, at tasks, at gatherings, some piece of me remained apart, terrified, while the partygoers went on unawares. In this I have always been strange. But now, as the commonplace horrors of the war encroach, you, too, all of you, the average, are set apart from the habitual mundane. You, too, feel horror, the same commensurate, explicable horror that is being felt in common by everyone around you. Well, I say welcome to it, because, you see, I am not surprised. I felt this horror as a child, just standing before a puddle in a garden path. I have felt it many times since, sitting in the bath or standing in a shaft of sun slicing through apple blossoms. But now, at last, blithe being has caught up to me. The outer and the inner crises have met. Now, when the horrors are everywhere, when the world is a whirlwind of shared distress, I am snug in the storm's eye. I am home."

Octavia can say nothing at first. She is caught by the pity of this, as Virginia intended her to be, humbled as if by a slap to the face. There is no refuting it. Here is a hell she has never known. Her clinician's hauteur shrivels under it, again, as Virginia knew it would. She is ashamed of having been angry, and perhaps unfair about the wounded men, but she is also irked by having fallen into the rhetorical trap that she sensed all along was being set for her. With Virginia, this always inheres. Octavia tries to weaken her resentment, and with it the underlying sense that they are in a battle of wills, but the stiffness is still there in her voice when she says, at last, "What is it, then, that you are asking me?"

"I was asking you about those men. Those particular men that you saw and knew and ministered to in the hospital."

Again Octavia cannot help prickling. "And what of them?"

They are back where Virginia wants to be, and it is infuriating.

"Did you never think . . . did they themselves at times . . . not ask you to desist . . . to mitigate their suffering by . . ."

But Octavia cannot let her go on. The point is too sore.

"You have not the first notion of their suffering," she erupts. "I will not speak any more of this."

Virginia is quicker this time. Having expected the outburst, she evades it in one turn, and presses on more surely.

"Then speak of *me*. Sufferings are not comparable, I do realize. I cannot know theirs, and they — you — cannot know mine. I am not asking you to. I am merely trying to find in your experience, your practice as a doctor, something to help you grasp —"

"I believe I can grasp," Octavia snaps, "and without your help, whatever it is that you have to say."

Virginia sighs and folds her arms firmly across her chest. She slides her hands into her armpits, trying again to warm them, and to ward off the worst of the misunderstanding.

"Then 'grasp' is not what I mean," she says more plaintively. "I cannot say what I mean anymore. Still, I must say this. I need to say this to someone. To you. I know that you will not want to understand it, but I am asking you to try. Please, Octavia. There is no one else."

The turnabout is sudden, and Octavia feels the pang of her own harshness, as well as the love that is between them.

"But how could I not want to understand? Have we not spoken together of many difficult things, Virginia? Have I not done so willingly? Usefully?"

"This is different."

"How?"

"It will be much more difficult."

"Tell me why."

"It will be difficult for you more so than for me, and — you are right, I said this stupidly just now — not because it is difficult to grasp, but because it is difficult to concede. I do know you, Octavia, a little. You will not agree, and that is the least of it. You will loathe this instinctively. You will not hear of it, and so, I fear, you will not hear it, and that is why you will not understand."

"So, you mean 'understand,' then, as in 'agree.' No, it was more than that. You said 'concede.' You need me to concede?"

"I need you not to act."

Octavia pauses to adjust to this twist. She knows, of course, what Virginia means, but she had not expected her to say it quite this way.

"I see," she says finally.

"Do you?"

"Well, it is only implied, as it ever is with you. You have not said the words. But yes, I believe I see where you are leading."

"And will you follow?"

"I don't know, Virginia. I really don't know. I can listen. That much I can promise you. I can talk, if that will be of use to you. And I can do so as carefully as I am able, knowing you, and knowing the perils of too forceful an intervention in your case. But I cannot say that I will sit by and nod approvingly at everything you say, or indulge you in these flights to which you are prone. I would not do so in any argument with anyone. That is my way. You know it. You expect it, and I think you respect me for it. You could not have come here thinking that would change."

"No. Indeed not. And that is why you are unique. The others are too close, too convinced of their clear-sightedness and my lack of it, to see clearly or discuss openly matters that frighten them, and which, in the end, are mine alone to decide. But you are just close enough, and just remote enough, to meet me where I am. Or you can be, if you are willing. I believe now that Leonard was right in this, after all. I did not come here thinking this, but I am beginning to see what it could mean. I know that what I will be asking you to do will not be easy for you, as my doctor and my friend. I know that you will fight it, because that is what you do, but I hope that you will do so in this room alone with me, without the threat of forceful intervention. I cannot have that. I have seen it done to other women, and I will not allow it to be done to me."

"So you are to dictate terms."

Octavia is turning pink around the eyes and nose. Her mouth is a tight line.

"If that is what you call it, then yes," Virginia says. "I say only this: Do not force me to Septimus's means."

"Do I understand you?" Octavia cries. "You propose to throw yourself from the window if I do not consent?"

"It is not a proposition."

"No. Indeed. It is a threat."

"Don't reduce it to the absurd, Octavia. You are not a simpleton."

"How gracious of you to say so," Octavia says, more acidly than she'd meant to. Hearing herself, she stops, and tries smoothing the taut front of her skirt. She takes several deep breaths to regain her composure, but she is too annoyed to calm herself fully.

"It is you who are behaving like a child," she says. "An adolescent, actually, a hormonal, histrionic adolescent. Are we still in Brighton, or have we been transported suddenly to the West End? It is too absurd, Virginia. There is no one watching. It is just the two of us here in the surgery. You cannot elevate this to a performance. You cannot supplant life with art, nor death for that matter. Do not gloss it simply to disguise the fact that you are doing nothing more exalted than playing the part of the thwarted ingénue who would have her way at any cost."

"No. Not my way," Virginia asserts. "My choice. I would have my choice. But you would leave me without one. That is the difficult fact that you do not wish to acknowledge. The point is not *that* Septimus threw himself from the window, but *why* he did so. So, I ask you. Think of it. Why did he? Well, his answer is mine. To avoid being committed."

"He *committed* the crime of self-murder."

"In defiance of the greater crime of committing a person against his will."

Exasperated, Octavia says, "Oh, Virginia, derangement deprives us all of choices. Doctors and patients alike. That, perhaps, is its greatest theft. I'm sorry, but there it is."

"But that is just it," Virginia says. "I am not deranged. Not now. I am on the verge of becoming so again. There is a great difference. These are not the arguments of madness. They are not crooked. They are not obscure. They are perfectly clear."

"And what precisely is it that you think is so clear — aside, of course, from your unwillingness to properly address your condition?"

"What is clear — and with invasion looming, it is clear to every man and woman in the street, but it has been clear to me all along — what is clear, Octavia, is that death is certain." Her eyes are immensely hard and shining, like polished river stones, and fixed on their target, boring into Octavia's own as if they would burn through.

"But," she continues, lifting her finger for emphasis — it is so wretchedly thin and pale that it has almost the opposite effect, but it is as steady as a spike — "if we are quick at the decisive moment, if we are not taken or struck down, and *if we have not been forced by those who would care for us,* then we may choose how we meet that certainty."

In the fervor of the speech she has dropped the instructing pose, and now both her hands are placed in front of her, palms up, in a strangely contrary gesture of decisiveness and supplication. "I am asking for that choice," she says.

Octavia is moved, but she will not yield or show it.

"And was it this same clarity," she insists, "this same argument that informed your previous attempts? Were you making the informed, the unforced choice when you threw yourself from the window as a young woman, or later, when you took the overdose of veronal?"

Virginia hardly pauses on the answer, which has a sudden coldness and finality that she has not shown before — not today, and perhaps never before between them.

"I knew then what I know now. I told you. I knew it when I was very young."

Octavia hears again the note of danger in these words, and knows, too, that it is new in their exchanges. But, she firmly reminds herself, she will remain as she is, whatever happens. She will not be drawn into panic, which is sitting there so oddly in Virginia, but as its more horrifying opposite, like a lizard, confident in the terror that it inflicts.

"And, for the simpleton, tell me again," Octavia says stiffly. "What is it that you knew?"

"That death is an embrace."

Virginia is abruptly softened by this pronouncement, which she has made dreamily, as if she were reading the last cozy line of a bedtime story to a child. She is looking off into her daydream, Octavia thinks, having scored the decisive touch, or so she believes. Octavia knows this line well, and will not rise to it, any more than she would to its saurian counterpart, which has just slithered artfully out of sight. If Octavia were not so alarmed, and if she were given to derision, she might be stifling a snort, but a kind of weary motherly displeasure is all that she can muster.

"My, how very dramatic," she says, almost drolly. "We are back to the footlights. That is worthy of Juliet."

Virginia looks back sharply at her, surprised and angered at being mocked. Octavia, fueled by the unexpected thrill of an advantage, rushes on.

"But even a simpleton can see through you," she says. "You have cleverly turned it all around, I'll give you that, but the truth is far less flattering than the guise. You were not a savant, and you are not one now. You have simply failed to grow up. The truer way of saying it is not that you have always known, but that you know now nothing more than you knew then. This is a child's romance, a child's rash and flamboyant method carried through intact to the fancies of a fifty-nine-year-old woman who, I might add, is far too intelligent and wise not to know better."

Virginia is strangely composed and, uncharacteristically, she ignores this insult.

"It's true that my courses then were not as well chosen as they might have been. I left room for error and interference. But, as you say, I was young. I was eager."

"Eager to escape," Octavia says.

"No, precisely the opposite. It was always life that was the escape for me. Sanity was the diversion."

Octavia is puzzled by this and almost intrigued, but she is also annoyed. To Virginia this has become a game.

"Escape? Diversion? From what?" she asks.

"Intimacy," Virginia answers, again in the dream voice.

This has ruined any intrigue there might have been.

"Oh, nonsense," Octavia says. "Romance . . . If you were so eager for this supposed intimacy, this embrace of death, then why did you not pursue it? Why did you not try again until you succeeded? Many years have passed since the last attempt."

"We are all susceptible to diversion, are we not?" Virginia says, a look of guilty innocence stealing over her face. The mix is typical and perfected, one of the ways Virginia has of conniving with paradox.

"And my diversion," she continues, now well in command, "has been perhaps more diverting than most. I was enraptured by it. I wanted to communicate what I had glimpsed, though I suspected from the start where this would lead. Expression, you see, carries the means of its own annihilation. Brought to its fullest consummation, its closest contact, it disintegrates. I have reached that point: the end of language. *The rest is silence.*"

Octavia has heard this before. It is a favorite when Virginia is depressed, intoned woefully at tea, the two of them consulting through the years, though not appearing to, just chatting as friends do, but with a purpose.

Octavia sighs. "You have said as much before, Virginia. Often, in fact, and for as long as I have known you. Each time you finish a book, you declare yourself mute and inert, and you fall into the torpor of this . . . this perceived ineptitude. It has always been the same."

"Yes, it has always been the same," Virginia agrees. "Because it has always been true, and I have always known it. That is what I want you to understand. The recurrence, and the when and the why of it, the coming back always to this single truth: The wholeness, the oneness, this way of being that I have intimated cannot be fully divulged. And all this writing, this fever to put it down, has only ever been a knowingly futile diversion from that inescapable, that scientific fact. It cannot be achieved. Not by our means.

Not in the confines of our minds, our language, our winnowing perception ... And all these times, you are right, always at the end of an attempt, because that was when I was faced yet again with the same evidence, I fell into this same silence. Always then, I knew again what I had known repeatedly before but had not yet been willing to accept. And so the cycle continued. I turned away. I scarpered back into distraction and forgot. I lived, striving to communicate this radiating significance that I had momentarily descried. I wrote and rewrote and revised until the last line, the last full stop. And then, feeling crushed, as before, I was back where I had started, newly failed."

She ceases abruptly, her breath coming full and almost chokingly fast. But she will not wait for Octavia to answer until she has said the remaining words, the whole in fact of what she came to say. She steadies herself with the dull determination of a furrower righting his plow, and finishes.

"But that is all over now. I have made the last cycle. I am done. I am ready. I accept. Hereafter, there will be no more leaving."

Octavia jerks forward and nearly stands, lurching up to the edge of her chair and slapping her hands violently against her thighs.

"Honestly, Virginia, you try me so. You prevaricate. Leaving is exactly what you would do."

The desperation in this, and the secret it reveals so unwillingly, that Octavia's grasp is slipping, rings between them like the distant wail of a child in distress.

"No," Virginia murmurs. "Not leaving. Going."

"Going? What do you mean, going?" Octavia is shouting now. "Into the waiting arms of the hereafter? Is that it?" Then, regaining at least a note of her adversarial pretense, if not her composure, she adds, "Hereafter. It is a telling word, don't you think? You said it a moment ago, you realize."

Virginia reaches for a cheroot and lights it, her hands as strangely steady as they were when they began this part of the conversation. She takes a luxurious drag, raising her chin imperiously to blow the smoke up and behind her. This is not meant to annoy, but it does, and Octavia again regrets that she is not better able to conceal her chagrin. Virginia looks at her kindly, or means to, though to Octavia it does not feel kind. Virginia crosses her legs and leans her elbows on her knees. This is the didactic mode again, as with the raised finger, one of her tricks, perfected at parties over the years. It holds her apart and safe from the messiness of contact.

"Now, my dear friend," Virginia says, "I think it is you who are being perhaps just a little romantic."

Octavia scowls dismissively, but says nothing.

"That is a Christian heaven you are thinking of," Virginia continues. "But you have it quite backward. The ancients had it closer, I think. In the East, I mean. Nirvana is not our hereafter. It is not everlasting life, or even life reincarnate. Extension is not the desire of going. Quite the opposite. It may surprise you to know that the literal meaning of the Sanskrit word *nibbana* is 'extinguished.'"

Octavia can contain herself no longer.

"Don't lecture me. The swastika comes from Sanskrit as well, and do you know what it means? 'It is good.' How do you like that? Oh, for God's sake, Virginia. This is madness."

"No. No, Octavia. Listen," Virginia says, patting the air with her hands in a calming gesture. "Not madness, but the relief of it, the completion of it. Don't you see? Madness is"—she raps her knuckles on her head—"this instrument overwhelmed. I am mad when the visions and the knowledge are most intense. I am *made* mad because I cannot accommodate the onslaught, because it is too much for my brain to take in or to put out. That is why the silence.

"Go back to what you know," she continues, determined to make this clear. "To Paul. The Bible. Acts, is it? His vision of heaven, you remember? He could not describe it. He was a man of many words, always instructing, always warning. Yet this he had no words for. And why? Because, as he himself acknowledged, it was indescribable. It could not be spoken . . . So it is with me. And no, Octavia, I am not delusional. I do not imagine that I am that pedantic lunatic Paul, or that I have seen heaven. There is no such *place,* no extra life. There is only the relinquishment, the happy, final throwing off of all these weights and frames that make me mad with incapacity: this body, these words, this hopeless bloody rock we are standing on. It cannot move fast enough. None of it. The light is shooting through and past us. We cannot catch up to it. And that . . . exactly that, this entrenchment while beholding the unspeakable . . . is why this consciousness is and has always been excruciating to me. I cannot do it anymore."

Octavia is staring at Virginia's face, which is flushed for the first time in months, possibly years. It is so incongruous, so unlike her normal state, Octavia marvels, that she looks like an old photograph that has been retouched, or a wooden doll whimsically painted to seem cheered. Pools of actual pink, deep pink, are dotted in the strangest places: on her left cheekbone but not her right, swiped across the forehead but not the chin. And the nose, the long, arrogant Stephen nose, is whiter than any of her has ever been, even at her sickest, and unreal, like putty, the flat colorless color of an object that defies the light.

Octavia is stunned by what she has heard. Won over, she might have said, except — she sees this at last — there is no contest. There

will be no more sparring—there never was any—no vain flour-
ishes of wit and frankness. Those were her projections. She has
had this wrong from the start, not superficially, of course—that is
all there, part of the veneer, and Virginia's ploy—but profoundly.
She has had it all profoundly wrong at the core of what, for Virginia, the whole purpose of this interview has turned out to be. It
has not, after all, been a debate staged between loving adversaries,
nor a tussle with an old friend. It has not been a consultation or a
medical call. It is simply a goodbye.

She cannot dodge the pain of this or stop the tears it brings. She
will not even try.

"And what of Leonard?" she moans. "Have you given him a
moment's thought in all this?"

"Of course I have. Always. We have been discussing this for a
long time."

"So you have talked of it?"

"We have talked of the ideas in it. Yes. But that was only creative flushing. The matter of it, the vision, has always been understood. He knows better than anyone ever could how the sickness
and the work have gone for me."

"Then why not tell him now?"

"Because knowing and hearing are two very different things. I
said so at the beginning of all this."

"I don't understand that."

"There are a great many things we feel and wish for that we can
never say aloud, often never admit to ourselves. Leonard is far too
moral and good a man to entertain a malignant thought, much
less have it set before him as a gift."

"Damn you. You are speaking in riddles again. How can you?"

"I'm sorry. Truly. I don't mean to. I am merely saying that without me Leonard will be free. Free to work, to live and love. And

this is a freedom that some relentlessly quashed and despised but deeply human and righteous part of him desires. Anyone would. And I want this for him. For years and years he has seen to me, watched over and cared for me, as well as talked with me, and been my dearest, most inspiring creative and intellectual companion. But I have been a burden to him. I have kept him back. He knows this, but his devotion will not let him see it, and his overbearing conscience will never let him admit it. To say it aloud to him, to drag it out glaringly into the light and name it, would be to insult him. To have it done, however, will be tenderly . . ."

"Tenderly what?"

"Anonymous."

"How typical of you. You will destroy him with this. It is not an act of love. It is nothing but an indulgence of pure selfishness and thoughtless disregard."

"Again you oversimplify. You forget that love is never one impulse, never one face, but many and varied and as conflicted as the truth always is. In my love for him, among many, many other contradictions, there is contained the cruelty of parting, and in his love for me, also many-faceted and at odds, there is the fulfillment of having me gone."

Octavia flattens one side of her mouth and shakes her head in disapproval. She is not remotely convinced, but she does not wish to wade any further into the double meanings of Virginia's marriage, if that is indeed what they are, or, and this is the more likely truth, into the rhetorical rings she runs round it to justify her will.

"And Vanessa?" she asks instead.

"She is my heart," Virginia says. "She will know."

What can she say to such a thing? Virginia has dismissed her sister's grief in two short sentences. It is like slamming a door. Octavia feels as if she is being systematically shut out, and there is nothing she can do but give in.

"What of me, then?" she says meekly.

"Oh, my dearest Octavia," Virginia says, her face melting into an almost unbearable kindness. "You are an oak. A sturdy, stalwart English oak. You will stand yet for a long time."

This reply is even more pat than the last. There is no way in. The conversation is at an end. Now all she can do is stall for time. She looks at Virginia once more, pleadingly, searching her face for some response, but Virginia is in a cocoon, her expression as blank and inaccessible as if it were wrapped in gauze.

"All right," Octavia says at last, sighing hugely and wiping the corners of her eyes. "I will agree to let you go and not to act. But on one condition."

Virginia says nothing. She merely tilts her chin to one side to indicate that she has heard. This hurts Octavia, but there is nothing for it. She can only finish her part of what is already done.

"That you promise to let me come and see you tomorrow," she says.

Virginia pretends to consider this for a moment. "The day after?"

"All right, then. The day after. It is a promise?"

"Yes," Virginia says, and smiles.

Octavia stands. "Right, then, let me get you your milk."

FRIDAY

SHE IS SITTING at her desk in the writing lodge at the end of the garden, looking down at the blotter where a stripe of weak sunlight is lashing across it at the corner like the ribbon on a gift. She has placed a piece of sky-blue stationery squarely at its center, and the pen beside it, stiffly vertical, like a display. They — the paper, the pen and she in the chair — have been here like this since just before six, when the night guns at Newhaven had finally gone silent and the swarms of Luftwaffe had buzzed back across the Channel, having laid their iron eggs.

Often now, it is the silence that wakes her, the cessation that is somehow more horrifying than the cannonade. This is what woke her again this morning. She crept down to the lodge immediately to write the necessary notes, just as the horizon was beginning to glow, the trees and the shrubs and the rooftops standing black against the rose quartz of the sky like chessmen, arrayed round the clearing in the orchard.

She sat here for a long time, watching the sun assert itself in lancing shadows and shafts across the grass, and feeling the room brighten almost undetectably, as if from within, each molecule its own source, slowly dialing up the light. Now the sun is well up and the first rays have begun to penetrate the foliage that surrounds the low triptych of windows behind her. She looks at her watch to confirm the hour. Five to nine. She can delay no longer.

Grasping the watch, anxiously twisting its face toward her, she thinks again of the guns, the cannonade and the hour. When it begins, when it stops, and the undissuaded dawn it leaves to ripen, festooned by a cacophony of birdsong. This is when the voices are loudest in her mind, shouting over the larks and the thrushes and the wrens like a rowdy parliament.

They are a predictable group, tailored for the occasion by the blights and scorns of memory.

There is her Tom, now Poor Tom, or Tom o' Bedlam, who comes ringing off the pages of Shakespeare with his penetrating nonsense, except that it is not really nonsense in the mouth of her stern, snake-eyed old friend, having, as it does, all the marks of his strict diction and the cold burn of his marmoreal skin. His is the dominant voice, her haunting competitor, here to the end, to beguile and torment her.

Then, for contrast, or because it makes a kind of twisted sense, there is her lovely gone Lytton, whose conversation she had craved so wretchedly every day of the last long nine years until he came alive again in this chorus this morning, shrill as ever, the quick dead Fool to Tom's Tom.

And then — because who else could be her Lear? — there is the old magus himself, Yeats, no longer the wan, dusty keeper of the curio shop, nor the suspiciously rosy beneficiary of a vasectomy. He is resplendent in his greyness now, both powerfully dull and shining, striated and smooth-edged, like an unfinished statue of the great poet himself, striding out of the sculptor's block, which is not marble or bronze, but one of those pure broadcasting minerals he had spoken of, titanium, perhaps, or zinc, hewn from the singing side of a mountain.

Finally, as always, there is Adeline, who is an angel of decorum, the Cordelia of this cast, speaking only when spoken to, or when the moment is perfectly right, the briefest, gentlest, most apposite words imaginable.

These are the personae — canonical, of course — that have come booming through her morning, just when the real cannons stop. From the canon for the canon's hour, she has aptly chosen *King Lear*. She saw *Lear* once in the West End with Tom, she recalls, years and years ago when they were young, and they had laughed, as the young do, at its tragedy, which at the time had seemed absurdly lachrymose and contrived. But now it has appeared, the real thing, like the ghost of irony personified, precisely on its hour to have the last laugh.

Yes, the canonical hour, she thinks. There is also that. Terce, is it? Nine a.m.? Tom would know. He had told her once in the full flush of his conversion, but she had not paid much attention, having been at the time too preoccupied with forced discretion, swallowing the quips and carps that had kept rising to her lips like the bile in her gorge. She had detested his weakness in going over to the Church, like a traitor to the other side. But then, she had known everything he was running from — Vivien's bane — and she had sympathized with him then, as she had sympathized all along. She had, she thinks now, always done her utmost to help him with the ill-starred accidents of his life, even as she had recoiled, and behaved every bit as badly as she had well.

Poor Tom, who had swallowed the catechism whole, and for what? To mark the hours in Latin? Or for comfort? To hide his furtive weeping boy's head in the clergyman's skirts? To pour all his festering confessions where they could never be retold?

Nine a.m. is Terce, says the pinching voice of Poor Tom. *The third hour. The hours are marked in threes. Six a.m. is the first hour, Prime. Nine a.m. is the third hour, Terce. Noon is the sixth hour, Sext, and three p.m. is the ninth hour, None. Pity your Latin was always so poor. But then, what can one expect of a woman, and self-schooled?*

She sighs at the old dig of this remark. It presses, as always, on the wound of insufficiency in her. It is the same thing again, the dread of being found out, or deemed an ignoramus by all those impeccable men who had come to her, armed to their gnashing teeth with all the academic rigors of their higher educations.

She unhands the watch and picks up the pen. Terce, then. She must be terse. Her eyes stray to the vase of the season's first yellow primroses that she has placed at the corner of the desk, and grimacing at the pun, she thinks sourly, This is something *he'd* have done. Joyce, the gaudiest by far of that baccalaureate lot. James Augustine Aloysius Joyce — she had seen the full train of his name in his obituary only two months ago, on January 13, just two weeks shy of her fifty-ninth birthday. She nods to her galvanized Yeats, as if to say, He was not my Irishman of choice.

Strange. Yeats, too, like Lytton, and like Joyce, had died in January, within days of her birthday in '39.

Bloody Joyce, that other creed-besotted sot and friend of Tom's. He'd have punned on "Terce," just as he had punned on a thousand other liturgical bug words, because, try as he might, he had never been able to get the Rome out of the boy. And Tom, the dolt, had put it (or its kissing cousin) willingly in, the mumbo jumbo of Canterbury.

It had been a bond in them, surely, the yoke of the Church, in the one case never quite thrown off, and in the other manfully taken on. It was all the same, a talking point between. She, too, had been a common subject for them to feast on, no doubt, as they were sharpening their knives on womankind. It was Tom who had told him, of course. Who else? "Virginia Woolf doesn't care for *Ulysses* — thinks you're a he-goat showing off."

Well, she *hadn't* cared for it, and he *was* a he-goat. So what?

She doesn't want to think of how the rest of that conversation must have gone. But it had registered, her remark, enough to warrant a retort from the he-goat himself. He'd put it in, amidst the other gobbledygook, in his final tome, his last inscrutable testament, *Finnegans Wake*, published of course by Tom at Faber, and the whole civilized world had promptly fallen before it, panting like a parish of evangelicals. It was almost beyond belief. The precious Irish choirboy, speaking in tongues, had paused to stick out his tongue at her. Well, well, she couldn't help but feel flattered. It was right there on page five, unmistakable (or was it?): "hegoak."

She hadn't read the thing, but Tom had shown her, pointing to it so fiercely on the page with his talon-nailed middle finger that he'd left a mark. He'd stood there with the book open, lavishing his oiliest scholar's smile on her, as if he'd just told her that he'd found a reference to her in the Holy Gospel itself, only this, of course, was the gospel according to James.

Oh, curse it, she rails: Why now? Joyce had had the indignity to die, and far from feeling the prick of schadenfreude she'd expected, she'd nearly broken down. She'd read the news in the paper and shuddered violently, almost epileptically, as if at a forewarning, then collapsed in a heap for the rest of the morning. Writhing in agonies of self-disgust, she'd lain on the floor for hours, filled with all the biting admiration she had not allowed herself to feel while he'd lived. In the envious throes of her imagination, his presence had always been too much, standing monstrous and grinning on the near side of the Continent, like a Cheshire colossus.

He, too—no, in truth, only he, not she, she could admit this now—had come to the end of language. He had flown. He had had the courage, the negation, to do what she had not: to fail flamboyantly.

That was the nut of it, and it was a truism worth proclaiming again, if only to these walls and these demons. She had said as much to Octavia yesterday, though in different words, and anyway, the stubborn, track-minded woman had not understood.

But here it was, she would repeat her summation, for herself and for Tom, Yeats, Lytton and Adeline, who were listening: All the greatest works of art were failures by definition. By design. This was the whole purpose and nature of art, to fail, for art was and could only ever be futile and moribund. That was what made it shine in the darkness.

Naturally. Of course. And why not? She would go on for a bit here, indulge herself as she used to, as if they were all still sitting around smoking and shouting and laughing: alive.

"Here," she pronounces, her mouth moving but no sound emerging, her eyes roaming the imagined group, "here, thrown up to a God who does not exist, are the brash and squandered valedictions of creatures who can make no sense of their predicament. And so they despair. Yet they choose to sing anyway, sing loudly and elaborately and gorgeously, unheard and unanswered, the dying anthem of the tragic human inability to communicate."

She sits up in her chair as if for applause at one of her lectures, and thinks, How about that for the scoffers? But then, just as quickly, she remembers her position—where she is, what she is and whom she is addressing—and she sinks back, defeated and ashamed, into the slouch she has been assuming all morning.

But Joyce—she cannot let go of this—however she'd grumbled over him, had done it. He had. He had sent up his beautiful, doomed, man-made flying machine, traced the arc of its brief flight and, with equal parts pride and insouciance, watched its inevitable crash. Yes. She could allow as much now. Daedalus, the master craftsman, was exactly the name; the creator and sire of Icarus, who flew on wings of his father's making and, flying too high, too human, fell to sea.

She has a moment of satisfaction over this, her, for once, resentless salute to the Artist, so called. But then, quick as instinct, the voice of Poor Tom is on it like a fly, blundering in from the farthest boroughs of her brain:

But you haven't done it. You didn't do it, did you? So, what of that?

And then, just as quickly, there is Yeats, fending off the assault, reciting the poem he once wrote for her:

We that have done and thought ... That have thought and done ...

Ignoring the old man, Lytton, ever naughty and loyal, elects his own way, and chides instead in her defense:

Here's a riddle for you, Tom. You'll like it. It's phil-o-soph-ic-al and topical, too. If an opus crashes in the desert and no one's there to hear it, or see it, or care one way or the other, does it make a sound? Not a bang, perhaps, but a whimper, eh? Just like our good old RAF in Africa, flying, rat-tat-tat, then down and—poof!—just a wee little handful of dust.

She smiles at this and barks a laugh, as if Tom is really in the room and she is just clearing her throat. Even now, she dares not appear too amused to hear his verses so maliciously lampooned.

But it is true. Poor Tom is right. She had not done it. She had not flown. She had reached her pinnacle in *The Waves,* the heights of translucence. But then she had lost her nerve and retreated, rushed back—like a woman?—to the sanctuary of the known world, to the writer's tidy workshop, call it, full of sawdust and lumber and glue, where she, along with all the other weary yeomen, had built solid, weight-bearing sentences with well-sanded corners and straight lines. Not a craftsman anymore, but a tradesman, she had churned out the riskless product in her later years, varnished, hidebound and safe as bloody houses. Even Leonard, in his own soft way, had agreed.

But—she catches herself—she had had her reasons, hadn't she? She had done it, written *The* (admittedly deadpan) *Years* and the overstretched *Between the Acts,* just to show that she could, and to answer her critics. Or that, at least, had been what she had told herself and everyone else when she could bring herself to say anything at all. Yet here, alone and not alone—damn these voices—the truth will out.

Those had not been her real reasons.

"I did it because I was afraid," she says aloud, furiously dropping the pen on the blotter, where she sees that the paper is still blank. How appropriate, she thinks. Not a word.

She looks at her watch once more and sees that it is almost nine-thirty. No matter. She will put down something for Leonard yet—she will—but the time will mean much more than the note. The note will be for the inquest, a document for him to show and be exonerated by, though by the authorities only. He will not exonerate himself. Never that. He is too hard, too exacting.

She knows that Leonard will go over this morning in his mind again and again, looking for his fault, and he will find it primarily in time, in vigilance. He will berate himself ceaselessly for falling asleep, or worse, losing focus on the watch, and he will rack himself for every minute gone.

This is where her wristwatch will do its work, a kindness she can show him, knowing him so well. She will be quick out the door and into the river. This she has promised herself for him. When they find her, he will have the evidence of the wristwatch, strapped to her, stopped at the wicked moment, and he will know then — he will have the needed proof irrefutably in hand — that it had not been long, not long at all, the time between her leaving and her going.

It would be noon at the latest.

Sext, says Poor Tom. *By Sext, thy will be done.*

Sexed at last, shrills Lytton, not to be outdone. *Our frigid blue-nose virgin-ia climaxes at last. And comme les françaises, no less, comme les françaises. Come one, come all, come comme les françaises and have your little death, or so they call it, la petite mort.*

Sext, Poor Tom says again, as if to obliterate this blasphemy. *By Sext it will be done, and by None they will know.*

Yes, she thinks, by three o'clock Leonard will know that what's done has been done, and he will know that he could have done nothing. That is all that matters.

The ceremony of innocence is drowned, says Yeats, reciting again. But this time, with the flintiest of smiles, he adds, *Surely the Second Coming is at hand.*

Soixante-neuf, squeals Lytton, delighted by his own invention and the chance to extend the ribaldry at Tom's and old Yeats's expense. *Between the soixante and the neuf falls the shadow of the slouching beast with two backs. What ho! He's coming again, and to Bethlehem.*

This is too wonderful to resist, and she explodes in sobs of laughter. These are the final outrush of all her rage and anxiety pent up. The surprise of this does not escape her as she seizes with mirth, her belly collapsing and distending painfully, the tears streaming down her face, her mouth a sloppy rictus, wailing of its own accord like an inconsolable child's.

Why is she laughing? How? But she knows why and how. She has done it before.

Suddenly and vividly she remembers her father's wake all those many years ago. Everyone had gathered in that awful, lugubrious sitting room, waiting to go in, the siblings and semi-siblings (except, of course, Laura, who had been sent to the asylum, and lovely Stella, who had died). There they had been, thrown together, the Duckworths, George and Gerald, and the Stephens, Thoby, Vanessa, herself and Adrian, all milling about and fidgeting in that dark closed space, desperate to escape the terrible knowledge that they felt freed, not aggrieved by their father's death, and now were strung up by obsequies that they could not properly bring off.

George, drunk of course, had broken the spell. Donning an absurd party wig he'd found in a trunk, he'd begun dancing on the furniture, singing sea chanteys in the style of a fishwife, his voice pitched like a corncrake's. At the sight and the sound of him, they had all broken down in fits of obscene merriment which had gone on and on, each of them feeding off the other, long after George had put his leg into an umbrella stand on an inadvisable leap from the chaise, and had clattered into the potted aspidistras in the corner. He had lain there for quite some time, moaning and giggling like a satyr in a pile of shards and scattered soil, and they had all gone on moaning and giggling with him until the doctor, or someone presiding, she couldn't remember who, had come in to shush them with a sour and scandalized face.

Laughter was not something one expected so close to the end, yet there it was, as akin to death as to madness — Poor Tom o' Bedlam, and the bedraggled Fool, poorer still, wailing and joshing on the heath beside their Lear, and all of them, like that other false man, Viola, *smiling at grief.* At last, the absolute, the perfect genius of that line rings true to her, like so much else that the Bard had just tossed off, the throwaway lines of his comedy, light fare, and the muttered asides that were there in every one of his tragedies, like darts. They had stuck in her and were twitching now like tune forks.

Absent thee from felicity awhile, quotes a wearying Poor Tom.

You are no Prince Hamlet, counters Lytton viciously, *nor were meant to be.*

And that, too, she thinks, is true, and Tom knew it. Poor straight Tom, forging his fraught poems on the anvil of his intellect, beating them till they shone and cut. He, too, had chosen the safe haven of the tradesman, yet not, she believes, as she had done, out of fear, but in rectitude. Emotions, though lodged in him viscerally to the point of impaction, had always been anathema to Tom, like a disease or a bad smell, and all the more so for being endemic. And, of course, the harder thing: They were so un-English. Yes, of course. English to the bone was something he had always so desperately wanted to be. And, through God knew what private scourgings and refurbishments, English he had damn well become — three-piece suit, wife, church, royal subject and all.

There had been a time, she recalls, when the most hurtful thing you could call Tom was a bumpkin, which Lytton or someone else had done repeatedly to rib him. Or you could break off humming the tune of "St. Louis Blues," another well-worn chaff resorted to when Tom got too high-stepping and forgot himself. He could talk, dress and wed his way to the core of proper English life, but there was just no sidestepping the old fact: He was a Middle American, born and raised.

But in the end it is immaterial, because Tom will be remembered. Yes, he will be remembered as well as — and this is the crucial difference — understood, because he is exactly what he'd always said he was, the prophet, not the god, the small man with a gift for sight and a talent for usefulness. Nothing more.

He will stand back forever in the minds of literary men, as he had always done, pointing at the spectacle, and doing so with such shrewd precision, with such cleverly veiled, yet niggling tenderness, that his works would shake men to their soles for as long as there were words and souls to hear them.

He will be that berated thing, a success, and so, not an artist, but an artisan, a virtuoso of the message that gets through, because it will have been sent from the sideline by a spectator who would not play in the endgame.

He will die standing, she thinks, the stony sage who has had the good sense not to alight, and I will die having dallied too long after my best, a coward. All of his predictions will come true. Fearing death by water, hearing human voices, I will drown.

She looks down at the paper and sees that, without knowing it, she has written most of the lines she intended for Leonard. Reading them, she sees that they are like something written in sleep — or in a lunatic trance of laughter and recrimination, more like — but they will do. She scribbles the rest perfunctorily, because she can do nothing else, hastily, obsequiously explaining it away in Adeline's voice, as if it were a piece of homework past due. But Adeline is good for this, diligent, repetitive, sincere. She soothes the injury by being daft. She cannot be held responsible for her crimes.

Yet the true crime is not lack of life, but of love. Nessa had been right. It is lack of love, the right kind of love, which Virginia has never shown to anyone. And in this Adeline has been as complicit as she. Indeed, Adeline is the author of it. Octavia had also been right. She, Virginia, has never grown up. Adeline is not her invention; she is Adeline's, just another persona in the array, and none of them capable of love outside the circle of themselves.

That much of what she has just written to Leonard is true. She has never been as good as he. She has never loved as he has, through acts and things done not from desire but out of care and at great cost.

Oh yes, of course, she has loved in her way, grandly, passionately, erotically, companionately, fraternally, sororially, filially, even spousally, to a point, but in all these ways she has only ever loved as a child loves, epiphenomenally, and without the dutiful giving back that truly adult partnership requires.

All those things she'd said and hardly meant, and all the people she'd said them to, just more words. But Leonard had not spoken. He had been. He had behaved as love does, and he had gone about it quietly, seeking no credit or reward, whereas she had blathered and bruited it to all comers, needing approbation, praise, adulation from each, and acting, if she acted at all, only in the thespian sense, or like a baby.

Certainly now she knows it. She has always known it, but here, at last, is the final sentence. This is the wrongdoing by which she is rightly shamed. She would embrace death, she had told Octavia, choosing it, the fullest silence, as she should have chosen it long ago, and that is the truth. But she cannot disown this last vanity: She is also going to it guilty as charged, head bowed, up the steps of the scaffold, like a queen condemned. That, too, is her truth.

Except that there would be no last words, only these execrable notes. No more descriptions, no faithful report of those perishing moments. These are all the things that she will never write. Yet they are all that she has ever wanted to communicate.

Absent thee from felicity awhile, echoes Poor Tom, *and draw thy breath in pain to tell my story.*

Where is my Horatio now? Lytton chimes, sounding far away and despondent for the first time. But it pains him—no, her—to be so sentimental—the dreaded thing—and so Lytton proffers a last emending jest, even though it tastes a trifle sour in his mouth as he says it. *My kingdom for a Horatio,* he burbles, but does not laugh, and neither does she.

My story, she thinks. What wash it has all been, and pompous, like Father keening over his wounds, solemnly gaping his waistcoat with both hands to reveal his sacred heart, throbbing in his desiccated breast. *We perished, each alone.*

Bosh! It is just Tom all over, the banker with the molten heart of fool's gold, locked in its safe, behind his façade. And it is Tom, no doubt, who will have the last word. Posthumously, speaking in the only language posterity can comprehend, and saying all the things that she has meant. Well, let him, then; she can write no more. In his beginning is her end.

In the disturbances of spring, moans Poor Tom in his own verse, *menaced by monsters.*

She looks down at the blotter and sees that she has dashed out the note to Nessa, again unknowingly, while she has been elsewhere, confabulating with fiends. This, at least, is in her own voice, not Adeline's, but it has rambled over the same ground: Leonard, his goodness, her state, and at the end, the frantic wave of recognition, like the flail of a drowning man.

Ah, well, the words she will leave her are of even less importance than those she will leave for Leonard. Between them, the closest of sisters, communication is not really verbal, after all. Never has been. Vanessa, congenitally wise, had chosen pictures, and she had chosen them very young, though she had not done so intellectually, but out of instinct and her natural self-confidence. She had done so knowing what she, Virginia, the younger sibling who chose words, had not known or been secure enough to accept until it was too late. The adage about pictures and words is too true. A single stroke of the brush comes closer to conveying the real thing than reams of written words can ever do.

Her best work has only ever been an emulation of her sister's art — indeed, the art of all the painters she admires — with its supple blurs and diffusions of the vulgar world, whose assortment of egos and objects is, to those who see through them, as idiotic and explicit as smut. They, the painters, have known from the outset that the almighty intellect is simply in the way. Direct apprehension is all. Adeline has known this always, too, but it has taken shriveled, striving Virginia a lifetime to let go of the pretense.

And now, to be reduced in the end, like this, to plaintive scribbling. Well, it is fitting. Back to the babblings of an infant, disenchanted with her own voice. And yet — again, she had told Octavia the same — Vanessa will know. She will know without being told, or in spite of being told *post delicto*. It is a meager insult that she will soon forgive.

The sun is high enough over the lodge that she can feel it, warm as a searchlight on her back, glaring through the windows. Yes, she thinks with a pouring relief, there will be no more planes, no bombs, no guns, no hot lights in the menacing dark. There will be none of these things anymore, only the lulling, purifying sound of water, and the end of everything.

She looks up and sees with a shock that it is already eleven o'clock. Through the pair of French doors at the front of the lodge, which she had thrown open first thing to catch the rasping of the natterjacks, she can make out Leonard, still some distance back, coming across the orchard lawn to fetch her, purposeful as ever in his country togs. She must meet him at the door. Rising from the chair, she pulls open a drawer in the desk, removes two blank blue envelopes and arranges them over the notes.

As she emerges from the lodge, Leonard is about to step up onto the wood planking that serves as a veranda for this retreat. There are two low-slung canvas deck chairs there, one on each side of the open doors. She and Leonard, or visiting friends, have often sat here for a smoke under the chestnut tree and whiled away the afternoon talking. But they will not sit there now. As she meets him, Leonard is already turning to lead her back to the house. Lunch will be ready at one, and he is insisting that she lie down for at least half an hour before then. He is going to finish some work.

She promises him that she will rest, but first she tells him she would like to take a short walk.

"I have been cooped up all morning," she says.

He gives her a look, but reluctantly agrees, and disappears again into his study. Once she sees that he has closed the door, she rushes out again to the lodge to retrieve the notes. She writes the names Leonard and Vanessa respectively on the two envelopes, folds the letters and puts each in its rightful place. Then, envelopes in hand, she scurries back to the house, straight up the stairs and into the sitting room. She places the envelopes side by side on the table, looks at them for a long moment, then pulls herself away and races back down the stairs to the hall. There she puts on her fur coat, takes up her walking stick and heads out again, this time down the garden path, out the back gate by the church and onto the path that leads to the Ouse. When she reaches the river, she walks a little ways along it toward the bridge at Southease.

When she is satisfied with the spot, she stops. Setting down her walking stick, she picks up a heavy, grimed mudstone from the ground and turns it over in her hands, rubbing portions of its smoothed surface with her thumbs to reveal the dark red and purple bands of clay running through it. She closes her eyes and brings it close to her face. Open-mouthed, she inhales the sweet reek of ferrous soil and roots and river water. She stands this way for some time, breathing in the stone. Then, from the left hip pocket of her coat she pulls a small vial that she has filled with some of Octavia's milk. Still holding the stone in her right hand, with the thumb and index finger of her left hand she eases the glass stopper from the top of the bottle. As she does so, she hears the dying voice of the old man, incanting her epitaph.

We that have done and thought . . . that have thought and done.

When she has it free, she lets the heavy glass stopper drop to the ground. She holds the stone aloft in front of her, and slowly, lifting the vial above it, she pours its contents over the stone. She watches as the thick, opaque whiteness of the milk drops onto the red and purple bands of the mudstone. Then, slowly, as it slides and dilutes, she observes the glaucous film it leaves behind. And she feels the cool, caressing drool of it dripping down her hand and forearm as the voice of the old man ends his lament.

We that have done . . . Must ramble, and thin out . . . like milk spilt on a stone.

She drops the vial, puts the dripping stone into the right hip pocket of her coat and moves forward. Taking Adeline's hand, which is frail and moist with trepidation, despite the look of radiant satisfaction in her eyes, Virginia moves to the very edge of the bank. The current is tidal here—mystic, as Yeats had said—and the freshet is high, rushing by with wild and vertiginous force. Yet, still, it sounds eerily far away, like the roar of the sea inside a shell.

There is a wind coming off the swell that chills her. She pulls her coat tighter over her chest and feels the weight of the stone shift from the awkward precipice of her hip to settle neatly like a tumescence in the lean concavity of her bowel.

The river is a strong brown god. Poor Tom's a-cold.

It is Tom's final call, but there is no Lytton now to goad. He is on his bed of loam somewhere, reclining, ignorant of this. And so, at last, in absolute quiescence, let him rest.

There is only Adeline to answer. Ever the dutiful schoolgirl, she has learned her lessons well. *Never twice, you infernal Greek!* she yelps. *Never the same river twice.*

She is trying to be brave, but there is a heart-rending tremor in her voice. Virginia gently squeezes her hand, in both reassurance and thanks, but she does not turn or look back. She must be firm, as decreed, *unvanquished and unyielding.* "Yes," she says, her face a mask of calm determination. She looks down at her wristwatch and sees that it is a quarter to twelve. "Never twice," she murmurs, and she steps into the river.

Author's Note

I consulted many primary and secondary sources while research-
ing this novel, but among them, far and away the most compre-
hensive and indispensable was Hermione Lee's biography *Virginia
Woolf*. I drew on it extensively for facts, dates and events, as well as
information about Virginia Woolf's relationships, states of mind
and works. I owe an immense debt of gratitude to Lee for giving us
such a full and detailed portrait of this remarkable artist.

I learned a great deal from Michael Holroyd's biography *Lytton
Strachey*, and from it (in the second scene of Act II, between
Lytton and Virginia) I have quoted Freud's letter to Strachey ver-
batim.

Also of great use to me in my research were Nigel Nicolson's
short biography *Virginia Woolf*; Stephen Spender's autobiography
World Within World; Carole Seymour-Jones's *Painted Shadow:
The Life of Vivienne Eliot, First Wife of T. S. Eliot*; Susan Johnston
Graf's *W. B. Yeats: Twentieth-Century Magus*; and Richard Ell-
mann's *Yeats: The Man and the Masks*. Finally, I made copious
use of the letters, journals and autobiographical works of Virginia
and Leonard Woolf, as well as the letters of Lytton Strachey and
T. S. Eliot.

Acknowledgments

I would like to thank my agent, Eric Simonoff, for his infinite patience, his friendship and his belief. I am also immeasurably grateful to my editor, Lauren Wein, as well as to my old colleague and friend, HMH honcho Bruce Nichols. Thank you for taking the leap with me.